THE COLONIST'S PETITION

BOOKS BY LORIN GRACE

AMERICAN HOMESPUN SERIES

Waking Lucy
Remembering Anna
Reforming Elizabeth
Healing Sarah

BRADFORD BRIDES

Rescuing the Sheriff's Heart
Bending the Blacksmith's Heart
Converting the Preacher's Heart
Healing the Doctor's Heart

HEIRS & HEROES

The Viscount's List
The Colonist's Petition
The Gentleman's Agreement (coming)
The Duke's Directive (coming)
The Captain's Letter (coming)
The Earl's Inheritance (coming)

STAND ALONE TITLES

A Little Clean Fun
Love in the Valley

ARTISTS & BILLIONAIRES

Mending Fences
Mending Christmas
Mending Walls
Mending Images
Mending Words
Mending Hearts

HASTINGS SECURITY

Not the Bodyguard's Baby
Not the Bodyguard's Widow
Not the Bodyguard's Boss
Not the Bodyguard's Princess
Not the Bodyguard's Bride
Not the Bodyguard's Angel

HASTINGS LEGACY

Too Much in Common
Too Far to Sea

MISADVENTURES IN LOVE

Miss Guided
Miss Oriented

SPELLBOUND IN HAWTHORNE

(with Maria Hoagland)
Taste of Memory
Sprinkle of Snow
Hint of Charm
Dash of Destiny
Stir of Wind
Essence of Gravity

Heirs & Heroes
BOOK TWO

THE COLONIST'S PETITION

LORIN GRACE

CURRANT
CREEK PRESS

To the forgotten
of Dartmoor.

ONE

June 1810

"Stop, stop! What are you doing, child?" Mr. Sprout hopped over a row of peas and skirted the herbs to reach the youth in question.

Using all her force, George brought the hoe down again, whacking the scrawny plant.

Mr. Sprout wrenched the hoe out of her hands and held it out of reach. "You are ruining my cabbages!"

"They do not look like cabbages. Cabbages are big and round." George used her hands to show Mr. Sprout the proper size of the vegetable.

The exasperated gardener dragged a faded handkerchief across his brow. "Miss Georgiana, what did I say last week when you wanted to dig up the roses?"

"I need to ask before using your garden implements."

Mr. Sprout's frown deepened the lines that creased across his tanned forehead. "That includes hoes. And what else?"

George looked down at her muddied boots. "You told me I needed to ask my governess."

"Did you?"

She twisted her dirt-smudged hands into the folds of her black dress. "She never allows us to do anything since Mother died."

"What if I taught you how to care for the vegetable garden, proper like?"

Raising her head, she met Mr. Sprout's eye. "Splendid, absolutely splendid."

"First, run and change your clothes. I will have no one upset with me over the state of one of your good dresses."

Georgiana looked down. "But I have to wear black."

"Perhaps you have something from last year that still fits you?" The gardener prodded.

"I have a grey dress." Grey was close enough to black, and a darker patch covered the tear from climbing a tree in a race against her friend Isabel. "I will be right back."

"Put a kerchief over your hair. Your governess will be less likely to notice if you look like you belong out of doors." The sun weathered gardener gave her a conspiratorial smile.

George scurried back into the house and up the servants' stairway. If she proved herself with plants in the kitchen garden, Mr. Sprout might let her take care of her mother's flower garden, not just watch him as he tended it. Since the bedroom she shared with her twin sister had been stripped of all but the black clothes she was to wear, George hurried to her mother's sunny sewing room, hoping the patched grey dress would be in the chest of clothes saved for her youngest sister, Rose.

Phil sat curled up on the window bench, holding a paper. She wiped her eyes with her sleeve before acknowledging George.

"What is wrong?" asked George.

"I have a letter from Alex."

"May I see?"

Phil sat up and patted the bench next to her. George read silently from the letter.

My dearest Philippa, Georgiana, Jane, and Rose,

(Grandfather insists I use your full names. Sorry Phil and George.)

After Father's visit, I feel I must write to reassure you of my health and that no matter what he says, I am not better off dead.

Please do not believe things are as dire as he may portray them to be—at least according to Grandfather and Aunt Healand. I will not lie and say I do not face great difficulties or that I am not in much pain. The pain is manageable with the drops the doctor gives me, although they make me sleep.

Aunt says I must stay here for at least two months since I have broken bones, including my arm, which is why this letter is not in my hand-writing.

Aunt says I must hurry if this is to go out with the day's post.

I love and miss you all. Grandfather promised to bring you here later this summer if Father agrees. I do not know that he will, as he fought with Grandfather and left for Town. Since Father is not going direct-ly home, I have no fear of this letter not reaching you first.

All my love,

Alexandra

A second signature in a shaky hand below the first—

Alex

A postscript followed.

Your grandfather and I feel we should tell you more than your sister dictated. In order to save her life, it was necessary to amputate Alexandra's right limb. We do not know if she realizes her loss yet, as the doctor is forcing her to sleep much of the time. She will need many prayers and all the encouragement you can give her. As Alexandra writes, we hope to have you visit The Willows soon.

Lovingly,

Aunt Healand

"Alex only has one leg? Like the old man who sits in front of the apothecary?"

"I assume so, only that man lost his leg in war. Father hinted at Alex's loss when he returned with Mother and William's bodies." Phil folded the letter. "I was not sure what he meant then."

George's eyes blurred. Blinking, she willed the threatening tears away. Father said crying was a sign of feminine weakness. She needed to be strong, especially for her twin Jane, who cried far too easily. "Do not show it to Jane. She will fret so."

Phil studied George—her gaze lingered on the dirty hands, muddied hem, and scuffed boots. "You have been in the garden again."

"Mr. Sprout said I could help him if I could find an old dress. I came to look—" George pointed to the trunk.

Phil stood and helped sort through the clothes. "What did our governess say when you asked to go to the garden?"

"After searching for Rose for only a few minutes, she told us to study quietly because she has a headache. So I did not bother to ask her." George held up the grey dress she found buried under several more colorful ones. It was shorter than it should be.

Phil stood. "Is Jane still in the schoolroom or out with the hounds?"

"I think she is in the schoolroom, working through a book of German folktales." The twins could not be more different in looks or interests, yet they were the closest of the five sisters.

"Put on your oldest shoes before you go out to the garden. I must go find Rose before the governess does."

If only the governess would resign. "You could let her go. Father left you in charge of the household and Mother told Lady Godderidge she intended to replace our governess this summer now that Rose has joined us in the schoolroom."

"I wish it was that easy. Then she would not be listening when we tell Jane and Rose of Alex's letter this evening."

"It will be better if they hear it from us rather than from Father." George envisioned her father delivering the news in his blunt way, labeling Alex as crippled or worse.

Phil paused at the door. "I hope Cook has ideas for something to make to soften the blow."

Food would not really help. No matter how many cakes and puddings Cook made, the pain of losing Mother and William lingered. Work—that was the remedy. If she worked hard, she would be too tired to think at night. George waited until her sister left to change without going back to her room and risk running into Jane or the governess. She raced to the garden where Mr. Sprout waited to teach her the mysteries of growing vegetables.

TWO

September 1814

So many carriages! Who would have thought that anyone lived in such extravagance? Carrying his portmanteau, Johnathan walked up the graveled drive to the enormous mansion. Unsure of his reception and unannounced arrival, he left his trunk at the inn where the post chaise left him less than an hour ago, before continuing the last few miles of his journey on foot.

While his grandpa called his ancestral home "The Willows," Johnathan did not expect a building roughly the size of a grove of trees. He heard of homes in Virginia being this big, but it easily eclipsed the size of any home he had seen in Boston.

There must be a mistake. As a farmer's son, even Johnathan knew he should not mingle with British gentry. Grandpa's revelation that he was in line to become a British Earl sent ripples of disbelief through the family. However, it was Grandpa's request that Johnathan travel to England to reconnect with the current earl that upended Johnathan's entire life.

No, his life was already chaos. He merely traded one kind of turmoil for another. Grandpa gave him a choice, as much as a man only four years from his century mark could give any grandson who loved him, so not much of one at all. That request placed him on the imposing doorstep of an earl. What was Grandpa thinking, sending him to England? What did he hope to accomplish? Weeks aboard a ship had not answered that question. Grandpa mentioned taking a wife, but there must be more to the journey than marriage.

Regardless, Johnathan came this far, and he would not let a score of carriages keep him from doing his duty. He lifted his hand to the knocker, but before he touched it, the door opened. People in fine clothing gathered around the doorway, including the man dressed in black who opened the door.

"Beg your pardon. Does Mister Whitstone, Earl of Ryeland, live here?" Johnathan waited for an answer.

The man holding the door lifted his chin. "This is the residence of Lord John Ryeland, Earl of Whitstone."

"Ah, that is what I meant. Titles are most confusing." People stared at him. Half of them were females of marriageable age, dressed in elegant gowns, making him very aware of his dusty travel clothing. Was one of them the woman he was sent here to wed?

The man holding the door sniffed. "Come back another day when you are not interrupting his granddaughter's wedding."

Perhaps while he was at sea, his distant cousin's problem of a husband for his granddaughter solved itself. Johnathan was not about to leave without discovering if his journey was in vain. "Will you inform him that Johnathan Whittaker, grandson of Nathaniel Whittaker, born Nathaniel Ryeland, heir to the sixth Earl of Whitstone, is here from Massachusetts to fulfill my grandfather's last request?"

The time he spent rehearsing that line during the walk from the inn was well spent. Even if it was likely not his grandpa's final request, it sounded important.

Those who had been talking in the background grew silent. A young man and a woman, who looked far too happy to be anything other than the bride and groom, stepped aside, and an older gentleman came through the crowded entry hall. He extended his hand. "You came at last."

Johnathan found himself scooted off into a side corridor.

The man who welcomed him spoke quickly in a low tone. "I am the Earl of Whitstone. I apologize for your welcome, young man. You have arrived at the most inopportune moment. If you will wait a bit, I will explain all."

"My apologies for interrupting the festivities."

"Not your fault. I must cloister you for now. There are those in attendance whom it is best you not meet." The Earl of Whitstone turned to the man who answered the door. "Show Mr. Whittaker into my study."

The man nodded. Only then did Johnathan realize the man in the dark suit to be a servant. A butler perhaps, since he was not liveried, like others wearing a deep shade of green around the edges of the room.

Johnathan followed the butler.

Three women giggled as he passed them. He judged them to be around the same age as his younger sister, Miriam, who had just entered her eighteenth year. He supposed at least one of those girls was among whom he was to choose a wife from. At first glance, he was not disappointed, but there was much more to a person than a pretty face.

The butler opened a door to an office. The smell of pipe tobacco in the room chased away the scent of flowers which perfumed the air in the entry. The curtains at the tall windows stood open, giving the room an inviting feeling despite the dark wood paneled interior.

"I will send in refreshment while you wait. Do not open any of the drawers or doors, or I will know of it," said the butler in a tone that indicated he thought Johnathan no better than a common thief.

Were all butlers so pompous? Johnathan had only met one other in his life.

Moments later, a maid dressed in black with a crisp white apron came in with a tray. She set down the food on a side table and left, closing the door behind her.

Johnathan picked up a tiny sandwich and ate it in one bite. He quickly followed it with another. The earl's provisions were much better than the fare he ate at inns since arriving in England, as it was not on the verge of rotting or over spiced to hide other defects. If money was not so tight, he would not have been forced to take such economies in choosing his meals. Although he suspected his accent betrayed him as a foreigner, ensuring that most fed him their poorest fare at any price. Until this moment, he was not sure the English knew how to prepare fresh food.

Laughter from the house beyond the door reminded him of the women he passed in the entry. Had he sailed around the world for one of them? Losing his intended to his older brother stung. An arranged marriage could not turn out any worse than what Johnathan planned for himself. If their grandfather was anything like his, his distant cousins would follow through on their promises and appear on their wedding day. Yet, there must be a better way for Grandpa to reconcile with his English relatives than by a marriage.

"Who is he?" Isabel asked, echoing George's silent question.

Jane shrugged. George searched among the crowd for her oldest sister. If anybody knew, Alex would. She was the granddaughter that grandfather doted on the most. None of the sisters felt slighted over grandfather's partiality as he was no miser when it came to any of his grandchildren.

Finally, she spotted Alex sitting on a brocade chair behind other well-wishers. Father stood in front of her, obviously giving the eldest sister instructions. As George approached, Father walked off toward the side table where a footman stood guard over the port and other libations for the celebration. Father poured himself a glass of amber liquid. George was glad that he was distracted for now, but knew that their trip back to Kellmore Manor would be much less pleasant due to her father's drink.

"Who was that man at the door?" asked George. Imagine arriving at the moment of Phil and Michael's send off. Most disastrous timing indeed.

Alex tapped her chin with her fan. "I assume he is Grandfather's cousin from America, but I thought his cousin was older."

Jane joined them. "Grandfather's cousin would be near a hundred."

"Obviously, this is one of his cousin's grandsons, or perhaps even great-grandsons." Alex stood when Isabel Godderidge, their neighbor, joined them.

"I've never seen such a firm chin. Is he a relative of yours?" asked Isabel.

George agreed the chin was as solid as the man. However, those searching blue eyes were far more attractive than a lightly stubbled chin.

"A cousin, of sorts, definitely." Jane's brow furrowed. Doubtless, she was trying to calculate the connection with little information. "Although not very near. No closer than a third cousin, but likely further. I don't see much resemblance to grandfather. No one has such full and mussy hair."

"Curly, would describe it better." Alex tapped her fan again. "I am under the impression that grandfather asked him here to marry one of us."

Jane gasped.

"However, after Phil's recent adventures, I believe grandfather feels he shouldn't force any of us into marriage. The poor man, to travel all this way and then..." A sigh that felt like relief followed Alex's statement. As the eldest, she would have been the one most likely to be offered such a match. Because of her injury, Grandfather set up a home in Bath and a fund so that she could live quietly near the healing waters for the rest of her life with no pressure to marry ever.

Jane was as silent as a statue around most men. An arranged marriage was likely one of her twin's deepest fears. Thus leaving it to George to wed the American stranger. At seventeen, she was still young and had no desire to wed anyone. Much less a stranger, even a handsome one.

Isabel fluttered her fan and looked toward the corridor leading to grandfather's study. "If he is not promised to marry one of you, would he be open to others?"

Rose let out a giggle. The youngest Lightwood sister joined them unnoticed. A rarity for the vivacious girl who longed for womanhood.

George took Rose's hand to pull her near. "He may not be here to marry at all. For all we know, he has a wife and children back in America."

Rose sniffed. "Did you see the way he is dressed? He does not have a proper valet at all, does he?"

Alex took Rose's other hand. "Darling, that is not how we speak of strangers. And it is unlikely that the man traveled all this way with a valet. He was likely two months at sea. We must give him leniency until we learn more."

"Well, I hope that if he marries somebody, he marries you, Alex. You should have been first." Rose's curls bounced as she spoke. With barely a dozen years to her name, her youngest sister did not understand the complexities of society. Nor why Phil was the first sister to marry.

"I believe he is the most handsome man I have seen in quite some time," declared Isabel. "I am glad that you have no arranged understandings towards him. Best of all, he is easily four inches taller than me, so few men are."

There was no reason for Isabel's musing to bother George. Other than for the first time in her life, she took notice of a man for his appearance. The tempting man wore a certain ruggedness about him. Which could prove interesting, *if one was of a mind to wed.* "We know very little of the situation. Or why he is here. I think it is best that we move our minds to other things."

"Like the harvest ball," said Rose. "Father said I could stay, but only for the first hour."

"He forgets you will be away at school. But I would let you take all my dances," said Jane.

The comment earned a pout from Rose. "I can't miss the ball. It is tradition."

The ball was part of the harvest fair and celebration hosted at the Godderidges's estate for all people of the surrounding area. It was not unusual for children as young as eight or nine to be allowed to stay for the first part of the dance, which was held for gentry and tenants alike.

George rubbed her sister's back. "There will be balls enough after you are done with school."

Rose frowned and left them.

"Isabel, how is the planning? I'm afraid with Phil's wedding we have not helped as we should." Alex sat back down.

"Since David will run Leadon Hill, he is in charge. Mother declared it was time for him and Susanna to carry on the tradition." Isabel leaned closer and whispered, "Still, mother is sharing her opinions freely."

"I am sure it will be a grand celebration," said Alex.

"Remember when our mothers spent hours together planning the harvest fair? And all the trouble we would find staying out of their way?" asked Isabel.

"I remember your brothers tormenting us," said Jane.

Isabel laughed. "Only Edward—" she stopped and looked at Alex.

"David teased us just as much. And the little ones they certainly tried." Alex's face showed no sign of pain at the memories. Before her accident, everyone thought she would marry Edward, but he married another, who was now Phil's sister-in-law. Odd how things connected.

"I am looking forward to the apple cider contest," said George, attempting to change the subject somewhat. "Our orchard has never looked so good. All we need is a fine frost, and we shall have the best cider in the county."

"How can you be sure?" asked Jane. "Everybody else just needs a fine frost, too."

Sometimes her sister possessed no imagination. George fought to keep the hurt out of her voice. "Well, we must hope ours is the best, Jane. Just because it is not practical for estates located in close proximity to experience different weather, does not mean it cannot be so."

"You know I am only teasing you," Jane smiled, one of her rare smiles in a public place.

Lady Godderidge came over. "Philippa's, I mean Viscountess Endelton's, wedding was absolutely splendid, and your grandfather provided the most excellent of breakfasts. Sadly, we must go. I should like to make it to Leadon Hill tonight. The inns along the way are less than I could hope for."

Isabel said her goodbyes and reminded everyone they should call as soon as they were all home as she must hear more about the colonist who had joined them.

Jane looked to where father stood with another drink

in his hand. "We must return to Kellmore so we can finish packing Rose's trunks for school. She leaves in three days."

Unlike the older sisters, Rose was to spend time at a finishing school. Time she much needed. Over the past four years, Alex, Phil, and now George and Jane attempted to educate Rose without the benefit of a governess or formal education themselves. Jane, whose love for books was only eclipsed by her love for her dog and sisters, was at her wits end, as Rose refused to do any of her schoolwork, and on those rare occasions Father was home, he liberated her from the schoolroom more often than not.

Alex stood. "We should see if Father is ready to leave. I have no more desire to stay in an inn than Lady Godderidge." She directed Jane to check on Green, their maid, and sent George after Rose. Their carriage was not as new as the Godderidges's nor their horses as fast. They would be fortunate to return to Kellmore before midnight.

Rose pressed her ear to the keyhole of grandfather's study.

"Come away," hissed George, not wishing to be found.

"But I must know," Rose protested.

"Grandfather will tell us in time." George grabbed Rose's wrist.

Rose twisted and slipped out of the grasp. "Do you not want to hear? He *is* our cousin, and he *is* from America."

"You have already answered what we thought we knew. Now come along. We want to arrive home before nightfall. You know how difficult traveling is on Alex."

Rose sighed. "Very well, but I will not tell you a thing that I learned."

George stifled a laugh. Anything that Rose learned would be told to all long before the carriage crested the first hill. And what she did not know, Grandfather would supply in his own due time.

THREE

The earl entered the room. Johnathan made to stand, and the man waved him down.

"I apologize. I needed to see to my guests first. Many of them are making preparations to leave. A footman will let me know if I need to give more farewells. I am Sir John Ryeland, the sixth Earl of Whitstone, as I assume you have guessed. And you are Johnathan Whitstone, correct?"

"Johnathan Whittaker. My grandpa is Nathaniel Whittaker. I thought he said he was in line to be the sixth Earl." Which meant Grandpa was not an earl—or was he?

"Nathaniel would have been fifth. My father took that title. The numbers can become confusing."

"Admittedly until last spring, I never thought of any titles beyond King." He tried to keep emotion out of his voice. King was akin to taking the Lord's name in vain. That men were given the title of lord, was barely short of blasphemy.

"Understandable. The colonists haven't held with titles for decades. Will calling me Lord Whitstone be difficult for you? Nathaniel refuses to use the title in his letters."

"I know I am expected to." Johnathan tried to keep his face from showing his discomfort, and failed.

The earl chuckled. "Call me what you will then. My peers call me Whitstone or Ryeland. Since you are a cousin, John is also acceptable. I am assuming you have letters of introduction with you?"

Johnathan pulled a packet of letters, including a sealed letter sent by his grandpa, from his breast pocket and handed them to the earl.

The earl set the papers on the polished desktop. "Your grandfather was my father's cousin. I was two years old when he left for America and have very little memory of the man, although we have corresponded off and on through the years. Most of my knowledge of him is what I heard rather than what I recall."

"Grandpa said you wished one of his grandsons here. Preferably the eldest, which I am not, as my eldest brother is happily wed and has no desire to leave Massachusetts, as did my elder cousins." He need not mention that his younger brother had also recently married.

"That will not matter." The earl waved the facts away. "Are you married?"

He would have been if—that tale was not one he needed to discuss with this stranger, cousin or not—"No, I am not, nor am I engaged. Grandpa surmised you wanted me to marry one of your granddaughters, although for what reason, he could not fathom."

"I will admit when I wrote to your grandfather of my plan for one of his grandsons to return to England, my initial hope was for a marriage to one of my granddaughters. However, recent events have changed my mind about asking you to wed anyone you do not wish to, or, more importantly, asking my granddaughters to wed anyone *they* do not wish to. Mind you, I will not be displeased if you were to fall in love with one of them, but it would have to be a love match on both sides."

"So what is it you want me to do? Fall in love?" Could any man find love twice in his life? Admittedly, the first time must not have been love on her side since she absconded to New Hampshire with his brother.

"I would like you to challenge the lineage to the Whitstone Earldom and become the seventh earl upon my death."

"I am American. How can I be an earl?"

"My understanding of the matter is you must pledge fidelity to the king, and then there is a lot of paperwork, persuading members of Parliament, and finally a vote. It will not be an easy battle. It shall take the better part of a year before we have an answer, assuming that I can get it brought up to the House of Lords this next spring."

"If I were to take such a position, would it be permanent?" Johnathan was not sure he liked the idea of not returning to America.

"You would have to swear you would hold the title of Earl of Whitstone until your death. The fact that your grandfather abdicated his post in the first place will not play in our favor. You did not fight against us in this current conflict, did you?"

"Keeping a promise to my mother, I did not. Yet I wished to."

"We will leave that last particular out. If you fought against our troops, it would have made things most difficult."

"You will excuse me for saying so, but I do not even know if I like England yet. Nor do you know if I would be a fit heir." Granted, his ride atop the overfilled post chaise did little to recommend the country. Nor did London, with all its soot and filth. The few days he spent in the Netherlands were much more pleasant. This house, if such a large residence could be called that, had much to recommend it. But he must know more before making England his home.

"You are blunt."

"It is better than beating about the bush when my entire future is in the balance."

"Yes, much better. I may not know you, but I can, without impunity, say that you would make a much better earl than my current heir."

"And what do you base that on?"

"Other than your unabashed honesty? You were raised in America and therefore have no expectation of earning anything which you have not attempted to earn by your own sweat and toil. Therefore, you would not be reckless with your stewardship."

"Even so, you do not know me. How do you know I would make a good earl?"

"Honestly, I do not, but I have letters, not a few over the past years, from your grandfather, and I have been able to sketch what kind of man he is, and I hope that any grandson he would have chosen to send over here would take after him. Do you?"

Johnathan thought. It was not a simple thing to answer. His grandpa was a pillar of a man who had seen so much of life, and possessed more wisdom than Johnathan could ever hope for. "Grandpa stresses we must have integrity in all things, and that we must follow God in our conscience. In that, I am trying to follow in his footsteps."

"That is noble enough. We will spend the next weeks touring my properties. I only have two entailed estates, The Willows, and Kellmore Manor, plus the house in London, so we shall not have to make an extensive tour, and obviously we will start here. Then we shall move on to Kellmore so we can celebrate the harvest fair with my granddaughters."

A tap came to the door. A footman entered. "Your granddaughters are departing, your lordship."

"Thank you. See Mr. Whittaker to his rooms. Johnathan, we will continue this discussion later."

On the way upstairs, the footman pointed out the portrait gallery and suggested that Johnathan might find enjoyment in seeing the earls that came before him. The assigned room was half the size of Johnathan's child home. Over the years several additions were made to the house his father built. Still, the papered bedroom with its thick rug and carved fireplace was more opulent than anything Johnathan imagined a guest could receive. He gave the footman directions to retrieve his trunk from the inn and cleaned up the best he could without a change of clothing. He thought over the clothing in the trunk. The finest he owned, still it was not as nice as the butler's suit.

With nothing else to occupy him, Johnathan set out for the gallery. Paintings of men in powdered wigs and large collars lined the walls. Brass plates affixed to the bottom of each frame named the various earls.

He found the man who he assumed to be his grandfather's father, the Fourth Earl of Whitstone. The painting did not reflect the stern man Johnathan created in his imagination. This was the man, his great-grandfather, who came to blows with his grandpa, pushing him to escape his earldom and heritage, and sail to Boston. The elderly man in the painting did not look physically strong, but then grandpa never said who won their fight.

There was an unlabeled painting with a man, who looked like his great-grandfather, seated with his wife and three children. Then there was another painting of his great-grand-father and a younger wife. The next painting was of his great-great-grandfather's father painted along with his wife. Followed by every earl back to the first Earl of Whitstone. It was rather astonishing, really, to see so many generations.

Johnathan hoped for a painting of his grandfather as a young man. The only portraits in grandpa's possession were small miniatures of his wives. It came as quite a shock to the family to discover that grandpa had two more wives than anybody knew of. Johnathan's own grandma died long before his birth, and he only remembered the Widow Black, as she was called fondly by all who knew her. Grandpa did not remarry after her death, likely supposing his death should not long follow. But at ninety-six, he was now determined to live to be a hundred—a wish which no one could be sure would come to fruition or not.

The earl joined him. "Ah, you have found the portrait gallery. Good. You will need to learn the history of the earldom. This is me, my two daughters, and my wife."

The daughters dressed alike in white, their hair in fancy bows with well tamed curls, sat on either side of their mother who had powdered hair and wore a blue dress, with the earl standing proudly behind his wife. The daughters, with their fair skin and luminous eyes, favored some of the women he had seen among the wedding party.

"Which daughter is which?"

"That is my youngest, Mrs. Healand. You will meet her at dinner, as she is staying the week." He pointed to a woman who could not have been older than fifteen at the time of the painting, then to the sister. "My eldest, Hannah. She married Felton Lightwood. Sadly, Hannah died in a tragic accident four years ago. It was her second daughter, Philippa, who married today."

"My apologies again for interrupting such an occasion."

"None needed. It is not as if you could have known."

"Do you have a portrait of my grandfather?" asked Johnathan.

"Oh, yes, but it is not in here. His father banished the painting. It was located in the attic a few years ago. Come, I will show it to you."

The earl entered a side chamber where a portrait of a young man hung. A young man who resembled Johnathan so closely that he gasped. "I feel as though I am looking in a mirror. If such a mirror had a powdered wig attached to it."

"Remarkable likeness. It was painted less than a year before your grandfather left England."

"From what he said about how angry his father was, I am surprised it was not destroyed."

"According to my father, the fourth earl was angered beyond measure by his son's disobedience and choice of a woman of, and I quote, 'inferior birth,' and subsequent abandonment of the family to go to the Americas. He would have destroyed it but for the love of his wife, who could not bear to part with it."

Johnathan studied the man in the painting. Did he have it within himself to be the earl his grandfather could not be? Did he even want such a thing? For the life of him he wasn't even sure what an earl was besides being a titled land owner who likely could vote in the House of Lords and was given his position by the luck of birth. Luck, that the Sixth Earl of Whitstone believed Johnathan possessed.

FOUR

re you going out dressed like that?" asked Alex.

A pair of trousers peeked out from under her old grey dress. George tied a knot in the skirt, raising it to below her knees, the same length as her apron. "It is the same as I wore for harvest the past two years. We are harvesting grain. You know how messy that is. Father is unlikely to come this many days before the fair, and Grandfather and his guest are not due until tomorrow. No one will see me who has not before."

"Last year you were younger. Trousers are hardly acceptable for a young lady out in society." The pleading in Alex's voice was not enough to convince George to give up her practical clothing.

"I cannot work without my dress riding up. At least this way my legs are not bare. The field workers wear thick stockings, I could borrow a pair. I think we used to wear them when we went out with Mother."

Alex sighed, whether from exasperation or memory George could not tell. "It was fun helping with harvest times, even if we only delivered cooled tea."

"You could come again. I have not seen you use a cane for days."

Alex patted her wooden leg. "Peggy, the IV is ever so much more comfortable and better balanced, but I would never wear it in the field. It will take forever to clean properly. Perhaps I will bring the cart and come out later. It is easier to carry the jugs with."

"Do you think Jane will come?" George's twin spent most of the day in the library or wandering the garden, followed by her faithful dog, Sir Galahad. If Rose were here, she would join George all too quickly and cause mayhem in the fields. As much as she missed her youngest sister, having her at school was best for all.

"I will drag Jane out if I must, which should not be hard, as she enjoys a walk in the orchard. And I can tempt her with an apple off the tree."

"I hope it freezes this week. I want the sweetest apples for the cider we enter into the competition." George waved to her sister and hurried off. The tenants would have started in the fields already. She had not missed helping with a harvest in six years and she would not let them down this harvest either.

This year, the wheat field in the southwest corner of the estate had produced more than ever. A miracle George partially credited to the new crop rotation plan she convinced Grandfather to approve two years ago after her father ignored her. A couple dozen people, including tenant farmers and their families, already were hard at work. Kellmore Manor participated in a friendly competition with Leadon Hill, owned by the Godderidges, and the other estates for biggest harvest per acre, first completed harvest, and other events. Prizes were awarded at the fair.

George tied a kerchief around her head to keep the chaff out of her braided hair. She joined in the gathering of the sheaves of grain, and the gossip and laughter. The sun played a game of hiding behind puffy white clouds, keeping the day cool without the threat of rain.

Just before noon, the sound of squealing pigs pierced the air. George turned as four pigs darted away from the pen on the far side of the field.

George dropped the sheaves she carried and, with the others, took off after the pigs. If the pigs got into the unharvested field, it would be a disaster that no one wanted. Her boots squelched in a muddy patch. Ignoring the splatter she ran on.

As if knowing how to create the most damage, the brutes zigzagged through the tall stalks of wheat, avoiding their pursuers. Glad her trousers made running easier, George chased after the smallest, who veered away from the other swine. The little squealer raced toward the stream dividing the wheat field from the orchard. Three of the older boys joined her as they raced to corner the pig. The pig splashed through the stream and into the orchard.

Screams of her sisters echoed through the trees. The pig was not the only creature seeking an apple. Jane would be terrified if the pig ran at her, as the beast likely weighed as many stones as much as her smaller twin.

Like the others giving chase, George sloshed into the stream. Her muddy boots slipped on a moss-covered rock, dropping her into the water with a splash that drenched her from face to foot. Sputtering and laughing, she pushed herself up. There was nothing to be done for her mud-covered clothes. This pig would make an excellent Christmas ham.

She dove into the orchard, dodging low-hanging branches laden with apples. The pig darted between trees, its pursuers always just out of reach. George's wet clothes clung to her, slowing her steps as she ran.

Rounding a tree, George's foot caught on a root, sending her face-first into the tall orchard grass, where the thick blades concealed fallen apples dissolving to mush. Slime sprayed onto her face. George used the back of her sleeve to wipe away the muck from her cheek. How many rashers of bacon would this pig provide as part of a breakfast come January?

"Got him!" shouted one of the older boys. Others joined in the triumph. The pig squealed his displeasure as they carried him off.

Laughing, George pushed herself up to sit on her knees. Three smashed apples tumbled down her front. Her laughter died as she saw her sisters' faces.

Alex and Jane were not alone.

Grandfather and Mr. Whittaker stood with them. All stared at George in various states of shock and amusement. Her cheeks burned as she realized what a sight she must be— sopping wet, covered head to toe in mud, grass, grain, and decomposing fruit.

Mr. Whittaker's eyes were wide as he took in her disheveled state. To be seen like this by the handsome American, who appeared more attractive in the fortnight since his arrival at her sister's wedding. Mortification upon mortification. If only the ground would open up and swallow her whole.

"I… I was jus…" she stammered, unable to meet anyone's eyes.

Grandfather cleared his throat. His eyes twinkled with laughter. "I see you have been practicing your pig-wrangling skills, Georgiana. Is there to be an event at the harvest fair?"

Mr. Whittaker stepped forward, a smile tugging at his lips, and thrust out a hand. "Allow me to assist you, Miss Georgiana."

George hesitated, acutely aware of the mud caking her palms. But Mr. Whittaker's warm smile left her no choice.

Allow him to play the part of the gentleman or snub him in front of the family? She placed her grimy hand in his, marveling at how easily he pulled her up.

"Thank you," she murmured.

To her surprise, his eyes held not disgust, but a hint of amusement. "Is this the latest in London fashion? I am still unfamiliar with things here."

Even Jane laughed at his comment.

"Only on harvest days when chasing pigs." George did her best to return his smile, hoping any red in her cheeks would be attributed to her exertion, not the humiliation she felt. This was not the first time she'd made a fool of herself. However, doing so in front of this man was many times worse for a reason she could not completely put to words. This was the kind of man she wished to have seen her at her polished best.

According to Alex, Grandfather did not want Mr. Whittaker to marry any of them out of duty. But if he had any interest in her at all, she crushed that thought like rotting apples at her feet.

"Excuse me, I need to—" George stammered, her cheeks warming further.

"Of course," Mr. Whittaker replied, stepping aside but keeping his gaze fixed on her with an expression filled with a friendly warmth, not the disgust she expected. In his clean hands he held a wadded handkerchief. When had he cleaned them? At least he hadn't made a show of it.

With as much dignity as she could muster, George trudged back to Kellmore Manor. Alex warned her not to wear trousers. Oh, what Grandfather and Mr. Whittaker must think, and poor Jane. In her way, her twin would feel even more humiliation than George could. If not for the pants, likely she would not have chased after the pig, and this would not have happened. There was no shame in helping with harvest, landowners participated from time to time. *Male* landown-ers. Father never would, so she must. No matter how she reasoned, each step of the soggy boots dragged her back into the depths of her humiliation. If only grandfather came alone. Why did having Mr. Whittaker see her so disheveled bring her to shame? A dozen men witnessed her in trousers—that morning alone—and it never bothered her before.

Johnathan chuckled to himself as he watched Miss Geor-giana scamper away, a muddy whirlwind in a country full of genteel decorum. This was not the image of a well-bred young lady he had been led to expect over the past weeks. Instead, Miss Georgiana appeared every bit the spirited coun-try girl, one much like he would find at home, or not. Most women of her age would not be chasing pigs. How did she survive in this country where everything was proper and poised? Both of her sisters presented all that was prim and prudent. "Your sister is rather… unconventional."

"Unconventional is one way to describe it." Miss Jane's comment was barely above a whisper. The delivery made it quite impossible to tell if the comment was in jest or in awe.

The earl laughed. "It is never dull around my granddaugh-ters. They have run Kellmore Manor for years with the help of an excellent steward."

This was not the first time the earl insinuated that his son-in-law and current heir did not take his responsibil-ities seriously. After seeing Miss Georgiana with trousers under her dress and covered with mud, he could not deny that there was something different about at least one of the earl's granddaughters.

Miss Lightwood motioned toward the pony cart. "If you would like, I can show you around our estate. Georgiana would do better, but I suspect it may be some time before she returns."

"I would enjoy that immensely, Miss Lightwood." This place felt almost like home. Farming was something Johnathan understood.

The earl helped Miss Lightwood back onto the cart. Johnathan caught a glimpse of the wooden limb she used. After a long discussion about the death of the earl's daughter and grandson, the prosthetic had been mentioned with strict instructions to ignore its existence unless Miss Lightwood required assistance or brought it up. In that, she was not unlike Johnathan's father. Though the wooden leg his father used was not as finely carved and much more obvious as it didn't fit in a shoe or boot.

Walking alongside the cart, Johnathan reached up to pluck an apple from a tree and offered others to Miss Jane, Miss Lightwood and the earl. Crisp and sweet, the apple did not disappoint.

The trees were older than the ones on the family farm in Massachusetts, but well maintained. "I must commend you on these fine trees. I can see care has gone into the pruning and cultivation of them."

Miss Jane looked up from her apple. "We have excellent orchard men. George helps where she can. Please do not judge her by how she looked—"

He waited a moment for Miss Jane to complete her sentence before he realized that there would be no more. "My upbringing was on a farm, not as grand as this. I understand how four-legged creatures can create chaos. Your sister has no need to be embarrassed."

The earl tossed the core of his apple near the base of a tree. "If it is not a burden, I would like to stay until after the harvest fair."

Miss Lightwood urged the pony cart forward. "Father intends to return for the fair."

The earl frowned. "I suppose it cannot be helped. He will realize what I intend to do by making Mr. Whittaker my heir sooner or later. May as well get it out in the open."

"I do not understand how changing the succession is possible." Miss Jane frowned and ate another dainty bite of her apple.

"It is not an easy process and not quickly accomplished. Parliament must vote on it before it can be taken to the king, who still may deny the application." The earl's explanation was much shorter than the one Johnathan received.

Johnathan suspected that the tedious process was partly to discourage the movement of titles over trivial disputes or revenge.

Wishing to turn the conversation away from his claims to the entailed earldom, Johnathan changed the subject. "Tell me about the harvest fair."

"It is a celebration of our yield and a way for everyone in the area to socialize. There are games, contests, and, of course, storytelling," Miss Lightwood explained, a twinkle in her eye.

"I like the storytelling the best," said Jane. "Grandmother Grimes can spin any mundane task into a story. She always wins."

Alex continued her description. "It ends with a dance hosted by the Godderidges. Everyone attends. The estate owners take on the role of servants for the evening. Although we still dance and participate."

"If I remember, the Godderidge estate is to the east. We passed it on our way here?" Several fine horses grazed in a meadow. Johnathan missed having his own horse.

The earl looked over the farm with a wistful expression. "Yes, that is Leadon Hill. When my daughter was alive, Kellmore took turns hosting the fair. I would like to see that happen again."

"Grandfather, it is not possible right now." Miss Lightwood's voice sounded pained.

The earl patted his eldest granddaughter's arm. "I know, I apologize. You should not be trapped in my regrets."

Miss Lightwood smiled back at him. "Thanks to you, none of us are trapped. No one could wish for a better grandfather."

Before the moment grew awkward, Miss Lightwood turned to Johnathan. "You said you have apple trees. What else do you grow in Massachusetts?"

"Flax, corn, wheat. We have a large garden with various vegetables, squash, and potatoes. We keep cows, chickens, and, of course, pigs." In his defense, Johnathan tried to hold the next comment in. "I do not think the latter would impress Miss Georgiana."

"As long as they are in their pens, I am sure she would have no problems with them." Miss Lightwood stopped the cart to watch the gathering of the grain.

Watching work, wearing the fine set of clothes the earl insisted he purchase, made his arms itch to be doing something useful. "I almost feel guilty for not joining them."

"If you wish, George can take you out tomorrow. I know she would be glad for the company. She tried to talk me into joining her this morning, even though she knows it is not possible." Miss Lightwood tapped her leg. "I assume Grandfather told you about Peggy the IV, my constant companion?"

"It has a name?" Johnathan stepped back. "Many pardons. I should not have spoken."

To his surprise, all three of his companions laughed.

"Naming her Peggy was a way to talk about my situation without having to call it all the difficult things. I am glad Grandfather told you. Now you will not think I am excessively forward if I grab your arm or make odd noises when Peggy claps." Miss Lightwood's smile was as natural as when she spoke about the orchards. "Most people in the ton refer to wooden legs as clappers."

"I have never heard of a more fitting name. My father used a similar device all of my life. I never knew him to name it." Father referred to his stump often enough, however that term was far from one used in proper conversation.

"Then you must not have met Jane's dog properly. Sir Galahad is as loyal as his name suggests," said Miss Lightwood.

The dog, a smallish hound, he met on his arrival was left behind for their outing. A wise choice considering the pig escapee. "I am afraid I did not spend enough time with him to learn his temperament."

As they continued their tour, Johnathan's mind wandered with the frequent mention of Miss Georgiana's name. Despite her unconventional appearance earlier, he found himself admiring her dedication to the estate. An esteem shared by the earl and her sisters. Curious about the muddy whirlwind he encountered earlier, he wanted to know more. "I would be interested to hear details about the everyday mechanisms of British farming. Perhaps Miss Georgiana would be willing to discuss them with me?"

Miss Jane muttered something that sounded curiously like, "If you can get her to stop talking is the problem."

FIVE

Carrying a bucket in either hand, George descended the servants' stairway into the kitchen.

The scullery maid looked up from the vegetables she chopped. "You do not need to do that, miss. I could have emptied your bath."

"You have far too much to do with Grandfather and Mr. Whittaker arriving a day earlier than we thought. My unplanned bath should not have put you out more than necessary."

"Are you going back out dressed like that, miss?" asked Cook, clearly concerned that George donned a clean day dress.

"No, they should return soon and Alex will likely call for tea." In truth, she embarrassed herself far too much for one day. George contemplated going out just so she could hide from Mr. Whittaker, but there would still be dinner. Putting off facing him again would only cause more difficulties. It should not matter, really. Everyone in the village knew that she helped with the harvest. Mr. Whittaker was a colonist, not a peer of the realm—at least not yet. For some inexplicable reason, Mr. Whittaker's opinion of her mattered far more than it should. Which was perplexing in itself. When Mr. Dalrymple took over the estate to the north this summer and every woman was all a twitter, except Isabel and Jane— Alex never was so she didn't count—George cared nothing for the goings on. Perhaps that was a poor example since her closest friends did not either. However, her other acquaintances could not stop talking of him.

She hurried back up the servants' stairway to her room to do something with her damp hair other than braid it. After several attempts, she managed to form a passable bun at the nape of her neck.

Sir Galahad dashed into the room, followed closely by Jane.

"Does Grandfather know he is not to be in the house?" asked George.

"Of course he does." Jane set her bonnet aside. "Grandfather does not care."

"I would be careful. Father is likely to show up without notice."

Jane shivered, no doubt remembering the last time Father banished Sir Galahad from the house with a swift, rib-breaking kick. The dog spent weeks recovering under the care of the master of the hounds.

Jane peered at George, her head tilted. "You did your own hair again, did you not?"

George puffed out a sigh. "That bad?"

"Sit, I will take care of it." With a few deft movements and far fewer hairpins than George used, Jane created a simple hairstyle that would be suitable for the rest of the day. "There, much better."

"I do not see what was wrong with wearing my hair the way it was. You always wear your hair in a simple bun."

Jane smoothed her grey dress. "I wear my hair in a way that suits me. You are not nearly so confined."

George bit her lip, wanting to ask Jane questions without raising suspicion. "How was the rest of the tour? Was Grandfather pleased at our progress?"

"Could not be prouder. Alex sang your praises too. Do you know the apples are almost ready?"

"Yes, they should be perfect for fresh cider at the fair. Did Mr. Whittaker say anything?"

A small smile lit Jane's face, and she sat on the edge of the bed. "He said many things on all manner of subjects."

"I mean about me, about how utterly wretched I am?" She must know even if it meant having her sister guess the possibility of interest in the man.

"You are not utterly wretched. I believe he found it refreshing that a woman supposedly out in society cared so much for her lands." Sadly, Jane was not one to elaborate or repeat long conversations. Where was Rose when her best skills were needed?

"He is a farmer, is he not?"

"I believe so. He talked of his farm. They also grow apples." Jane petted her dog, which jumped up beside her. "Alex has ordered tea. I was sent up to find you."

George stood and smoothed the day dress she rarely wore. "Is my dress acceptable?"

"Of course it is," Jane replied, turning to her dog. "Go to the kitchen."

Sir Galahad left ahead of them as they exited their room. After the dog slipped through the door to the servant's stairway, Jane closed it. "I thought it best that Galahad not come to tea. While Grandfather might tolerate him, our guest might mention later that the dog was there."

Even with Father absent, the fear of him hung over their heads. George was about to inquire more of Mr. Whittaker when the man arrived at the top of the stairway at the same time they did.

He nodded at both of them. "I see you have recovered from wrestling that swine."

"Yes, I, um, usually I am not..." George's mouth refused to work. Where were her words?

"Of course you are not." He offered each sister an arm as they descended the stairway.

It was not fair for men to have such sparkling blue eyes. It made them far too handsome.

He continued talking. "But some things happen on farms that city folk can't comprehend."

"Yes, they do." Jane agreed, surprising George with the ease with which she spoke around a stranger.

They found Alex and Grandfather already in the parlor.

Grandfather stood as they entered. "There is my girl. I must say, I have not seen the harvest at Kellmore look better than it has this year."

Heat rose in George's face. Why ever was she blushing at Grandfather's praise? She mumbled a reply citing the steward's excellent work and sat next to Jane on the settee.

Mr. Whittaker, like Grandfather, took one of the wingback chairs. Immediately, the maid brought in the tea cart. Alex directed Jane to pour, as she often did, as it was a way to include the least talkative of the sisters.

The cup shook as George took it from her twin. What was wrong with her? She was so agitated that she was sure to spill. Usually, it was Jane who showed signs of nerves around people, yet she seemed quite at ease around Mr. Whittaker. Could it be that this man would be the exact type of husband her twin needed?

An uncomfortable sort of lump lodged itself in George's chest. As much as she dearly loved her twin, there was some bit of her that did not like the notion of Jane with Mr. Whittaker. Although, once Mr. Whittaker obtained the earldom, assuming Grandfather's plan came to fruition, Jane could live the quiet life she wished to. The same sort of life her grandparents had led. For it was possible for an earl to live with some degree of solitude without judgment from the ton.

Jane would make the better match if one were to be. In time, these odd palpitations George experienced in Mr. Whittaker's presence would fade. She was only seventeen, anticipating her first Season, likely this attraction for a man she barely knew would occur again. Why was she even pondering marriage? It took months for most plants to grow into usefulness. A single embarrassing day did not signify if one was growing toward a lifelong attachment.

The earl kept the conversation going through teatime, a tour of the manor house, and into dinner without it growing stale. Johnathan never once felt unwelcomed by his three new cousins who wove their way in and out of the rooms and conversation. Despite the earl's caution that Miss Jane was quiet around people, Johnathan discovered that Miss Georgiana was the least likely to respond to a general question. An oddity both Miss Lightwood and the earl commented upon. Perhaps her day in the fields exhausted her.

The difference between the girl—no, woman—he witnessed chasing after the pig and the quiet one who barely contributed to the dinner conversation, despite a good deal of it being about the harvest, piqued his interest.

When they retired to the library after dinner, Miss Lightwood pulled out the cards and proposed a game. "George, Jane, one of you must partner with Mr. Whittaker."

Neither twin looked overly happy at the declaration. Miss Georgiana volunteered and sat next to Miss Lightwood.

Miss Lightwood sat and indicated he should take the other chair next to her. "It is not fair to anyone to have the twins as partners when we play. I have never figured out how they do it, but they win every game."

"We do not cheat," said the twin sisters in unison.

Miss Lightwood shuffled the cards. "I did not say you cheated. Only that when teamed together, you two win the vast majority of the games. I believe being twins gives you an unfair advantage."

Miss Jane frowned before answering. "Perhaps it is because we play so often. There must be a finite number of card combinations, and even though that number is well beyond my calculations, I believe we have played them all."

"You play that often?" asked Johnathan.

"It is my fault." Miss Lightwood passed the cards to him to cut and deal. "I was nearly a year in bed, and I would beg my sisters to come play anything with me. Phil is particularly good at chess. Rose trounces us all at vingt-et-un. And any game involving partners, George and Jane are nearly impossible to beat."

"My apologies, Miss Georgiana, if I put you at a disadvantage this evening." Johnathan's comment was met with a raised brow.

"I do not believe the point of the game is to win as much as it is to entertain ourselves before we retire." Miss Georgiana looked at her cards. Her face showed no reaction.

Miss Jane sorted her cards, not looking at anyone. "We could retire and read, but that would not be very sociable. The library here at Kellmore is not as extensive as the one at The Willows, but it should provide you with ample reading material."

"You will make Mr. Whittaker think he is unwelcome." Miss Lightwood delivered the reproof with a smile.

"Oh, no, I did not mean that at all! I am nearing the end of the most delicious novel, and I—" Miss Jane blushed a deep shade of scarlet.

The earl came to stand behind Miss Georgiana. "It has been some time since I have played a hand. Perhaps I could take your place, Jane. I doubt your sister will relish having you burn a candle half the night."

Miss Georgiana gasped and held her cards to her chest as she turned to her grandfather. "You saw my cards."

"Of course. How else am I to cheat?" The earl's laugh matched that of his granddaughter's.

The sound brought a wave of homesickness that made Johnathan feel both alone and welcomed. If it were possible to feel such opposite emotions at once.

The game proceeded with each of the teams winning a round. As far as Johnathan could tell, no one cheated, though the teasing continued. During the third round, Miss Georgiana hid one yawn, then another, behind her hand. They lost the round spectacularly.

"My apologies, Mr. Whittaker. I cannot keep my eyes open. Will you excuse me?" Miss Georgiana stood, when no one responded. "Good night."

"Will you be concluding the grain harvest tomorrow?" asked Miss Jane from her seat near the fire.

"Yes. I will try not to disturb you." Miss Georgiana yawned again as she left the room.

Miss Lightwood gathered the cards. "I am surprised she stayed awake that long."

"Did my presence deny her sleep?" asked Johnathan. He was not tired, but he should follow suit since he planned to observe the harvest in the morning at the earl's invitation.

"No, mine did," said the earl. "I am afraid I forgot Georgiana keeps farmer's hours most of the year."

"Her first Season will be difficult for her, with so many late nights and nothing to plant." Miss Lightwood stood, balancing herself with a chair back.

Johnathan scrambled to his feet, belatedly realizing he failed to stand when Miss Georgiana left the room. His mother taught him better.

Miss Lightwood shook her head at him. "Mr. Whittaker, we are not so formal here. If you got up every time one of the three of us stood, you would not be able to accomplish anything all day. As you are to be with us for several days, there is no need to play the Jack-in-the-box here."

"Will you forgive me if I do? My mother spent hours lecturing me on the practice, and I am still learning to make it a habit. As I have already proven tonight, when I did not stand for your sister, I have far to go in formal manners."

Miss Lightwood tilted her head. "As you must, then. Only if you are to follow George about the fields, please do not act too gentlemanly. She does not like it when others treat her like the lady of the manor."

"I shall endeavor to remember that." Johnathan looked uncertainly about the room. Miss Jane was intent on her reading. The earl moved to the chair nearest the fireplace. Miss Lightwood returned the cards to a box on a shelf and crossed the room to Jane.

Johnathan moved the chairs back into place. "If you do not mind, I shall retire as well."

At the top of the stairway, a low growl met him. Johnathan took another step, which was followed by a sharp bark.

"Sir Galahad. Bad dog!" Miss Georgiana rushed down the corridor, her mob cap askew, white gown billowing behind her, and bare feet slapping on the carpet. She stopped short of him, her hand clasping the shawl around her shoulders. "Oh, no."

Johnathan turned his attention to the growling dog. Anything to keep from staring at Miss Georgiana in a nightgown looking all soft and adorable.

"Come, Galahad." Her command was sharp.

The dog lowered his tail and slunk past Johnathan. He heard rather than saw Miss Georgiana scoop up the dog.

"No more barking at Mr. Whittaker. He is a friend." She cleared her throat. "My apologies, Mr. Whittaker. I will talk to Jane, and her dog will not bother you again."

Johnathan waited until he heard her retreating footsteps to look back in her direction. The most delightful ankles peeked out from under her nightdress. Miss Georgiana was the most interesting and unexpected thing he had seen in England.

SIX

Dressed before the cock crowed the first time, George hoped to leave the house unseen by anyone. Sir Galahad raised his head but remained curled in a ball at Jane's feet. She did not need a light to find the servants' stairway and make her way down to the kitchen.

Cook looked up from the kettle she placed over the fire. "I did not think ye would be this early. The farmers are not even out."

George cut herself two slices of bread and a hunk of cheese and wrapped them in a cloth.

"Is that all you be taking?"

"I will grab an apple too."

"I have cold chicken if ye like."

"I know the chicken is grandfather's breakfast."

"There is enough. Ye take some."

George shook her head. "I should be going."

"Not without some food in ye. Now sit down and I will get you an egg and toast." Cook gave George a shove toward the table in the corner.

A stair creaked. George looked that direction, hoping it was one of the servants.

"But I must go."

"Not before ye eat." The cook turned to the fireplace as the scullery maid entered the room.

George let out the breath she held. Mr. Whittaker would not come down the servants' stairway, would he? Did they show him how to get to the kitchen yesterday? She missed as much of the house tour as she could to limit her interactions with the newcomer.

Cook set down a pewter plate with a clatter.

George jumped.

"What has ye all worked up? Nervous as a rabbit in Mr. Sprout's garden, ye are."

"Nothing." George stuffed a bite in her mouth large enough to earn a frown from Cook.

"It would not be that handsome young man visiting with his Lordship, would it?"

Unable to talk because of the food in her mouth, George shook her head. That was not a lie if she did not speak, was it?

"Hmm. Either my eggs are too hot, or ye have developed a penchant for blushing."

She was tempted to agree with her father for once—she was too close to the servants. But Cook helped fill the emptiness after mother died. "It must be the rush to get to the fields."

"Are ye not supposed to take that fine American visitor with ye?" Of course Cook knew.

"Grandfather did not say all day."

"Then why did that nice Mr. Whittaker ask what time would be convenient for an early breakfast?"

"Maybe he is accustomed to eating early?"

Cook crossed her arms. "He will be down to eat in a half

hour, as he refused us taking up a tray. I expect you to take him out with ye for the harvest."

The very thing she wanted to avoid. Arguing with Cook would be pointless.

"Now I need to prepare his food. Make yourself useful and peel ten of those apples." Cook pointed to the basket in the corner. George finished her egg and started in on the apples, playing a favorite game of trying to peel the apple in one long string. The longest string peel yet broke as Mr. Whittaker stepped out of the vestibule of the servants' stairway.

"Good morning. I suspected I would have to get up early to go out with you, Miss Georgiana. Apparently, I was not early enough." The clothes he wore were much more suited to a gentleman farmer than yesterday.

George nodded his direction and picked up another apple. "I was awake earlier than usual."

Mr. Whittaker looked from the cook to her. "If you have an extra knife, I can help."

It was Cook's turn to blush. Served her right for interfering. "No, it would not be fitting for a guest to help in the kitchen doing scullery work."

"But—"

Seeing where his objection was taking him, George interrupted. "Cook said that you were coming and suggested I wait. I could not sit here doing nothing."

"And I have your breakfast ready for ye." Cook set a large plate on the table that included stewed apples baked with egg and crumbed bread—not quite a pie nor a pudding. George's stomach rumbled at seeing the treat. "Would ye like some, miss?"

"Please."

Cook gave her the scantest piece. Having already finished one breakfast, she could have not eaten more anyway. Still, what if Mr. Whittaker thought she was one of those women who would not eat in front of a man because she wished to be dainty?

They finished breakfast in silence, owing to Cook's excellent fare and George's concentration on not allowing last night's embarrassment to surface. Her nightgown. What had she been thinking to leave her room in her nightgown? She had not—her first thought was that father returned, and she needed to get the dog out of the house before father could kick him down the stairway again. Could she never appear before Mr. Whittaker with some sense of decorum?

Cook set a bundle of food on the table. "I assume ye will not be back before teatime. If ye would have another bushel of apples sent to the house by noon, I would be happy for them."

"If Miss Georgiana approves, we can pick them on our way to the fields, and I will bring them back straightaway."

"That would be too kind of you, Mr. Whittaker." Cook blushed again. Those eyes must affect everyone.

George muttered something completely unmemorable in her mind and headed for the back door. Mr. Whittaker brought the empty apple basket with him as they left the kitchen.

Dawn lit the grounds in a cool grey light as the sun tried to break the skyline. Oranges and lavenders colored the soft clouds as the eastern sky melted into golds. She would have paused to watch the sunrise, but that might lead to conversation. To her chagrin, Mr. Whittaker stopped.

"Is it not wonderful how God gifts this view to everyone no matter where they live?"

"I have never thought of that."

"I did not until we were in the middle of the ocean and there was a spectacular sunrise, and I thought that my family would not see it for hours yet, and then that it had already been seen in England."

"What a thought. I rarely think of anyone not in England, so I have never thought of them being at a different time than us."

He stepped closer to her. "I had no occasion to either. I knew England existed since I was a lad and saw a globe. I learned when it was day on one side of the world it was night on the other, but I never put it all together until I experienced it."

"Is it difficult for you to be here when our countries are at war?" Where did that question come from? Instead of safe subjects she asked ones requiring long answers.

"I came over with a delegation that is hoping to sign a peace treaty. We have lost more soldiers to illness than anything else, and we just want to end this and have our prisoners of war back before they die, as well. No doubt there are those in England with the same wish."

"I am surprised you are not fighting."

"My father lost his leg near the end of the Revolution. He lived for many years after, as you can guess, since I exist. After he died, my mother extracted a promise from me that I would never go to war. I kept it. There is no honor in dying of dysentery."

George shuddered at the thought. "I doubt there is any honor in war anywhere."

"It would depend on what you were fighting for. My father fought for freedom to make his own choices."

"Do women have that freedom, too?"

"Not yet. Maybe someday. My mother says Abigail Adams asked her husband to 'remember the ladies' when he was helping frame the Constitution. In time I believe it will happen."

"That is forward thinking of you. Even though a queen once ruled England, women have no say in most matters." The sun finished cresting the horizon. George turned to the orchard. "We should pick those apples."

"I believe women should be considered. My mother's opinion is invaluable to the entire family."

Refreshing. Women were as capable as men in many respects. She knew Jane's "novel" last night was more likely some treatise written in German by a scientist than it was some romance. And with the way Jane enjoyed learning facts, she could have been an excellent solicitor. Then she would not have to think on marriage ever. Granted, she could live with Alex in Bath. A townhouse with no garden to speak of, George would go out of her mind with only a window box to tend. She stopped at the edge of the orchard. Being in charge of her own farm was an impossible dream. At least Mr. Whittaker didn't dismiss women.

"Any particular tree?" Mr. Whittaker set down the basket bringing George's thoughts back to the present. "I am partial to the Pippins." George pointed to a tree not far from them.

It took only a few minutes to pick a bushel. Mr. Whittaker consistently picked apples higher than George could conveniently reach.

She set a nearly perfect apple on top. "That should make Cook happy."

"I hope so. I feel I must stay in her good graces. She was not pleased that I refused a tray. I did not want anyone to go to extra work, and when I learned you ate in the kitchen, I decided to as well."

"I will not ask who betrayed my hoydenish ways and allowed you to reject her hospitality. You have seen enough of them yourself that I wonder if I have not appalled your sensibilities."

"If you are referring to your chasing of animals, I find nothing amiss with it." He shouldered the basket. "And rescuing your sister's pet, I found it quite charming."

George stayed a step behind him so he would not see the blush. "A gentleman would not recall that he saw me last night."

Though Johnathan could not see Miss Georgiana's face, he knew he embarrassed her. "I have yet to be accused of being a gentleman. I am not sure if a colonist can truly be one."

"If you are an earl, you will be one like it or not. Of course, I would prefer you acted the part as well. It would never do to have a cousin who was a rake or a scoundrel." Miss Georgiana continued to walk just far enough behind him that he could not see her face without turning.

"Is that your opinion of me?"

"No, if you were either, you would not have turned away last night when I appeared with so little decorum." She paused. "Thank you for that. You must think me the least genteel of ladies."

"On the contrary, I find your devotion to your home and your sisters most amiable."

The footfalls behind him stopped. He turned. Miss Georgiana stood as straight as a tree.

"You do not think me next to heathen?"

"Not in the least."

"Then you have given me hope."

"Hope for what?"

"That not everyone will find me unfit for my first Season."

"Autumn?"

The corners of her mouth turned up, and she resumed walking. "The Season in London. A time to find matches, which usually starts after lent and runs until the parliamentary session ends. There are balls, dinners, and musicals most evenings."

"There is a time to find a spouse?"

"Some call it the marriage mart. In England, as I assume it is everywhere, the type of husband one can obtain determines a woman's future."

"So everyone goes to London for a Season to search for a spouse?"

"It is one way it has been done for decades. My sisters and I are fortunate that my grandfather purchased Alex a home in Bath and left a legacy to care for it. Still it will go further if it does not support all four of us. Anyway, I digress. There is also The Little Season and one in Bath, but they are not *The Season*. That is the place where most matches are made, as the men of any consequence are in Town during the parliamentary session. This spring, Jane and I are to have our Seasons. Some women go for several Seasons, but father has declared we are only to have one. Phil and Alex went this past spring."

"You are two years younger than your next sister, the one who married." He was not sure what he should call the wife of a Viscount. "Should you not wait for a year?"

"Since father lowered our dowries already, we do not dare put our Season off. As charms do not go far in finding a good husband. We are of age to marry, and father is determined that we must capitalize on Phil's connections. It is better we choose for ourselves than have father manipulate our lives for us. Phil and Alex agree we should take this chance."

"Why do you call them that?"

"Call who what?"

"Your sisters with the masculine version of their names?"

Miss Georgiana laughed. "Until our brother was born, Father always called us by the masculine. Once William started walking, he stopped. However, those are the names to which we were accustomed. We even convinced the Godderidge children to use them. Alexandra, Philippa, and Georgiana are such a mouthful, do you not agree?"

Johnathan, whose own name often felt longer than it should, could not help but to concur.

"Jane is fortunate to have such a short name. If it bothers you, I can use our full names."

"No need, however, whenever you are called George, it brings to mind my eldest brother. Who, of course, is named after President Washington." They reached the kitchen. Miss Georgiana opened the door, and he set the basket inside and waved to the cook before heading in the direction of the fields.

"I did not realize you had a brother named George. I think you only mentioned a sister. I can ask my sisters not to call me George if that helps."

"Not necessary. Miss Georgiana, I was just curious."

"As we are cousins, it is not necessary that you call me Miss Georgiana all the time."

"As long as you refer to me as Mr. Whittaker, it is."

"Are you so terribly formal in America?" She sidestepped a puddle bringing her closer to him.

"Not as formal as I've seen here, at least not with family."

"Since you are family, I propose we drop the formality when not in company." She looked to the fields bustling with activity. "Which is not now."

"So you will call me Johnathan?"

"Only if you wish it. I assume you would not call me George."

"No, I do not believe I will."

"Is your brother nice?"

"Sometimes. Older brothers can be difficult."

Georgiana laughed. "All siblings can. Older and younger."

They reached the edge of the field, and Georgiana found Mr. Rhodes, the steward, who directed Johnathan to where he could help. Georgiana waved and went to join the women working at the far end of the field. His thoughts followed her.

In Massachusetts, a woman working the harvest would hardly warrant notice. But here, watching Georgiana interact with others with such natural ease, he could not help but admire how she balanced between the two worlds. She knew every worker's name, understood the land intimately, yet could transform into a proper lady for dinner. Nothing like the simpering misses he expected. Not that he should be comparing her to anyone. He was here to consider becoming Earl, not to notice how the sun brought out golden highlights in her hair which by its lightened color was not a stranger to the sunlight.

The wheat harvest was in, and judging by the gathering clouds, none too soon. The wind tugged at George's hair. She tucked it away only to have a strand fly back into her face. She should have braided it instead of only tying it back.

Johnathan crossed the field to meet her. In his shirt sleeves, it was easy to tell he was as muscled as any other worker. Did he understand he could not be just any other laborer? That his new station would make his working as inappropriate as her own?

She watched him throughout the afternoon. Not once did he shirk the back-breaking work. The men around him warmed to his laughter. Johnathan—she was glad to think of him that way—fit him much better than Mr. Whittaker did. How would he be as Earl of Whitstone?

"Will I offend you if I do not put my coat back on?" he said as he reached her.

"Not in the least. Enjoy it while you can. Once you are titled, you likely will not work in the fields."

"I will not?"

"Perhaps in dire circumstances, but not day by day." Thoughts she suppressed came to the forefront of her mind. Perhaps her sister and others were right. "No. As loath as

I am to say it, this is likely my last year. I am no longer a child, and my presence causes some discomfort, and I hold no title of rank. I doubt the farmers would feel they could talk and act freely."

"Are you sure?"

"It is an idea I am trying to accept. Though it has been told to me for years. However, today I think I felt a little of it for the first time."

"How so?"

"There is a new bride among our tenants. Her husband grew up here at Kellmore and is used to me joining in, as is her mother-in-law. Every time I came near, she curtsied and grew silent, even though all of us assured her she has no need of giving me deference. If I marry, I will move away. Even if my husband allowed me to go to the fields at harvest time, his tenants, assuming he has them, will not accept me among their ranks as readily as the ones here at Kellmore. And my sister is correct. I am too old to wear breeches under my dress." She kicked her leg out, showing the soiled cuff.

"I think it is an ingenious idea."

"It has saved me some scrapes and scratches. However, if I had been pursuing more appropriate pastimes, I would not have been in a position to be injured."

"Like chasing a pig?"

"Will you not allow me to forget that moment of indignity?" She willed the heat in her cheeks down.

"I will not mention it again, but I cannot forget one of the dearest memories I have of this country so far." A short chuckle marked his words. "It was the first time I thought I might be able to overcome my homesickness and stay."

"You realize that women of any rank rarely chase after errant pigs? Likely you will never see such again in your life?" She tucked her hair back again. The gesture allowed her a moment of reprieve from his gaze. Perhaps forgoing braids that morning was a wise choice, even if it would take forever to brush out her hair.

"Yes. But up until then, my visit had been all bowing and politeness and I was not sure I could be in a country where people do not laugh."

"We laugh." She could not say for sure about all her countrymen, but she was sure that they laughed. Otherwise what was the point of the jesters or the many amusements?

"Politely." His point was well made.

"We are to do everything politely. Not that I have ever experienced it, but among the ton, if one has offended, they might receive the cut direct. Which is simply a look and turning away without words. Which is more polite than harsh words."

"Hardly. If I offended someone, I would wish for words so I can fight them or defend myself."

"But that could cause a scene." She answered as her Aunt Healand would.

"It could create a memory. If everything is all stiff politeness, how does one remember one event different from another?"

"I assure you, I have plenty of memories." Perturbed, George sped up, anxious to reach the house and to change out of her soiled clothing.

He caught up with her easily. "I was not implying that you do not have fond memories. I am not explaining myself well."

She whirled to look him in the eye. "What do you mean, then?"

He ran a hand through his already unruly hair and looked at his feet. "I do not know how to explain myself. It is a difference between here and home. And I miss all I knew."

Something tugged at her heart. She felt loss before—like nothing would ever fit again. Although he had not lost his family to death, he had to distance. It was unlikely after he was made earl that he would visit the Americas more than once, possibly twice, in his life. She reached out and touched his arm. He raised his head. As their eyes met, something material passed, almost like a silk rope linking them. She dropped her arm, but the feeling did not leave.

"Then do not try. I am sure if I went to America I would have the same feelings of sorts. Come, we have already missed tea. If we are fortunate, Cook will have saved us a biscuit we can eat as we prepare for dinner."

"I hope it is more than a biscuit. I am famished."

George laughed. The invisible silk rope slipped away, and they were back on friendly terms. "Cook always has more biscuits if you know where to look. And it is your lucky day. I know all the good hiding places in the kitchen."

SEVEN

Picking apples was the most familiar thing Johnathan had done since leaving Massachusetts. He assumed the technique was the same the world over. Grasp, twist, pull, repeat. The apples were cool from the overnight frost. His mouth watered at the thought of cider, and pies to come. The sack hanging across his chest expanded until it would hold no more fruit. Johnathan took it to the waiting wagon.

"Mr. Whittaker, you may be the fastest picker working in the orchard today." Dressed in a faded dress, without men's clothing underneath, Georgiana did not climb ladders, as he suspected she might have done if her grandfather were not in residence. Instead she helped transfer apples from sack or basket to crates which were stacked in the wagon beds.

"It has always been one of my favorite parts of the harvest." Johnathan exchanged his full sack for an empty one.

"Why is that?"

"Because it leads to warm cider and apple cakes." He could not help his smile, the apple and egg concoction the cook made again for breakfast this morning was still on his mind.

"Then you shall enjoy the harvest fair. There is an award for the best of the apple puddings, pies, and cakes."

"Do we get to taste them to see if we agree?"

"Of course." Her smile brightened the almost perfect fall day. Not many people could radiate that much joy.

Halfway back to his tree, a female rider galloped into the orchard scattering workers. The woman rode a sidesaddle in a fine habit. He recognized her from the wedding. She stopped short of the wagon. Georgiana met her, hands on hips.

"Isabel Dawn Godderidge, you know better than to come galloping into an orchard full of people."

"I was up at the ruins." Miss Godderidge said breathlessly. "Your father is coming."

Georgiana's fists dropped to her sides, gathering her skirt. "How far?"

"His carriage was just entering the village." Miss Godderidge soothed her horse's neck "Did you expect him today?"

"We knew he would come before the harvest fair." Georgiana looked down at her dress. "I suppose I should change. Mr. Whittaker!" His name started as a shout but faded when she realized he still stood close enough to hear. "My father is coming. He will be in a sour enough mood after realizing Grandfather is in residence. He will be even more upset if he realizes I have put you to work."

"Shall I return to the house?"

"I think it would be best if we both returned."

Miss Godderidge turned her horse. "I will take the long way home, so he does not see me."

"You just want to spy on the rest of our harvest." Georgiana made a face.

"I am sure David and Father will ask for an update when they learn I have been here."

Georgiana tsked. "Do not give me cause to think you are cheating."

Miss Godderidge laughed. "We can talk later. You best hurry."

"Come, Mr. Whittaker." Georgiana took the empty sack from him and set it back on the wagon. "If we go through the kitchen, we should be able to get changed before Father finishes greeting Alex."

"Your father does not approve of you working in the fields?"

"Of course not. The only thing he approves for his daughters is making matches that have the potential to fill his coffers."

Georgiana lifted her skirts and sprinted. Johnathan followed on her heals. They burst through the kitchen door, startling the cook.

"Is he here yet?" asked Georgiana, panting.

"Who?" asked Cook.

"Father. Isabel saw him."

"Not yet." The cook turned to her scullery maid. "Run and tell somebody above stairs to be prepared."

Georgiana grabbed Johnathan's elbow and tugged him towards the servants' stairway. "This way."

He followed her up the stairs, passing no one as they reached the floor where his room was. Georgiana opened the door to the corridor and peeked out before opening it wide. "I will see you in the parlor shortly."

"Are you sure I should come down?" Witnessing a family reunion was not his place as a guest.

"Please do. It may keep him from coming to blows with Grandfather."

Johnathan turned the opposite way from Georgiana and hurried to his room. He made quick work washing in a bowl and changing his shirt. His half-tied cravat hung around his neck when the earl's valet entered the room.

"I have been instructed to help you dress."

"I am mostly done."

The valet's lips formed a thin line. "Hm. Best let me do that, sir."

Johnathan dropped his hands and allowed the valet to tie the cravat and adjust his coat.

The valet stepped back. "Oh! What is that?" He reached and plucked a leaf from the back of Johnathan's head. "Do turn around, sir."

Johnathan turned slowly for the valet to inspect. The valet ordered him to sit in a chair while he repaired his hair.

"I believe I straightened everything out. You no longer appear as if you have been in the orchard. His Lordship said he would await you in the library." The valet picked up Johnathan's discarded working clothes and left the room. Johnathan glanced in the mirror before following. How did the valet get his hair to lay so smooth? It did not look like him at all. Johnathan ran his fingers through the top of his hair. The bit of curl the valet restrained sprang back into place. There—he looked more like himself, even if it was not properly British.

Over the last few weeks, the earl explained very little about why he did not get along with his son-in-law. Snippets of Georgiana's conversation and her flight from the orchard spoke volumes. Though he tried not to, Johnathan found he formed an opinion most decidedly against the man. It was not fair to Sir Lightwood to so soon create a negative opinion, but there was no help in how he felt.

As he reached the top of the stairway, the front door flew open.

"Why were you not waiting?" Sir Lightwood thrust his hat at the butler.

The butler did not answer.

"I heard Whitstone is in residence. Where is the old scoundrel hiding?"

This was the first time Johnathan heard anyone call the earl by just the last part of his title. A baronet was lower than an earl, was it disrespectful? Labeling his father-in-law a scoundrel certainly was.

"I believe his Lordship is in the library." The butler answered with a dignified air.

"And my daughters? I am assuming they are out in the fields?"

"Miss Alexandra is with the housekeeper. Miss Jane is likely in the library—"

"And Georgiana? Please tell me she is not disgracing herself for all the county to see."

Behind Johnathan, there was a rustle of skirts. He stepped back from the railing to allow Georgiana to pass.

"Stay up here for a minute. Step back into the shadow," she whispered.

She descended two steps before calling out. "I am here, Father. Welcome home."

Unable to see from the spot near the wall where Georgiana directed him, Johnathan waited until he heard her shoes on the marble entry floor before moving forward.

"You almost look as if you have not been out in the fields today." Sir Lightwood's voice dripped with disdain.

"I have not been in the fields."

Johnathan leaned over the rail to watch the exchange.

"You are lying. You never wear gloves unless going to church or you are hiding filthy and ragged nails." Sir Lightwood grabbed for Georgiana's hand, but she stepped back quickly.

"I was in the orchards. I did not lie."

He lifted his hand as if to strike her. "You forget yourself. Next time you will be punished for your insolence. Tell your sisters I shall be in residence for the week and I am expecting a guest. And you are all to show respect."

"A guest?"

"Yes. Have the rose room prepared."

"Rose's room?"

"No, your mother's room. The primrose room. The sickening color she liked."

"Mother's room? You cannot put anyone in there."

"I can and I will."

"Your guest is not a woman, is it?"

"My guest, is none of your business. Tell your sister to adjust the menus accordingly. I wish for a bath. If you see your grandfather, tell him I have no intention of talking to him."

There was a mumbled response before Georgiana turned down the corridor. Johnathan stepped back into the shadows. If he had not created a poor opinion of his absent host before, the threat to slap Georgiana would have done it for him. Fathers should not treat children, especially daughters so. Meanwhile, Georgiana's handling of the situation only increased his respect for her. When he saw her with the pig, he thought of her in the same category as his younger sister. However, after watching her in the fields and with her father, he found her more mature than her years would have suggested.

The heavy footfalls of a man coming up the stairway meant he would soon be face-to-face with Sir Lightwood. Given what he heard, avoiding Georgiana's father at this point would be the prudent course. Johnathan turned down the corridor, hoping to reach either his room or the servant stairway before Sir Lightwood reached the landing. No such luck.

"You there! Is my bath prepared?"

Drawing a bath in mere minutes was impossible. What a demand. Johnathan continued walking away.

"You! Stop when I talk to you!"

There was no one else about, so Johnathan slowly turned.

"You are not dressed like one of my footmen!"

"No, I am not."

"You must be one of the earl's servants. You do realize the valet should not be in the main corridor?"

"Yes."

"Go on about your business. I don't wish to see you again."

Johnathan entered the nearby servant stairway to leave the man's presence before he realized his mistake. By using that stairwell, he all but proved he was a servant. He reached the library through the circuitous route as Georgiana and Miss Jane were exiting. He nodded to the women and let them pass.

"Ah, there you are," said the earl. "I assume you have heard that my son-in-law is back in residence."

"I believe he thinks that I am your valet."

"My valet? That could prove interesting. Georgiana told me he does not intend to visit with me for a while, which suits me fine. Although he has upset her by putting a guest in her mother's room, he forgets I own this estate and he is only a caretaker. There will be no guest staying in my daughter's room. Especially not the mistress who broke her heart. For I can think of no one else Felton would want in an adjacent room. There is not a single widow of means in the ton that will even look his direction."

What sort of man brought his mistress into the house where his children lived? What family spoke openly of such a woman? That was worse than Mr. Hamilton publishing his letters in the Reynolds pamphlet, was it not? If gossip here was anything like it was at home, the whole of the county would learn that the mistress was here. That could not possibly reflect well on his cousins. Johnathan did not make any comment, as it was not his place.

The earl beckoned him. "Well, do come in. I will deal with that woman if she comes. How was your apple picking?"

As they conversed, a palpable tension rose in the house, carried in first by the servant who brought in tea. It grew with the sound of each door shutting or footfall in the corridor.

The rantings of Sir Lightwood through the door of the library reached them moments before the man threw the door open with such force that it banged upon the wall. "See here, old man, I can put my guests wherever I choose to."

"Felton, you forget I own this property, not you. You live here out of my goodwill. And if, as I suspect, you have brought your mistress here, the last place she will stay is in my daughter's room. Unless you have gone and married the woman."

Sir Lightwood scoffed. "Married? Why would I marry her?"

"Why would you bring her into your house?"

"That is none of your business." Sir Lightwood leaned menacingly over the desk where the earl sat.

The earl looked as if the invasion of his person meant nothing. "I am afraid it is very much my business. I remind you the only reason you are allowed to continue our agreement made upon your marriage is for my granddaughters' sake."

"I spend enough time here."

"Really? How many bushels of wheat did the farm yield this year?"

Sir Lightwood stepped back from the desk. "I do not know. I have yet to meet with my steward."

"You mean *my* steward. And Georgiana knows. If you would take time to be a proper caretaker of what you have been entrusted you would know that."

"Of course Georgiana knows. You allow her to go gallivanting around the fields when you are in residence." Sir Lightwood paused his rant to glare at Johnathan. "What is your valet doing here? My servants know better."

The earl nodded at Johnathan. "Mr. Whittaker is not my valet. He is my cousin."

"What kind of cousin?" Sir Lightwood's eyes narrowed.

"One of close relation."

It was as if the world stopped in that moment, and no sound could be heard for the distance of an eternity.

Jane jumped—a needle pricking her finger—when their father's bellow echoed from the library.

Alex sighed and set her stitching aside. "I hoped he would last longer. I will make sure that tea is sent in and try to separate Father from Grandfather. Do you think it is best that we coax Mr. Whittaker out?"

Jane's hand shook as she set her needlework down. "You have not shown him the cider press."

Raised voices continued to come from the library.

"Hurry. It is best Mr. Whittaker not know the full extent of Father's wrath," Alex limped toward the library. She had not limped in weeks. Could father have that affect on her?

A footman stood just outside the partially open door, ready to intervene if necessary.

George nodded at him as he opened the door for her and her sisters. Jane hung back as they entered the room.

"Welcome home, father." Alex stood in front of him, forcing him to acknowledge her. "I trust you will find everything in order. Did you get tea? Cook has made the most delightful apple tarts."

"From fruit your sister picked, no doubt."

George signaled behind her back for Jane to come further into the room and took Alex's place in front of her father. "Have you settled in?"

It was the wrong question to ask.

"No. I have been informed the maid will not make up the primrose room as requested."

"The blue room is available," said Alex, not even earning a glance from her father, who scowled at Jane.

"Do not hide behind your sisters. Step up." Father's tone lacked any note of kindness.

Why must he always take his anger out on Jane? George stepped back and allowed Jane to greet Father.

"I thought I told you to wear anything but grey and brown. Our guests will mistake you for the staff."

The footman brought in a fresh pot of tea and a tray of tarts, saving Jane from an answer. The scent of spiced apples filled the air.

Alex took her place on the sofa and nodded to her sisters to sit on either side of her. "Cook is outdoing herself this year. Two new offerings to tempt us."

The nudge George received was not necessary. Keeping the conversation centered on food was the best course. Jane even managed a compliment.

Father glowered as they ate but did not start or continue any further arguments.

George set down her half-empty cup. "Mr. Whittaker, I have not had a chance to show you the cider house. Would you like to accompany me on a tour of it this afternoon before the pressing starts?"

A nod from her grandfather was all it took for Johnathan to accept her invitation.

"We should start now so we can finish before dusk." George stood, and Johnathan followed her lead.

Jane accompanied them out of the room. She paused at the end of the corridor. "I am not going with you. I only thought it was best that Father not have reason to think about a chaperone. I mean, um—" Jane turned away. "You should have one, or maybe not, with absolutely everyone outside harvesting, you will have more than enough."

George touched her sister's shoulder. "Thank you. Are

you sure you do not want to come?"

Jane shook her head. "I am going to check on Sir Galahad. I sent him out with the hounds."

George put on her spencer as the afternoon had cooled. The three walked in silence until they passed the stables where Jane took a different path. The tension from the library silently followed them.

"I must apologize for my father—" she began with no ending in mind.

"Why must you?" asked Johnathan.

"Well, he will not beg forgiveness himself, and I do not wish you to think we, my sisters and I, agree with his actions."

"I have been here for three days and have felt your welcome. I do not hold Sir Lightwood's volatile personality to your control. Despite your warnings, I did not expect—"

She cut him off. "No, nobody ever expects. But it is the lot we have been given. Father and Grandfather will be discussing things for some time, and we thought it best you not be stuck with them."

"So, the cider press? There is nothing better than fresh cider."

"As you have mentioned. There is not much to see since it is not working at the moment. The morning of the fair they will press fresh cider for the contest. Most of the pressing will not happen for another week or so after the apples are sorted."

They reached a damp section of the road, and George lifted her skirt to keep the hem from the mud even as it coated her nicest boots. Ugh—it would be a mess to clean off.

Johnathan slowed and studied George. "Do you need to return and change your clothes?"

George looked down at her dress. "It is finer than what I normally wear out here, but it will do. I will be very careful to avoid pigs."

Johnathan's laugh was tighter than she expected. No doubt having to endure her father's tirade so soon after meeting him added to the tension. "I am going to pretend for a moment that I am the uncouth colonist and ask questions that I probably could not in London's polite society."

George tilted her head and raised a brow, allowing him to continue.

"Is your father always so—so?"

"Do you mean loud and argumentative? No. Sometimes he can be quiet. Very quiet. But he and Grandfather do not get along well. They have not since my mother's death."

"And why is that?"

"Father blames Grandfather for allowing Mother to leave, although he was the one that demanded she return, rain or shine."

"Leave?"

"Oh, I am sorry. Do you not know the whole of the story?" At his shrug, she continued, "Four years ago, my mother took Alex and my only brother William to visit at The Willows. After a sennight, they were to return, but they extended their stay almost a fortnight as the weather was quite wet that spring. Father sent an express demanding that they return home. And the next day, being rainy, again, Mother thought not to delay her return to Kellmore. They were not but two miles from my grandfather's estate when my father's carriage lost a wheel as they rounded a turn, and the carriage tumbled down an embankment. My mother and brother did not survive the resulting crash. Alex, as you know, ended up with her friend Peggy. Then, as you learned today, there is the matter of my father's paramour whom he has kept for more than a decade. I think Grandfather blames my father for many things, not the least of which is breaking my mother's heart. Father is not the most discreet of men."

Johnathan walked along silently.

"Did I shock you, cousin?"

"I did not believe you would talk about your father so openly."

"Father's reputation preceded Phil and Alex to London and kept doors closed to them. Phil's husband was forbidden to court her because of it. I believe it is far better to acknowledge impediments than to pretend they do not exist. And as you have witnessed for yourself, an explanation is in order. Especially if you are granted the earldom. There are also financial arrangements between the men that have changed over the last few years. Father has less say in the doings at Kellmore than he once had. I am not privy to them all, but there will likely be an argument over that issue as well."

They passed the fence surrounding the press house.

Johnathan paused at the gate. "Pardon my asking, but I am of the opinion that faithfulness among your British peerage is not exactly expected."

"It is hoped for." She searched her mind for a way to defend her countrymen. "And I know there are some happy marriages. The Godderidges, for example, are one that is quite happy by all accounts, and none of the children are aware of any infidelity."

"Would they speak of it?"

"Isabel is a particular friend. There are few secrets I think she would hide from us, although she is closer in age to Phil. Are American men faithful to their wives?"

The skin around his collar turned red. "I cannot speak for all. In my community we are taught to cleave to our wives, but not all do. I believe the expectation is that we will."

They stopped at a shed where barrels full of apples waited. George opened the door. "Here it is. Our cider press which is probably as old as your grandfather. He may have even drank cider pressed by it."

"That is as odd a thought as realizing when I stayed at The Willows I slept in the house he was raised in." Johnathan walked around the large cider press. "Impressive size!"

"It is the largest in the county. After we press our apples, we allow our neighbors and tenants to use it as well."

"That is the same as we do in Massachusetts, only we are usually third or fourth to take our turn, as the press is not ours."

Georgiana gave the handle a turn to see if things were in proper working order. The recently oiled mechanism turned perfectly.

"Do not tell me you run the press as well." Johnathan examined the screw mechanism.

"No, once it is full, I hardly have the strength," she admitted, stepping back at the same time Johnathan did, accidentally bumping his side. He grabbed her elbow to steady her. The same awareness she felt of him yesterday filled her, as did warmth that radiated from where he cupped her elbow. Perhaps she should have forced Jane to join them. But then she would not feel this delightful and perplexing draw to have his hand remain.

EIGHT

Johnathan released Georgiana's arm and stepped back. Although the press house was huge, the space felt smaller with her in it. She moved past him, demonstrating the machinery's workings. He caught the faint scent of apples and lavender. He should focus on learning the estate's operation. Instead, he watched her hands as she explained. How could such delicate fingers manage such hard work as she did?

Cease these thoughts. You are here to save her from her father's poor management, not to... What? Court your cousin? Return to America with an English bride? Both ideas were equally impossible. Were they not?

Their talk of fidelity had him thinking of matrimony, and the woman who stood near him was a more than interesting prospect. Did she have any idea what thoughts filled him when she looked at him with that soft innocence? He was not even entirely sure, but he did not want to let such thoughts grow without more answers. Under the guise of inspecting apples, he walked out of the shed to give their situation more propriety. The last thing he wanted to do was anger Sir Lightwood or the earl by a perceived insult to Georgiana's character.

Georgiana closed the door behind her as she exited. She looked back towards the manor house. "Have you seen the ruins?"

"No, I have not."

She pointed to a hill in the distance. "It is about a two-mile walk. Usually, we go there on horseback. It is too late in the day to go now, but if you wish, we can make a plan to go next week after the fair."

"Do you think I will be at Kellmore that long?"

"I do not see Grandfather leaving before father does. And father will want to make a point." Georgiana sorted through the apples until she found two that looked pristine. She handed him one.

Johnathan took the proffered apple. "I am confused. Your father is a baron, correct?"

"No, he is a baronet, which is lower in rank."

"Still then, should your home not be part of his estate?"

"There is a small estate in Yorkshire where my father grew up. It is what belongs to his title. His widowed sister lives there. By agreement Grandfather allowed him to run Kellmore since it would be Father's one day and Grandfather wanted my mother closer than Yorkshire."

"How long has your Aunt been widowed?"

"Her husband was killed when a French frigate attacked some six years past. He was in the Navy."

"Your father did not ask his sister to come live with you after your mother passed?"

Georgiana looked at him as if the idea had never occurred to her. "Father has never gotten on with his sister. I doubt such an invitation would have been made. Even if she did not have a child of her own."

"A cousin?"

"I have never met him. I think he is seven or eight."

"Surely her living here would have made everyone's life easier. Your aunt could have taken on much of the responsibilities you and your sisters must have. And she—pardon, I over step. I was raised with the notion that family cares for their own." All of his cousins, aunts, uncles, and even Widow Black's children were in and out of each other's lives and homes as often as not. Until his brother had eloped on Johnathan's wedding day with his bride, most of his cousins didn't even bother knocking before entering a house. If he were to court another woman, it would be a very long courtship. He took a small step further away from Georgiana.

She finished a bite of her apple. "I have only seen my aunt once, when my grandfather died, and Father took us to Yorkshire. There was a terrible row between them and my grandmother, for what reason I know not. I was only five then and my aunt was not yet married."

"Help me to understand, if your father is to inherit a title from your mother's father, are they cousins?"

"Distantly. A rather convoluted connection that Jane could unravel for you. It goes another two generations further back than the connection between us. It is not uncommon for much nearer cousins to marry."

It was not that uncommon in America either. As far as he knew, his church did not forbid cousins from marrying, and neither did the church in England. Although nuptials of close cousins were not encouraged by many families. Rumors suggested that marrying into the same lines repeatedly caused madness. "I have heard of cousins closer than us marrying."

"It is hard to think of you as a cousin at all when you are American."

"Admittedly. If it was not for the earl asking me to take his place, I would have no reason to even ask if we could be related." As Jane explained at dinner last night they were third cousins once removed, although most would simply call it fourth cousins.

"True. However, you favor your grandfather's portrait, so I might have wondered."

"You have seen it?"

"I found it in The Willow's attic when I was about ten on one of my expeditions."

"You played in the attic?"

"Grandmother's old dresses with their panniers," George held her skirt out to either side to mimic the style of hoops that sat above each hip, "were so fun to dance in. We mostly tried to knock each other over on turns. I learned to dance the Minuet in them."

"I do not know how to dance the English dances." Johnathan felt heat rise in his neck at the admission.

"Are they greatly different from American dances?" A vee of birds flying overhead caught Georgiana's attention. She stopped to look up.

"I would not know. I have never been to a ball here. I'm afraid I'll embarrass the family at the Harvest Ball."

"The Harvest Ball is much less formal than even one at the Assembly rooms. Have you danced at all?"

"I have attended several dances, but not for some time, and never a ball." The recent war had curtailed all but a few events and festivities—something he doubted she would understand, as it seemed as if English society carried on despite the many wars the British were engaged in.

"We can show you the popular dances tonight. Alex plays very well, and Jane and I often partner. I am afraid I am much better at the men's steps than I am at my own."

"Your sisters would be willing to help me?"

"Of course. It would be much more pleasant than playing cards, especially if father is in a mood."

They returned to the manor house sooner than he thought they would. As they approached the front door, a carriage stood in the front drive. The wails of a woman crying emanated from it. The earl stood at the top of the stairs of Kellmore's entrance flanked by two footmen. Sir Lightwood leaned in the door of the carriage. Georgiana grabbed Johnathan's hand and pulled him into the trees. Silently they circumvented the residence and came round by the stables, entering the house by the door into the library. Miss Lightwood and Miss Jane sat holding books in their hands, but clearly focused on something else.

"Are they still out there?" asked Miss Lightwood, closing her book.

"They were a moment ago." Georgiana sat next to her twin on the settee. She motioned Johnathan to be seated.

"That woman arrived a half hour past. The shouting only lasted for a moment. I am surprised Father has not left with her," said Miss Lightwood.

Miss Jane whispered just loud enough to be heard. "I am surprised Grandfather is still out there."

"Should I do something to aid the earl?" asked Johnathan.

"No!" the sisters answered in unison.

"I am afraid there is nothing that can help when two stubborn men are locked in battle," Miss Lightwood picked up her book again, "except read."

"Or pray," muttered Miss Jane.

The bang of the front door echoed through the house. A moment later, the earl came into the room. "I hope you do not mind. I have called for tea again. I find that I am in need of refreshment. Alexandra, will you tell your housekeeper Sir Lightwood will be staying at the coaching inn and requires his bag be sent over?"

Miss Jane stood. "I will go."

The earl took the seat closest to Johnathan. "I do not wish to pressure you in your choice to seek the earldom, but clearly you can see why I cannot allow my son-in-law to inherit."

After dinner, they convened in the music room where Jane and George, with the help of Johnathan and a footman, moved the furniture out of the way.

Alex sat at the pianoforte and thumbed through her music. "Let us start with this one. It is a simple country dance, and you may be familiar with it."

"Would you like to watch first?" asked George.

Johnathan nodded, and George stood with Jane and worked through the steps of the dance.

"Oh, I know that one!" His excitement filled the room, chasing much of the tension away.

"I was sure you would know some of them," said George as she hopped the next step.

"Are you in need of practice?" asked her grandfather.

Johnathan shook his head. "No, not on that one."

Alex stopped playing. "Here is another dance." She struck a tune.

Johnathan tapped his foot. "I may not be in as much trouble as I thought. This one is familiar to me too."

The very suggestion that George feared came too soon when Grandfather spoke. "You should dance with Georgiana to be sure."

They took their places. Georgiana stumbled more than once, having been so used to dancing the male part. Grandfather partnered with Jane and danced a more sedate version. Thankfully, Alex skipped most of the song, keeping it to the essential steps once through.

For the better part of an hour, they continued through the popular dances. Each time, Johnathan was familiar with the steps, although sometimes with slight variation.

Alex shuffled through her music again. "I do not know that there will be a waltz. Have you ever danced one, Mr. Whittaker?"

"I have."

Grandfather declared in no uncertain terms that Mr. Whittaker should practice in case it was different as well. George looked to Jane, hoping that she would dance this time as his partner. But Jane gave the slightest shake of her head, and George could not ask it of her. Alex started the music, and George was left to dance with Johnathan again. She hoped he would not notice through her gloves that her palms were damp. Finally, she found a reason for gloves that made sense. The waltz, while a lively dance involving several skips and hops, put her face to face and hand to hand with her not-so-mere cousin, more times than she was comfortable with. She hoped all in the room thought the high color in her cheeks was simply from the exercise and not the fluttering that filled her veins.

The final notes played, and Johnathan bowed and thanked all in the room profusely for their help. He waited for George and Jane to sit before he did so.

Alex returned her music to its folder, said something about checking with the butler, and left the room. Grandfather declared it was long past his bedtime and left also, leaving Jane, George, and Johnathan alone.

"I declare you should have no problem at all at our Harvest Ball." George's voice came out much more breathless than she wished.

Johnathan leaned back, looking untouched by the exercise. "I am surprised that I knew so many of your steps. I thought it would all be the minuet and other formal dances."

"There is an occasional minuet or allemande at more formal balls, but this is to be a country dance, so the dances popular in my grandfather's time are not as likely to be played."

"I am glad of that."

Jane looked around at the furniture. "I suppose we must return the furniture to its proper place."

Johnathan helped to move the settee back into place. Jane fetched a footman to help with the other pieces. When the room was set to rights, Jane covered a yawn. George stifled one herself. Johnathan took the hint, thanked them again, and left for his own room.

George checked the front door to be sure it was locked before following Jane up the stairway. Not that she did not trust the butler. With all that had happened, she just wanted the extra warning if father was to return.

"You danced with him all evening. What was it like?" asked Jane.

"Only because Grandfather made me." George opened the door to the room, happy to see a cheery fire waiting for them.

"The two of you made a fine pair."

"Nothing shall come of it. Grandfather has been very clear to him that there is no pressure to marry a granddaughter. That he is to choose for himself. I cannot think that Mr. Whittaker would choose a father-in-law such as our father." The words were meant for herself more than Jane. It had occurred to her that Grandfather was playing the match-maker despite his promise.

Jane sat at the dressing table. "What will happen to us if Mr. Whittaker becomes the next earl?"

"I have not asked. I assume Father will lose whatever agreement he has to live at Kellmore. Likely, he will be forced to move back to Yorkshire. Alex's home in Bath has room for us and Rose. Phil will not forget us, either. However, until we reach our maturity, where we live will be Father's choice. He would be foolish to remove us from Grandfather's influence, if he wishes us to find good matches." As she spoke, a sense of peace filled George. She had not realized she carried some of the same fears as Jane for their future.

"Bath is nice. I suppose Alex and I will be two lovely spinsters."

"Why just you and Alex? I have little chance of finding a match. Our decreased dowries and my hoydenish nature are not in my favor."

Jane brushed out her hair. "Caring for tenants and the land is not hoydenish. You should marry."

"And why not you? You are excellent with the village children."

"Only because they are kind to me. I shall not find a man with the same forbearance."

"Jane, do not think so. We are barely out. We have not even had our first Season. Michael is as kind to you as he is to Phil. There must be other men like him." Johnathan was kind to her as well, but Georgiana could not bring herself to say so.

The hairbrush dropped with a clatter. "I cannot do a Season, George. Father will force me to marry one of his odious friends. I know it, and I will not have the backbone to say no. And since I can barely talk to a man without blushing, how am I to fall in love like Phil? Even if there is another kind man like Michael."

Having no answers, George knelt next to Jane and pulled her into a hug. "Well then, we will be three very merry spinsters, because I refuse to leave you alone."

"Promise me, George, if you find love, you will not keep such an oath."

George leaned back and settled on the floor. "I am loath to promise it, and leave you alone."

"I will not be alone. I will have Alex. And she must have someone to keep her company. Please promise you will not pass on marriage for my sake."

"For your sake, I will promise, though I think my prospects unlikely. If only we were as pretty as Rose. I have no doubt that Rose will be married her first Season, if not before."

Jane picked up the brush and resumed brushing her hair. "I am sad she will not be here with us for the harvest fair."

"Could you imagine her flirtations? Our cousin would not know what to make of her I think."

"We would have both been spared dancing tonight." A smile returned to Jane's face.

They readied themselves and climbed into the large bed they had shared since leaving the nursery. George could not fathom being without Jane. A marriage to someone from a distant part of England and leaving Jane behind would break her heart. However, when she dreamed that night, she dreamed of dancing with a tall colonist with blue eyes and enjoying it far more than she should.

NINE

The sun filtered into Johnathan's room before he dressed. He had debated far too long into the night about whether it was appropriate to don his working clothes again. That is in the few moments when he had not been pondering on the dances with Georgiana. Between the two thoughts, he had lost enough sleep that he ended up sleeping in later than he had done in years, resulting in a series of dreams before finally waking. Dreams which included dancing in his work clothes and not being able to find anything to wear and still dancing, which was much more embarrassing.

He had not been asked to help in the orchards today. At the same time, he had not been told he could not. Better to be out of the household than inside, especially if there were to be a repeat of yesterday. The paper on his desk fluttered as he passed. Unable to sleep last night, he had tried to make a list, Benjamin Franklin style, of the pros-and-cons of becoming an earl.

By the light of day, it offered no more solution than it had by candlelight.

Pro:

1. *Help G. and her family.*
2. *It would help the farmers who would suffer under Sir Light-wood.*
3. *Introduce concepts of the Constitution to England through Parliament.*

The last was a long shot. He was not an expert on the Constitution, or anything for that matter, but he felt compelled to add it after the conversations he had had, and overheard with the treaty delegation.

Con:

1. *Unlikely to see mother and siblings more than once again.*
2. *Will not be able to do physical labor.*
3. *Must promise allegiance to a king?*

It was difficult to weigh the list. The thought of abandoning Georgiana made his gut twist almost as much as not seeing his mother and sisters again. That was perplexing in itself. While she was of marriageable age, she was young. Nearly a decade his junior. Even younger than his former fiancée, Prudence. The thought of her name didn't bring the pain it once had. Prudence, her father had not named her well. Though two years younger than Prudence, Georgiana seemed wiser. He had not missed Georgiana's blush as they touched while dancing. That, along with the moment in the cider house, was enough to make him want to swagger a bit at the thought that she might have feelings for him. Despite what his Prudence said, someone found him at least moderately attractive. Though why Prudence chose to elope with Elias— hearing his brother's name didn't hurt as much either—he'd never fully understand. Perhaps Grandpa was correct, in time they could be friends again. Though if he stayed in England, he would never know. Was that a pro?

The whole king and Parliament went against everything his father fought for. If only he were still alive, so Johnathan could ask an opinion. His grandpa had been of the opinion that sending Johnathan to England was the best choice, but did he understand the earl's plan? Likely not. Grandpa seemed to think this was more about a marriage. During the long voyage made longer by seasickness, it had never occurred to Johnathan he would not be returning. Although there had been a moment or two when he wondered if he would survive the voyage at all. The thought of going back was not pleasant.

No one was in the breakfast room when he arrived, so Johnathan made quick work of an egg and a delicious bun. He was somewhat disappointed that the cook's apple and egg concoction was not among the fare. As he was leaving, a maid entered with the very thing on a plate.

She set it in front of him. "Cook sent this up for you, special."

"Thank you. Send her my compliments."

The maid's face pinked before she hurried away. Perhaps he was not meant to thank her.

After finishing, he hurried to the apple orchard which buzzed with industry. He did not see Georgiana or her sisters.

The steward stood near the wagons tallying the apples. "Mr. Whittaker, I did not expect to see you this morning."

"It seemed like a fine morning for apple picking."

"That it is. Lucas can direct you." The steward nodded to a lanky man Johnathan had met in the fields.

Johnathan fell easily into the work. Picking bushel after bushel. As the sun reached its zenith, Lucas whistled for everyone to take a break. Since he had not asked the cook for a meal, Johnathan kept working.

"That means you too, Yankee Doodle." Lucas stood at the bottom of Johnathan's ladder.

"I came out late. I have no need to stop."

"Maybe so, but the lads wish to ask you questions. Come down."

Johnathan joined the others at the side of the orchard where they sat eating. One man scowled and turned away. Lucas leaned close. "That be Jack. His son was pressed into service two years ago, and he is afraid he is dead."

"Lucas, keep my business to yourself," Jack growled without looking up.

"My condolences. I too know the fear of losing loved ones." Silence met Johnathan's statement.

No one spoke for several minutes.

Lucas spoke up. "Come on, lads, you have been asking questions all week. Now's yer chance to ask them without the earl or the ladies about."

"Is it true that ye come to take the earl's place?" asked a man with carrot colored hair.

"I came because my grandpa asked me to. It is true that the earl hopes to make me an heir."

The men looked sideways at each other. One whispered loudly to the carrot top, "I told you to start with the Indians."

Another man leaned forward. "How can ye be an earl when you are not born here?"

"I have wondered about that myself. I have to swear fidelity to the crown and renounce my American citizenship. It is not going to be an easy process."

"Why would you do that? I heard you say you had your own farm there, and you are more like us than the gents."

"A very good question. May I ask you one in return? I am aware that if I take this radical step, I will be your landlord. Would you want a man who was willing to work alongside you?"

"'Tis not right. We do not mind you now, but it should not be done if you be titled," said the red-haired man.

"I will have a hard time sitting inside watching you work. I suppose there are other things I can do."

A woman sitting on the edge of the conversation stood. "I do not care if ye work with us. Only that ye are honest with us like Miss Georgiana and her sisters."

"I will do my very best." Johnathan nodded at the next man.

"What about those Indians? I heard they shoot people with bow and arrows."

"I have heard the same, but I have never met one in war." Johnathan continued to answer questions about farming and land ownership the best he could throughout the meal.

When lunch was over, he found himself pondering the entire British system. Rents? Tenants? One person owning land they never worked. Of course, he was aware of the practice in some areas of America, especially the southern states where they relied on slavery. Was tenant farming any better? While it was possible to free one's slaves, how did one free their tenants? He could not sell the land that belonged to the earldom. If he didn't employ them how would they live?

"Have you seen the blue buntings?" asked Isabel from behind an armload of red cloth.

"No," answered George, "but there was some green in the crate near Jane. You would think after years of hosting the harvest fair, we could put away the buntings in a semblance of organization."

"We say that every year," said Alex from her seat where she was repairing a ripped cloth, "and every year we tear it down, saying we are so tired, and never do a very good job of it."

Lady Godderidge entered through the porch door. The sounds of hammering filtered after her. "Do you have everything sorted yet?"

"We are still missing the blue buntings," replied Isabel. "And the new ones we ordered are in need of ironing."

"Nearly finished," called Jane from where she stood near the fireplace helping a maid iron out the wrinkles. In theory, they were to be setting up for the harvest fair without the help of maids, yet no one really wanted to see Lady Godderidge, her daughter, daughter-in-law, or the Lightwoods ruin something because they had not developed the skills to perform daily tasks.

"It looked like they had new lumber this year. Are they building new booths?" asked Alex.

Lady Godderidge sorted a pile of ribbons. "Susanna has decided to add a few new ones this year."

Isabel snorted and looked heavenward. She found her eldest brother's wife to be far too prudish for country life. Susanna seemed nice enough, but she was a bit more fastidious than any of the Godderidges. She frowned whenever someone didn't use George's or Alex's proper names.

"I saw that, young lady," said Lady Godderidge. "Susanna and David will be responsible for the harvest fair after your father and I are gone. And you will be married and likely living far away. It is best she learn things now."

"Mother, do not talk that way," Isabel protested. "It is not like you and Father are old and decrepit at all. You just choose not to live here at Leadon Hill and pass on the tradition."

"We do live here," Lady Godderidge corrected. "We just do not live here all year. Your father is spending more and more time in London, even when Parliament is out of session, and with your youngest brothers at Eton, it hardly makes sense for us to—"

"I know, Mother, you have explained it before," Isabel interrupted, "but I am glad we will be here at least through Twelfth Night. I prefer Leadon Hill to anyplace in England."

"That you may, but it will not be your home for long, as you must go where your husband lives. Girls should never grow too attached to their childhood home." Lady Godderidge's warning hit George. How could she live anywhere else?

"But I—" Isabel's protest fell short due to Susanna entering from the corridor, followed by a footman carrying a crate.

"We found another one," Susanna announced.

Isabel set aside her armful of buntings. "I hope it contains the blue buntings."

Georgiana bit her lip and looked at Jane, who also held back a smile. Isabel's exclamation upon opening the crate filled the room. It was as if, for a moment, the blue buntings were the most important thing that there ever was.

"Ouch." Jane blew on her finger before sticking it in her mouth.

The maid hurried to Jane's side, removing the iron from the fabric before inspecting the burn. George hurried over, followed by everyone else.

Susanna took charge. "Come, our cook will have something for that burn."

Isabel sighed. "I suppose that means one of us will need to take Jane's place."

"I will." George volunteered, more to avoid the making of the fabric rosettes. George folded a cloth to wrap around the iron's handle, picked up the iron, and started where her sister left off.

"You are so good at that. I am afraid I have no aptitude for that at all. Last year, I put so many scorch marks in my first bunting that mother told me I was never to touch an iron again. I would be in so much trouble if I fell in love with the stable boy. His clothes would be burned through, and we would starve as I do not know how to cook," said Isabel.

Lady Godderidge clucked her tongue. "Isabel, what a thing to say."

"It is true. I read a novel only last week where the heroine ran off with the farmhand, who fortuitously was an heir to a large fortune, as she burned their very first meal. He was rather mean not to tell her for a week that he was a gentleman, and she was in tears. They had eaten nothing but porridge. I decided then and there that I would have left him after a day. I could never love someone so much that I would go hungry for a week trying to learn how to cook."

Alex set aside her sewing. "Then you would not be truly in love, would you? If you are not willing to go through the hard things as well as the easy."

"I could be in love, but I might kill him with my attempts to cook. Then where would we be?" said Isabel.

Everyone, including the maid, laughed at that.

George switched out her iron for a hotter one. "Before I ran off with such a man, I would learn all I could from Cook and the maids."

"You are far ahead of me on that count. You can cook eggs and porridge," said Alex.

"I can churn butter, too. Cook gave me that job often enough. None are skills that will help me during the Season, will they?" George didn't look up from her ironing.

"What skills?" Susanna asked as she entered the room with Jane whose hand was wrapped in a white cloth.

"Cooking and cleaning."

"Why ever would you think of such a thing?" Susanna sat and immediately started making rosettes at an astonishing speed. "There are much better topics to discuss. Did I tell you that my David visited with Mr. Dalrymple yesterday, and he is coming to the harvest fair?"

"Of course he is coming. He would be a fool not to." Isabel's tone held an uncharacteristically derisive tone.

Alex stood and shook out a bunting. "He seemed very amiable at church."

"Was he the one with the blue waistcoat?" asked Jane.

"Sardinian blue to be exact. He does not have the height for that color," said Isabel.

"Isabel." Lady Godderidge's sharp rebuke was enough for even George to stop her work. "I did not raise you to find fault."

"I cannot help it, mama. He is so short." Isabel was not usually so negative.

"I thought he was almost as tall as Father," said Jane.

Isabel stood. "I am as tall as your father. I abhor looking at a man and seeing the top of his head."

"Come now, at most he could not be more than this much shorter than you." Susanna held up her fingers a hair's width apart.

"He was wearing heeled boots."

"As were you. If you would listen to me and have the bootmaker give you lower heels, you would not be as tall." Lady Godderidge walked to Isabel's side and lifted her skirt five inches. "There is no reason for heels that high. This Season, we are not commissioning any boots with a heel of more than an inch."

"Mama." Isabel stomped her foot.

George covered her mouth to keep from laughing.

Lady Godderidge waved her daughter back. "Enough of this. If you do not wish to dance with Mr. Dalrymple, then who?"

"Mr. Whittaker is on my list. He is tall enough for all of my shoes."

"The American?" asked Susanna.

Isabel twirled across the floor. "Of course. Have you seen his strong chin?"

George looked down at her ironing.

"Isabel!" snapped Susanna. "That is not proper."

"What? Dancing with a guest?"

"No. Associating with an American. How could you?" Susanna rushed out in a flurry of skirts.

George felt as stunned as Jane and Alex looked.

Lady Godderidge sighed. "Forgive her. Her brother died two years ago fighting in the war."

Obviously, Johnathan was not responsible for any war, or killing, but how many would blame him anyway?

TEN

Johnathan's shoulders burned. After only 15 minutes of cranking, the strain from the old apple pulper pressed his arms to his limit. Such a small pulper was inadequate to feed the press, which Georgiana had shown him two days past.

"Put your back into it!" yelled Lucas.

Johnathan's muscles strained as he attempted to speed up the pulper. Someone switched out the bucket below, and the kid in charge of dropping apples into the funnel dropped them faster. Johnathan switched positions.

"Hey, Yankee Doodle, tired already? Faster. Got to get the press going."

Johnathan tried to smile, instead, his jaw clenched. A burning sensation started to fill the muscles in his right shoulder. He adjusted his position a bit more to put more of the strain on his left. He would not stop.

"There you go, that's it. We might get a gallon by the end of the day."

"You need another pulper," Johnathan said, pausing between each word.

"What Yank?"

Johnathan dropped the handle and shook out his arms. "You heard me. The first thing I will do if I become earl is buy you a new pulper."

Lucas slapped his leg and laughed as Johnathan rubbed his shoulder. The other men joined Lucas's laughter.

"You do not need to do that, Yankee Doodle. We already have another one."

"What?" Johnathan asked, incredulous.

Lucas pointed to the other side of the shed. Where a two-man team cranked on a large pulper that allowed the apples to be mashed and ground in preparation to meet the cider press by the bushelful."

Johnathan let out a laugh. "So that little pulper you had me working on?"

"As useless as a dull ax," said Lucas.

"Then why?"

"A test of your fortitude." Lucas said with a grin. "All the new lads take a turn."

"Did I pass?"

Lucas slapped Johnathan's back, and a muscle retaliated. "You did well Yankee Doodle."

Johnathan windmilled his arm backward, trying to relieve the strain on the muscle. "Now?"

"We give you the honor of pressing the first apples—the ones you pulped," said Lucas.

Johnathan scooped up the bucket of apple pulp using his left arm and walked into the cider shed, where he dumped it under the press.

"Hey, lads!" called Lucas. "We're ready to start."

Everyone gathered around the mouth of the cider shed. The sounds of the pulper outside ceased. Johnathan was surprised he had not heard the sounds of the larger apple pulper while he had been grinding with the small one.

Johnathan grabbed the handle that Georgiana had shown him the other day. Lucas clucked and shook his head.

"No, not that way. It'll take us forever." Lucas inserted a large handle into another port. "Now we work together."

At Lucas's signal, Johnathan pushed his end as Lucas pushed the other. Gears ground, and the familiar squish and squeak of the apples filled the air as the first stream of cider ran down the funnel into the waiting cask. A cheer went up. Lucas and Johnathan proceeded to turn the crank until it would turn no farther.

They reversed direction, releasing the pressure, and a woman used a long stick to adjust the fabric-wrapped apple pulp, and the men repeated the process of pressing the apples. After a fourth press, Lucas determined there was no juice left to extract. He took a tin cup from the wall and poured fresh cider into it.

"Well, Yankee Doodle, I do not see Miss Georgiana about, so I think you should have the first drink," Lucas handed him the tin cup, and Johnathan swallowed back the sweet cider. Holding the cup above his head, he declared, "Best I've ever had."

Everyone shared a laugh as they passed the cider around in four or five cups. Just then, Georgiana rushed around the building, slightly out of breath.

"Did I miss it?" she asked.

"You would just be in time for the second cup," Lucas said with a grin.

Johnathan filled his cup again and passed it to Georgiana.

"Second cup?" she asked, raising an eyebrow as she accepted the newly filled mug.

"Why, yes," Lucas said with a chuckle. "We decided Yankee Doodle deserved the first after we had him grind apples on the old grinder."

"You did not!" she exclaimed, her eyes twinkling with amusement.

"Had to test his mettle, Miss." Lucas replied with a wink.

Georgiana lifted the cup to her lips and drank deeply. As she did, her gaze flicked to Johnathan over the rim of the cup. Did she realize her lips were now touching the same spot his had just been?

"Delicious! Best yet!" She held up the cup in triumph before passing it on. A drop of fresh cider clung to her lip before her tongue flickered out to remove it.

A wholly inappropriate desire to taste the cider on her lips welled up in him. He turned away, banishing the thought. But like Lady Macbeth yelling at her laundry, the image refused to fade. Seeing that the small pulping machine he used earlier stood idle, he strode over to it. Perhaps another burning muscle would banish the thought. Just as he reached the machine Georgiana's voice stopped him.

"Mr. Whittaker?"

He turned.

"Grandfather asked that you come see him as soon as is convenient."

"I should clean—" he waved his hand at the pulper.

"No need for that. The younger boys will be working it," said Lucas.

"Thank you for the honor." Johnathan nodded at the work-hardened man.

Georgiana waited near the road. Something struck him as different. The breeze lifted a strand of her hair and she tucked it out of her face. Her hair was not in braids or tied back and her dress was a proper ladies gown. Or at least it resembled what her sisters wore. The pale green suited her.

She fell into step beside him. "I'm glad to see they like you so well."

Still washing out the image of kissing her from his mind he did not answer.

"Lucas would not have put you on the old pulper unless they accepted you."

"Were you there?" He would have noticed her.

"No, I arrived after the first cider came out." She stepped closer to him.

Her hand was within a hair's breadth of his. He widened the distance between them. "I am surprised you were not helping earlier."

"We are off to Leadon Hill to finish preparations. I wanted to stay and help Cook, but Alex says I am expected."

That explained her nicer clothing. "I should not delay you."

"I have to wait for Alex and Jane to finish packing the tart boxes. I am not allowed to help, as I have a tendency to eat too many. I do not think trying one of each flavor is too many."

He could not help himself, he laughed.

"Are you mocking me?"

"No, not at all. I agree with you. It is necessary to try one of each kind."

"I knew you would understand." She touched his arm.

He smiled down at her. No, he did not understand at all. What was it about Georgiana that could drive every other thought out of his mind?

It was well past dark when the Godderidge's carriage returned George and her sisters to their home.

The butler met them at the door. "His lordship retired shortly after eating. I believe Mr. Whittaker has as well. Do you require anything?"

"Just my bed." Jane stifled a yawn.

Alex rubbed her hip again. "If someone could send up some of Mrs. Green's tea, please."

"Shall I ask them to draw you a bath as well, Miss?"

"No. But I would not mind a poultice if it is not too much trouble." The exertions of the day strained Alex. Tomorrow would be worse.

"I will see that everything is sent up immediately." The butler turned to George. "And you, Miss Georgiana?"

She gathered her sister's wraps and hung them over another chair. "I agree with Jane. All I require is my bed."

George held out her arm for Alex. Jane moved to her other side. Together, the three climbed the stairway.

"I did not know it was possible for anybody to be so particular about rosettes," sighed Jane. "I will be happy to never see another one again in my life."

"Agreed," George said.

Alex giggled. "Poor Susanna. She's beside herself trying to put this together. We must be kind to her."

"I find it terribly hard to be kind to her when she's being so rude about Johnathan." Sometime in the past day, Jane started referring to their cousin by his Christian name.

The particular connection George felt with him faded, knowing that her sister also shared the privilege of no longer keeping to formal names.

"Whom we're quick to defend. But Susanna lost her brother and must still be grieving for him." Alex's strained voice betrayed the pain she felt. She should have agreed to a bath.

"His death is not Johnathan's fault." How many times had George repeated the statement in her mind today?

Alex stopped halfway up the stairway, clenching both her sisters' arms tighter. "I know, however, all she sees is Johnathan being an American."

When had Alex commenced using his name? Perhaps there was no intimate connection at all.

A sound in the corridor above them made the three sisters look up.

"Sir Galahad, is that you?" asked Jane.

A moment later, the dog appeared.

"There you are, you naughty boy. I suppose you have already been sleeping in my bed."

The sisters continued to the top of the stairway. George was sure she heard something down the corridor, but she saw nothing moving in the shadows. Light spilled out from under Johnathan's door. He must still be awake.

They turned to Alex's room. The need for Mrs. Green's tea must have been anticipated, as Mrs. Green herself brought it. A steaming bath also awaited Alex. Protests or not, Alex needed to allow the servants her grandfather paid handsomely to nurse her when necessary.

"I'll see to her now. Go get your sleep," Mrs. Green said as she ushered Jane and George out of the room.

"I still think Susanna's being terribly unfair. She's never even met Johnathan." Jane flopped down in the dressing chair to remove the pins from her hair.

"We can hardly change her opinion of him."

"You did precious little to change her mind. You left me to defend him."

"I saw no reason to interrupt. You were laying out our cousin's cause admirably."

Jane turned in the chair. "You know him better. You should have defended him more."

Not possible. If she had, then Isabel, Lady Godderidge—or worse—Susanna might have seen the blush from the heat of her cheeks. "I defended him yesterday when the subject came up."

"Barely that. At least she did not have him uninvited. For a moment this afternoon, I thought she would."

George stood behind Jane, removing her own pins. "She might have, if Lady Godderidge had not been there. Do you think he will face this often? Anger because he's an American?"

"Likely. That's going to be one of Grandfather's most difficult things to explain in Parliament, is it not it? Convincing them that an American should be an earl."

"Better him than Father."

"If Johnathan is declared an earl, then Father will be unbearable." Jane set her brush down. "I almost wish Grandfather had not started this."

"You have seen how Father mishandles this estate. If Grandfather had not taken back many of Father's responsibilities, the place would be in ruins. Can you imagine Father managing the entire earldom?" George picked up the brush and ran it through Jane's hair. "We all know exactly what type of earl Father would make, and it would be a disgrace. Which is why Grandfather cannot let it happen."

"Can you be sure?"

George could not answer Jane's question. She did not truly understand nearly as much about financial affairs as Alex did. If Grandfather's plan failed, Father would became the next Earl of Whitstone. She would beg Father to allow her to stay at Kellmore and oversee the farm and tenants as she had been doing. It would be odd for a woman to do it, but Father had proven he did not care enough to do it himself. And he would live at The Willows, since it was a day's journey closer to Town and the more opulent home of the two. That would be one way to save the land and people she loved.

With Jane's hair finished, they traded places so Jane could brush out George's tangles.

George continued with her thoughts. It would be much better if Johnathan succeeded. But where would that leave her? And this growing infatuation? If only she could have been more ladylike, such as her twin.

She looked at Jane's reflection in the mirror. Johnathan must have a care for her as well if Jane called him by his name. She had not heard Johnathan refer to her sister as anything other than "Miss Jane." However, she was not always with them. Perhaps Johnathan had private moments with Jane too. A moment when they nearly touched and anticipation filled the air. It hurt her heart to think–

Jane must like Johnathan or she would not have defended him. As much as George wished to scream at the unfairness of both of them liking the same man, she was the eldest of the two of them and she promised to see to Jane's happiness after Mother's death. Johnathan was a good man. George loved them both enough to step aside for Jane.

ELEVEN

cock crowed. The desire to hide under his covers
flickered through Johnathan's mind. The days spent
working to help bring in the harvest had taken a toll
on his body. He had become soft on the journey to England
and the time not laboring while at The Willows. Some of
his aches could be attributed to the pulper from yesterday.
They were worth it—every ache was worth it—especially
for the acceptance he had found among the earl's tenants.

He sat up and placed his feet on the cool floor. The fire
had not yet been lit, so perhaps he had not slept in as late as
he thought. As he stood, a throb in his toe reminded him of
his hasty escape in the corridor last night and the side table
leg that nearly led to his discovery. However the Lightwood
sisters had not heard him—or at least not seen him. He was
sure George had looked his way.

His mother always said that eavesdroppers would come
to no good. The throbbing toe served as a painful reminder
of that. It was not a lesson he would soon forget.

Nor was he likely to forget the pain of realizing that a near
neighbor had lost a brother in the same war that he had

avoided. It was understandable that whoever this Susanna was, she was not in favor of him being here.

Would the members of Parliament who needed to approve him side with those like Susanna? Had they lost their own children and brothers in the wars?

How could he overcome that obstacle?

A tap on the door paused his musings. The young house boy, who had started his fire the last few days came in.

"Sorry, Mr. Whittaker. I meant to be here before you woke."

"Not your fault. I have always been an early riser." He almost added that at home no one ever started a fire for him as there was no fireplace in his attic room.

"I'll bring some water up in a moment. Should I fetch the valet?"

"I only need water. Thank you."

The boy nodded and left.

Johnathan looked at the clothing the earl's valet had laid out for the harvest fair. A new white linen shirt and pressed cravat? There were supposed to be contests, archery, apple bobbing, and others. How could he participate in any of the festivities dressed in fine clothing? Maybe he was not meant to participate. Georgiana said something about competing in an archery contest, so contests were not closed to him. He searched for one of his older shirts. He could wear it for the day and change for the dance. Hadn't Jane or Alexandra mentioned taking a second dress?

Squeals of children mingled with those of the small bovine as the race began. George watched, remembering her own recent pig chase. Never again.

"It looks like they're getting practice in while they're young." Johnathan followed the sisters, carrying a crate of pies. George tried not to notice how his arms flexed with the weight, or how his colonial accent had grown rather pleasing to her ear.

"Perhaps that was my problem the other day—I did not start young enough." George carried a basket of baked goods in her arms. "I must get these over before the judging commences, or Cook will burn my food for the next month."

"She would not really do that, would she?" Johnathan's blue eyes twinkled with amusement.

"Likely not, but I do not want to find out for myself." George looked away when she caught Isabel watching their exchange with interest. She did not need her neighbor making assumptions, especially when she expressed an interest in Johnathan.

From the balcony of Leadon Hill, Lord Godderidge and his wife observed the race. Susanna stood next to David Godderidge, doing the same. Susanna glanced the direction of the newcomers but did not acknowledge them. Isabel made up for her sister-in-law's snub, waving at George and her sisters. Alex, being less encumbered than Jane or George, raised her walking stick in response.

After the sisters dropped off the baked goods at the various tables, they went their own ways. Alex joined Lady Godderidge, where she would be safe from being toppled by running children. The vicar's wife whisked away Jane to help with some item or other. Leaving George to escort Johnathan.

Isabel hurried across the lawn to join them. Her smile reflected the surrounding excitement. "So glad you are here! Welcome, Mr. Whittaker. George, the archery competition is in half an hour. Are you going to participate this year?"

"I believe I have a title to defend, do I not?" For the last three years—to her father's annoyance—she had won no less than third place from shooting an apple off a post in homage to William Tell. Last year she took the first place prize.

"You only won because Edward was not here last year." Isabel worked her way between George and Johnathan.

"I only win because the huntsmen have a contest of their own. I could best Edward if he were not at sea."

"When my brother returns, we shall have to host a competition to see if you have really gotten better than him." Isabel turned her attention to Johnathan, laying a hand on his arm. "What about you, Mr. Whittaker? Do you think you could best George?"

George's stomach tightened at Isabel's familiar gesture, though George could not quite explain why. Perhaps it was due to the fact that she was quite sure Isabel and Johnathan had never been formally introduced. Something George was not going to remedy.

"I do not have a bow."

"Oh, we have several. You must try! I'll show you." Isabel took him by the arm and marched across to the archery field, leaving George to retrieve her own bow from the Godderidge's footman.

The familiar curve of the bow brought back memories of her mother, who had arranged for Lady Godderidge to store the finely crafted bow after Father had snapped her first bow in half when she was eleven. What would mother think of her now? Would she shame her for competing against men? Likely not. If only Mother were here to help sort out George's feelings around Johnathan. Mother would see the wisdom in arranging things between him and Jane. Perhaps that is why seeing him with Isabel pained her, because it would hurt Jane. George shook the thought away. If she pondered too long upon mother, she would be unable to concentrate on her target.

The archery competition began with the children aiming at large paper targets. When they finished, the adults aimed for a single apple on the top of a post. It took some time to give each person a turn, even with five targets. Johnathan's form was excellent. His arrow pierced the center of his apple.

"Yes!" Isabel cheered the loudest as Johnathan returned to the line of archers.

When George's turn came, she felt unusually nervous.

"You will not win it from us again this year, Miss Lightwood," said a farmer George recognized from church.

"I can only try." She nocked her arrow and aimed, acutely aware of Johnathan's presence. Her hands trembled slightly as she steadied her bow. Ridiculous. She had shot hundreds of arrows. But never with those intense blue eyes watching. She was not trying to impress him. Still, her heart leapt when she heard his quiet "well done" after her shot.

The fourth round narrowed the final competitors down to five; Johnathan, the farmer who had spoken to her earlier, Mr. Dalrymple, Lucas, and her. They let their arrows fly. Mr. Dalrymple missed, leaving four. It took two more rounds before Lucas missed his shot, leaving three.

"Miss Lightwood, ye will not be winning today." The farmer's jovial teasing brought a smile to her face.

David Godderidge shouted for the three remaining archers to take their places. The farmer went first, his apple exploding upon impact.

"Way to show him." Father's booming voice shattered the moment. When had he arrived? And obviously in his cups. "Cannot let that troublesome American win, can we?"

Next to her, Johnathan stiffened, his perfect form faltering. His shot went wide, and something in George's chest ached at his defeated expression as he stepped away.

George took her place. The fun was gone. If she missed, the farmer would win and his family could likely use the prize more than her. A win by the farmer would help others forget about the American comment. Her mind made up, George nocked her arrow and aimed. The crowd quieted. She hit her target. The arrow stuck in the post an inch below the apple. The farmer was the first to shout his joy.

George could not help but smile at him. The footman collected her bow, and she turned to accept Jane's condolences. Instead, her father rushed between the twins and grabbed George by the shoulders.

"Where did you get that bow? I shall break it in two!"

"I am enjoying the fair. As for the bow, the Godderidges's footman has already collected it along with most of the others." The half-truth tasted bitter.

Father dragged her toward the targets, away from prying ears—including Mr. Whittaker's concerned gaze. "Do you realize the scandal if you had won again? No man wants a wife who can best him at a man's sport."

Her thoughts flew to Johnathan's appreciative "well done." There was one man who would not care. Reasoning with Father that there were many ladies of the ton that excelled in archery would not help. George bit her tongue.

"I have half a mind to send you home for the rest of the festivities. However, you are the only one who can catch Mr. Dalrymple's eye. I just learned he has over eight thousand a year. If you can catch him, I can save on not sending you and Jane to Town for a Season. Sending Jane is a waste, anyway. Our Lady of Perpetual mourning will never catch a husband. Just as well. I need someone to care for me when I grow old." The stench of drink wafted off of him.

George's stomach churned at her father's casual cruelty toward Jane. It was father's fault she wore only colors suitable for half mourning. If George found a husband—one of her own choosing, her mind whispered traitorously—she would make sure Jane was welcome as often as she wished. That might be her best reason for marrying. Or she could find Jane a suitable husband. Johnathan would be just that for her twin. The irony of Jane becoming a lady above father's station would be all the better.

"This is not a total loss." Father spoke more to himself than to her. "Mr. Dalrymple has taken notice of you. You will spend the rest of the day ingratiating yourself to him."

"Why should I?"

"Because you could spare your sister a Season. One you know, she would rather not take. Although there is another option in Yorkshire." Father's tone hinted at something neither she nor her sisters would like. Father's description of the home of his youth was as cold as he was.

Send her sister away? Jane would cower at that idea. They had never spent a full day apart. How would Jane fare such a separation? Father was not supposed to arrange marriages, but he may find a way around the Duke of Aylton's threat made the night Phil escaped from the inn. The thought that their father was tricking his cousin into marriage outraged the duke. Phil's integrity and bravery so impressed the duke that he had become her champion.

"I will do my best." For Jane. There were worse ways to spend the day, she supposed. Mr. Dalrymple's interest could not last that long if she managed to capture it. But would it last long enough to keep her sister from being sent away?

TWELVE

lthough he could tell the status of the harvest fair attendees by their clothing, Johnathan was surprised at how, at least for the moment, the classes mixed. His understanding was that the peerage had little to do with those of lower social standing. The earl sat among a group of men near his age who appeared to be mostly farmers and tradesmen. Perhaps living in England would not be as isolating as he thought. He had much more in common with the men who worked for their living than he did the likes of Mr. Dalrymple, who was the only single man of elevated status near Johnathan's age. The gentleman held himself aloof, not mingling with anyone. Oddly, Miss Georgiana seemed determined to cross the man's path at every chance.

Thus Johnathan was left to the attentive Miss Godderidge as Jane and Alexandra were occupied elsewhere. Which, all in all, was not a bad position to be in. She did not rush him as they moved from booth to booth. A table laden with pies caught his attention.

"Mrs. James won this year." Miss Godderidge drew his attention to the pie in the center. "She claims her recipe is over two hundred years old. However, I prefer Mrs. Lamb's pie, she is more liberal with the cinnamon. Truly, none of them are ever bad. I believe the judges rotate through the winners because they cannot decide."

"What are those?" Johnathan nodded to the spread beyond.

"New recipes. Scones, biscuits, cakes. Most of them are more experimental in nature. As a child, I chose one with currants..." Miss Godderidge shuddered. "I became ill from the alcohol-soaked fruit, causing me to miss the ball."

Johnathan found his attention wandering to where Miss Georgiana stood, laughing at Mr. Dalrymple's side. The sound carried across the festival grounds, musical and light. What could be so amusing about the dour man's conversation?

"I'll choose with care. Did you make any of these?" he asked Miss Godderidge, forcing himself to focus on their conversation.

Miss Godderidge hid her shock quickly. "I have never learned to cook or bake."

Of course not. Of all the ludicrous questions he could have asked. He caught another glimpse of Miss Georgiana, who was now walking with Mr. Dalrymple toward the storytellers' area, her hand resting lightly on his arm.

"I suppose every woman in America cooks?"

"My mother employs a girl who helps with meals and cleaning. We purchase our bread from the baker. But yes, my sisters are all well versed in the basics of baking and cooking, as am I."

"You know how to cook?" Full of disbelief, her wide eyes mocked him.

"Enough to survive on my own."

"What a peculiar thought."

Not to learn how to take care of one's basic needs, or that

one would want those skills? A question he did not dare ask.

The announcement of the storytellers starting their activities saved him from further awkwardness. Johnathan sat on a blanket with Miss Godderidge, Alexandra, and Jane. Several children joined them. Miss Georgiana, however, chose to sit in the chairs near the back of the field with Mr. Dalrymple. Johnathan found himself straining to hear her reactions to the stories over the general murmur of the crowd.

The first tales were brief—a massive pumpkin that became a seaside house, ghosts in potato bins, and talking rabbits. Then Grandmother Grimes took the seat, holding up a single red apple. Her tale of a determined little pig seeking apples brought laughter from the crowd, especially when she acted out the pig's failed attempts at flying and his final mad dash through the orchard chased by a lady. Everyone looked at Georgiana who blushed, her eyes meeting his for just a moment before she looked away, her cheeks coloring slightly as she turned her attention back to Mr. Dalrymple.

Of course, Grandmother Grimes won the prize: a bushel of apples, which she promised not to feed to any pigs.

Johnathan spent the rest of the afternoon wandering through the stalls, trying various delights and occasionally catching glimpses of Miss Georgiana through the crowd. He made the mistake of asking a woman for her tart recipe. She brandished a fork in the air as she informed him that no American could ever make her dessert.

A little boy tugged at his pants. "Is it true you're from the colonies?"

"Yes."

"Did you come to invade us?"

"No."

"Then why are you here?"

In England? Or at the fair, where he was far too distracted by Miss Georgiana giving her attention to Mr. Dalrymple?

The boy would not have been interested in the long answer, so Johnathan had kept it simple. "I am here to try your cider. I've heard it is the best in all of England."

"It is the best. My father helped make it." The boy ran off.

Johnathan smiled after him. The question, "Why are you here?" was never quite far from his mind.

The last of the afternoon sunlight reflected off the white furniture trimmed with gold in Isabel's bedroom. George sat as Jane reworked her hair. What would she do without her sister? The thought hurt too much to contemplate. Tonight she would do her best to flirt again with a man she knew by little more than name after her efforts this afternoon failed. Mr. Dalrymple spoke little and seemed to endure her presence out of good breeding. How much longer could she keep throwing herself at him? There must be a better way to fulfill father's request. How did the ladies of the ton flirt? Not for the first time that hour, George wished for the guidance of her mother.

Isabel entered wearing her favorite blue dress from last Season, and her abigail followed. "I cannot believe you three are not putting on different gowns."

Alex looked up from the novel she borrowed. "There is not much of a point for me. It is not as though I collected much dirt, and I will not be dancing, anyway."

"Jane and George, you brought a change of clothing," Isabel pointed out.

"Yes, we did," Jane replied, "but after Father commanded I change and try to ensnare Mr. Dalrymple, I have no desire whatsoever to do his bidding."

George dropped the hairbrush. "He asked you to engage Mr. Dalrymple too?"

Alex slammed her book shut. "Father's not supposed to be arranging anything. He cannot force Mr. Dalrymple to choose one of us."

Jane adjusted a pin in her own hair. "It is not as if he would be interested in me when he has you."

"Just because he's not supposed to arrange anything does not mean he will not. We should know that by now," George balled her hands into fists. Since Jane seemed so unconcerned, had father issued the same threat she received? Should she tell?

"I do not see your problem. He is taller than either of you and handsome enough, I suppose," said Isabel, whose height nearly matched the man in discussion. "And you would be living in the county. According to my maid, Mr. Dalrymple intends to stay here for the more part of the year."

"I have no interest in him." Jane brushed an invisible bit from her skirt. "It is wrong to capture his attentions when I do not want them."

"How can you know if you want them if you have never spoken with him? You pass judgment, yet, if we had judged Michael by our first conversation, Phil would not be married now." Alex crossed the room to her sisters and put a hand on Jane's shoulder. "You should change, if nothing else, so Father believes you are trying. I do not know what game he is playing. Mr. Dalrymple is not one of his gaming friends. It will not hurt either of you to at least converse with the man and dance a single dance."

"I had not planned to dance at all. I only brought a gown to please grandfather since he had it made for me." Jane lifted the palest of grey dresses from the bed. So pale, most would call it white.

"Did father threaten you?" asked George as she smoothed out her primrose gown.

Jane held up her new gown, hiding the brown one from view. "No. Sir Galahad is safe."

"One dance will not hurt you. If Mr. Dalrymple is a gentleman, he will ask each of us to dance. Including me." Isabel lifted her skirt. "I suppose I should put on my low-heeled boots. At least we are out of doors or mother would insist on slippers. Your cousin is taller than me. I must say, he's probably the most handsome man here."

"Is he?" George feigned ignorance.

"Of course he is. Even you should be able to see that. Do you have any claims on him?" asked Isabel.

"Definitely not." Jane carried her gown to the changing screen.

"You know I have no claims on anyone," said Alex.

"And you, George?" asked Isabel, pressing the idea more than she should.

"How could I? He's only been here a few days." It was good to remind herself of that truth. Johnathan should be Jane's. Isabel's abigail helped George switch dresses.

"But you have spent the most time with him." Jane's muffled words came from behind the changing screen.

"Of course I have. Grandfather has had me showing him all of our farming methods. Things he absolutely must know if he is—" She trailed off. It was common knowledge that Grandfather intended to see him into the earldom.

"Is to stay in England. That's what your grandfather intends, is it not? For him to stay here and take his title?" asked Isabel.

"You know?" said Alex.

"Of course. Your grandfather was talking to my father. He is a member of the House of Lords."

"I did not realize that they would be discussing matters so soon. Will your father vote for him?" George held her breath, waiting for the answer.

"He has not said. But I think if Mr. Whittaker proves himself to be a gentleman, Father would prefer him as a neighbor to your own father. No offense meant. Susanna would persuade him otherwise, but Father explained Johnathan was not responsible for the whole of the wars the Crown fights. Father says he will wait to see if the young colonist"—Isabel's voice took on a deeper note—"is worth his salt."

George could not help but laugh. "Well, if it's of any help, I do believe Johnathan—"

"On first names already?"

"We are cousins," George defended herself. "Anyway, as I was saying, Johnathan understands crop rotation, planting, and he has been very good with our tenants. They're not sure what to make of him. Whether that's because he's American or supposed to be a gentleman, I am not sure."

"You're positive you have no claim on him?" asked Isabel again.

"Why would I?" George answered a question with a question.

"Then I suppose you shall not mind if I dance with him this evening," said Isabel.

"As Alex has already pointed out, a gentleman would dance with every lady he could this evening."

"Does he understand the expectations of the evening?" asked Jane.

"I'm not sure." George assumed he would know.

"Did you not explain when you were teaching him to dance?" asked Alex.

"You taught him to dance?" Isabel sat for her maid to change her shoes.

"He already knew most of the dances." George did her best to deflect any questions Isabel might have about such an endeavor, for if her friend thought long upon the matter, she would certainly realize that George taught the majority of the steps and danced with one man for an entire evening—something that simply was never done.

The memory of their dance practice flooded back unbidden—his hand at her waist had felt different from when she practiced with her sisters. Warmer. More... Present. She tried to push away thoughts of how his eyes crinkled slightly at the corners when he smiled, or how secure his grip felt when he turned her. Or how she had nearly forgotten the next step, distracted by his proximity.

The first strains of a violin tuning filtered in through the open window.

Isabel stood and shook out her skirt. "They must be gathering. We should go. We do not want to miss dancing with the children."

"That is my favorite part," said Jane.

George allowed Alex to re-tie her sash. With each note of music, her heart sped up. Was this what facing a gauntlet felt like?

THIRTEEN

Lord Godderidge's study became a dressing room of sorts for the men for the evening. Johnathan was not the only one who brought a fresh shirt for the dance. Farmers and gentlemen alike shared the space. David Godderidge handed out hot damp towels to all who needed one.

Lucas took a towel. "Too bad Sir Lightwood yelled when he did. I was certain you would best Miss Georgiana. I cannot believe she missed her shot, too."

She hit right where she aimed. Johnathan was sure of it. He was not positive why. Was it so the farmer could win the pig? Which may have been the same one that she chased into the orchard. Or was it because of him? "She's good with the bow."

"Last year she won by another five paces at least. Only person I've ever seen best her is Mr. Edward, the Godderidge's second son."

Johnathan finished dressing and tossed his used towel to the basket.

Mr. Dalrymple arrived at the door at the same time. "Whittaker, correct?"

"Yes."

The man thrust out a hand in greeting. "I know we have not been formally introduced, but after losing to you on the archery field, I do not think introductions are necessary."

"I agree, Mr. Dalrymple."

"You are American. Your speech betrays you. I had not quite believed… How strange for you to come over in the middle of a war."

"Not the middle, surely. I traveled on the same ship as the peace delegation. I believe we wish an to end this."

"True. True. It seems England is always at war, the French, the Americans… Enough of that, the women would have our hides if we discussed such things during the festival."

"I believe you are right."

"I am curious about the Lightwood sisters. I understand you are a relation?"

"Distant cousin. I've known them less than a fortnight. I doubt I can answer your questions." Nor did he want to. Georgiana's interest in Mr. Dalrymple rankled.

"What can you tell me of Miss Georgiana? I found it peculiar that she would compete against the men."

"I thought many women in society practiced archery."

"As they do, but not in competition with men."

Johnathan tempered his wish to defend her. It would do neither of them good if he showed his feelings. "Perhaps if more of the ladies had participated, they would have had their own category."

"And her sisters. The eldest is a particular beauty but I have been told she, well she is—" Mr. Dalrymple lowered his voice, "—damaged."

"Miss Lightwood is particularly delightful and honest to the core. I am sure she will dissuade you of any false notions you may have."

"Interesting you use the word false, as I have been told her leg is precisely that."

"Then you are well informed." Johnathan stepped to leave.

"And the other one, is it true she is a mute?"

"No. Miss Jane is certainly not a mute. If you will excuse me. I hear musicians tuning their instruments and I promised to be on hand to help with any carting of the refreshments." What an odious man. The more Mr. Dalrymple had pressed about his cousins, the more Johnathan wished him gone. What had Georgiana seen in him to spend the last two hours in his presence? Not that she had been with him exclusively, but near often enough. Mr. Dalrymple was not the man for any of his cousins if he was so shallow as to try to glean information in such a manner.

He needed to keep Mr. Dalrymple away from the Lightwoods.

The Harvest Ball was unlike any other. It was George's favorite evening of the year.

The sisters and Isabel hurried down the stairway and through the ballroom, whose doors stood fully open to the patio and makeshift dance floor on the grounds. As the evening went on and the group got smaller and the night cooler, they would move inside.

Lord Godderidge, acting the role of his butler, announced a jig. The girls went their separate ways to find partners. George caught sight of Johnathan watching the proceedings with keen interest before a twelve-year-old boy from the pig chase approached her with a bow.

"May I have this dance, Miss?" he asked, his cadence missing most of the country accent he usually spoke with.

"Why, of course. I would be delighted." She followed him out on the floor as he forgot to offer his arm until they had reached their places.

"What of Grandma Grime's story?" he asked as they began the steps.

"It was obvious she was talking about our pig. I am glad that none of us were named."

He smiled mischievously. "Everybody knew the lady had to be you."

"You only know because you were there." George caught Johnathan's eye above the head of his partner still in braids. At least Grandma Grimes left out the part of the story where the lady was helped to her feet by a handsome newcomer. She looked away before a blush could rise.

"Everyone's talking about how you chased the pig. We'll all be sad when you leave. Me mum says it's time for you to go off and be wed. I wish you would not."

Was he flirting? George was not sure how to respond to such a young man. Thankfully, the next moment took her away from her partner. When they were reunited, she asked him about his favorite apples.

The next dance was with a lad of thirteen whose enthusiasm made up for his missteps. As she guided him through the figures, she noticed Johnathan attempting the English country dance with surprising grace. Their eyes met briefly as the dance brought them near, and she had to remind herself to focus on her young partner.

During a break, George sought out Jane at the refreshment table serving fresh cider. Johnathan joined them, standing close enough to make conversation unavoidable.

"This is excessively delightful. You told me it would be, but I was not prepared."

"I'm glad you're enjoying your evening." George ignored how her heart beat a jig when he spoke.

"I have met some of the most exceptional people. I received a treatise on weaving from an eight-year-old, and a lecture on what I did wrong in the footrace I participated in this morning from her sister.

The musicians relocated themselves closer to the house. Mr. Dalrymple and Isabel joined them at the refreshment table. Mr. Dalrymple took a sip of his cider.

"Do you know which of the houses produced this cider?"

Isabel answered before George did. "It came from Kellmore. George can tell you all about it."

The man turned to Johnathan. "I thought your name was Johnathan?"

"Oh, sorry," said Isabel. "I meant Georgiana. You do know Georgiana Lightwood?"

"Of course. I was unaware—" Mr. Dalrymple stumbled on his words.

"An honest mistake anyone could have made." George explained as quickly as she could about the names.

When Mr. Dalrymple requested the next dance, she accepted with practiced grace although her heart sank as Johnathan immediately turned to Isabel. Her friend set her hand on Johnathan's arm and looked up at him with a bright smile that did not merely feign interest.

The dance with Mr. Dalrymple proved interminable. He spoke little, just as he had earlier that day, leaving George to guide the conversation and express interest for Jane's sake.

Attempting to move the conversation away from farming, George asked, "Why did you choose this area?"

"It had much to recommend it, however a hundred and thirty miles to Town is a difficult thing to traverse. There are far fewer trees than I thought there would be here."

"This is not the Cotswolds," Georgiana replied dryly.

"Apparently not."

"If you are disappointed, why did you choose to live here?" she asked again, trying to steer the conversation.

"The price was right. An investment."

"Do you not intend to live here? You have excellent lands."

"Oh, I will live here most of the year. I shall likely have a steward see to matters of farming. I have no skill for it. After tasting the cider here, I think there is some room for improvement. I could be successful at that."

"Room for improvement?" Georgiana repeated, her tone sharpening.

"Well, yes. Would you say the cider we had today at the table was overly sweet?"

"No, I would not." George caught sight of Johnathan leading Isabel in a perfect turn and forced herself to focus on her own partner.

"Well, believe me, the taste was far too sweet. Whoever made it had the wrong mix."

"I would like to remind you, sir, the cider was provided by our estate. And it is known far and wide to be the best in the area."

"My pardon. Miss Godderidge mentioned something of that sort, before we were distracted with the names. Well, to each his own, then. It seems that most everyone is delighted with it. I did not mean to offend." He bowed ever so slightly.

Pompous man. George fought to hide her irritation. His dismissive response sealed her opinion of him. Father's wishes and Jane's future notwithstanding, she could not imagine encouraging this man's suit. Watching Johnathan dance with Isabel would be preferable to enduring Mr. Dalrymple's company — though the sight of her friend's hand on Johnathan's arm still made her stomach twist uncomfortably.

When the dance ended, George made her escape to the vicar's wife, whose dower presence was preferable to the conversation of Mr. Dalrymple.

There must be a way to prevent Father from manipulating their futures. But when she caught sight of Johnathan again, still entertaining Isabel's giggles, she wondered if her heart had not already chosen a path that would complicate everything.

FOURTEEN

Miss Godderidge was a lovely dance partner. Her conversation witty, and her rapt attention caused Johnathan's chest to expand. A year ago, he believed he would never have that feeling again. In the space of a fortnight he experienced it twice. Even if this second was not nearly as strong as the first. The dance brought Georgiana into his sight, she turned her face away further than the dance called for. His chest deflated.

"You really must tell me more about America," Miss Godderidge's eyes reflected the light of the lanterns. "Jane read us the most fascinating accounts when we were children."

Johnathan obliged, keeping away from politics, aware of the tensions lingering between their countries. Isabel proved an attentive listener, asking clever questions that showed genuine curiosity about his homeland. Yet his gaze kept straying to where Georgiana danced with Mr. Dalrymple. A frown flashed across her face. Good, she did not like her partner any more than he did.

The dance ended. Miss Godderidge's next partner swept her away before Johnathan could return her to her friends.

Movement near the refreshment table caught his attention. Jane stood alone near a potted tree, her pale grey dress standing out against shadows. He changed direction to join the quietest of his cousins.

"Miss Jane," he bowed. "I believe you have denied me the pleasure of a dance this evening."

She startled slightly. "Oh! Mr. Whittaker, you need not feel obligated—"

"I assure you, I wish this dance with you." He offered his hand. "Unless you truly wish to refuse?"

A ghost of a smile crossed her face. "Very well."

As they took their places for the quadrille, Johnathan caught Georgiana watching them. Her expression softened as Jane moved through the first figure with surprising grace. Jane proved to be a skilled dancer and a thoughtful conversationalist once he coaxed her into talking. The more they talked, the more being with Jane grew comfortable, like talking to his sister Miriam. If they could meet, he was sure they would get on famously.

"Thank you," she said quietly as the dance ended. "It's been some time since I've participated. Father mandated I must dance tonight, and you have given me courage."

"Then the loss has been everyone else's." He bowed over her hand, pleased to see her genuine smile. "It looks as if the musicians are taking a break."

"They are moving inside. I should find Alex and help with the refreshments."

Johnathan joined the other men in moving chairs and tables. The musicians began tuning again. Whispers rippled through the room, carrying an edge of excitement. The waltz. Johnathan learned it was still considered somewhat scandalous in some circles, though his dance lessons with Georgiana prepared him well enough.

He turned to find another partner. Georgiana stood near

the doors to the garden, the gas lamps reflected off the sun kissed highlights in her hair. Before he could think better of dancing the waltz again with her, his feet carried him to her side.

"Miss Georgiana." He bowed, noting how she started at his use of her full name. "Would you do me the honor?"

She hesitated, and for a moment, he thought she would refuse. "I... Yes."

The first notes filled the air as he led her to the floor. When his hands grasped her gloved ones, he felt the same jolt of awareness he experienced during their practice sessions, only now it seemed magnified by the intimate nature of the dance and the gathering darkness beyond the windows.

"You have been quite popular this evening," Georgiana said as they turned a half circle, her voice carefully neutral.

"Miss Godderidge has been very kind in helping me navigate English society." He guided them through a turn, acutely aware of how perfectly she moved with him. "Though I am still struggling with some aspects."

"Oh?" Her eyes met his briefly before darting away. "You seem to be managing quite well."

"Perhaps." He tightened his hold slightly as they navigated around another couple. "Though I'm beginning to think I've misunderstood something rather important."

"What might that be?"

The waltz brought them close enough that he could see the faint freckles across her nose—proof she was as involved in the harvest as any. "The need for new boots to be properly tested and tried."

He was rewarded with a smile.

"That can be a difficult lesson to learn."

"Indeed. I wish someone warned me."

"Are you in much pain?"

"Nothing that a pan of warm water will not solve."

"There, you might have a problem. Our staff is off until morning." Her laugh told him he had no need to defend himself.

Still, he did. "Fortunate for me, I am unaccustomed to having staff."

"A thing I think you will always remember?" The corners of her mouth turned up.

"I hope I do."

"Then I will not worry about Kellmore when I am gone."

But I want you to stay. The words came into his mind with all the force of a cider press. There was only one way that she could stay on land entailed to the earldom. They made the final turn of the dance and he pulled her closer than the step required. Georgiana did not resist.

As Johnathan escorted Georgiana from the floor, Jane met them at the edge of the dancers. "Alex and I are leaving with Grandfather. Are you coming or will you stay until the end?"

"Is Alex well?" asked Georgiana.

Jane's worried eyes gave the answer. "She says she is fatigued."

Georgiana took her sister's hands. "I'll stay. We said we would help to clean that which cannot wait until morning. I assume Father has left?"

"I have not seen him for sometime. He could be playing at cards. I worry about you coming home so late."

"I've done so a thousand times."

Johnathan cleared his throat. "I too have promised to help afterwards. I will see your sister safely home."

Jane smiled at him. "Thank you cousin, I would not leave, but with no staff…"

"Mrs. Green set out a poultice for Alex. All will be well." Georgiana let go of Jane's hands and sent her off.

An hour later Johnathan worked opposite of Mr. Dalrymple in moving tables to where Lord Godderidge indicated.

"I see why they ended the ball early," said Dalrymple.

"Early? It is nearly midnight." After all the work they accomplished this week Johnathan was more than ready for bed, even if he did not get his foot soak.

"Balls in Town usually go well into the night."

Lord Godderidge joined them. "The late Lady Lightwood and Lady Godderidge decided years ago that the festivities should end early so that we might have time to clean up, and that everybody could be rested for church in the morning."

"A perfectly reasonable decision," said Johnathan.

Mr. Dalrymple did not respond.

After they packed up the tables and chairs, Johnathan found Georgiana coming out of the kitchen. "Are you finished?"

"Quite so. Have you been waiting long?"

"No."

She started down a path that did not lead to the road.

"Are you not going the wrong direction?"

"This way is much shorter, and I do not know about you and your new dancing boots, but my feet would prefer a shorter distance."

"An excellent idea, although—will it not cause a scandal, since we are walking without a chaperone?"

"Likely not. Most will have assumed we've taken a carriage back."

"I'm surprised the earl did not send one back for you."

"Considering there would have been no one to drive it back—other than himself—I am not surprised at all."

Apparently, when everyone received the evening off, they meant everyone. "So, who took care of the horses?"

Georgiana laughed. "Our stable master, undoubtedly. He cannot handle seeing the mistreatment of any animal, and I'm sure he would not have let Grandfather take care of them."

"But I thought he would have the time off."

"He did. He was there, dancing and enjoying the day as well as any. But like Cook, who made all of her goods in advance, there are some things staff do not trust us to touch."

"That makes sense. But will you mind terribly if I check on the horses before retiring?"

"Of course not. I take it you care for your own horses at home?"

"Yes. One of my earliest memories is of mucking out stalls."

High above them, an owl hooted. Georgiana turned her face up, looking for the animal. "Good night, Sir Owl."

The owl hooted back before the flutter of wings filled the air.

"Do you often speak to the owls?"

"Not often. I am not out late enough."

They reached the stile which although well-kept looked steep with its three stairs. Johnathan extended his hand to help Georgiana over, though he was sure she did not require it. At some point during her cleaning, she had removed her gloves. Her hand was soft and warm in his. He wished the stile was wide enough to otherwise accommodate them both, so he need not let go. He scrambled over and he would have offered his arm to her but she stepped back far enough to make the gesture awkward.

"I saw you dancing with Isabel. Did you enjoy her company?"

"Are you seeking out tales? I am almost positive I danced with more partners than there were dances."

"I only want to ascertain, if you have found somebody to stand at your side once you obtain the earldom."

"I may have." Johnathan slowed his step. Georgiana took a couple of others before realizing she left him behind. She stopped, turned to him, and tilted her head.

"Isabel?"

Johnathan took a step forward, closing the gap between them.

"No."

She tilted her head. How could she not know? He stepped closer still. "I have taken a keen interest in someone who far better suits me."

Georgiana searched his eyes. Her lips parted in a silent gasp.

Johnathan lifted his hand and rubbed a thumb across her cheek. He should answer her in words.

"Me?"

His head lowered an inch, as if propelled by his heart more than his mind. "Georgiana..."

Above them, the owl hooted again. A scolding sound, giving his mind greater control. He stepped back. "There is another thing I must know about your British customs."

"What?" The single word fell breathless from her lips.

"Should I seek permission to court you?"

Georgiana turned. "I do not think that's a conversation we should be having alone in the dark."

She was right. He never would have thought of kissing her if they were properly chaperoned. Well he would've thought of it, just not started to act upon his thought.

Georgiana pointed to a path that took off a few feet in front of her. "That will take you to the back of the stables. Good night."

She hurried off.

Johnathan waited for a moment before he followed her. He wanted to be sure she made it safely to the house. He watched from the shadows as she entered the kitchen door before heading to the stables. As she said, the horses were properly cared for. Still he checked each one before returning to the manor.

In the kitchen, he found a steaming kettle on and a foot bath half full in front of a straight back chair. For him? Finding no one else about, he pulled off his boots. Foot falls on the stairs stopped him.

A robe covered Georgiana's nightdress. She stayed in the shadows of the doorway. "Good, you found it."

"You set this out for me?"

She nodded. "My father."

Sir Lightwood would not have left anyone hot water. "Pardon?"

"You should speak with my father." Georgiana fled up the stairs before Johnathan could move.

Did that mean she approved? He pondered the idea as he soaked his feet. She prepared him a footbath. That signified. The water grew cold. He lifted his feet out and paused.

No towel.

He dried off the best he could with his stockings.

Maybe the foot bath did not signify as much as he thought.

FIFTEEN

"Miss Georgiana," said the footman, "your father wishes to see you in his study."

Johnathan spoke to her father so soon? When? Father returned home after services, partaken of the small repast, and retired to his study. Jane asked Johnathan to come see the new pups in the kennel. Johnathan must have returned without her. Yet it was scarcely a *quarter of an hour past since Jane and Johnathan had left. She made her way as slowly as she dared to her father's study hoping to spy Johnathan on her way.*

The moment she stepped inside, Father barked, "Shut the door!"

Click. Nothing she detested more than the sound of the study door closing.

"Sit down and explain yourself."

"Explain what, Father?"

"Why did you not make a bigger effort with Mr. Dalrymple? You allowed Isabel Godderidge to flirt with him."

Isabel flirt with Mr. Dalrymple? Unlikely. She must have danced with him as it would have been expected. "I can hardly attempt to stop a dear friend's enjoyment of the dance."

"But he only danced with you once."

"Yes, he promised dances to other women." It would have been odd for him to dance with her more than a single time especially since she spent so much of her day obviously following him around. One dance was more than acceptable.

"He danced twice with the vicar's daughter! She is far below you in station. I am excessively displeased with you. I am even more displeased with your dance with Mr. Whittaker. A waltz! You know he presumes to supplant me as heir to the Earl of Whitstone, and I will not have it." Father brought his fist down on his desk. The builder of the desk must be commended as after years of fist pounding it still stood.

George kept her mouth shut as her father ranted.

"And your grandfather is still here. Well, I am finished with it. That colonist shall have none of my lands, my title, or my daughters. What does he have for himself? Nothing. Nothing but my fortune, the fortune that will be mine. I forbid you from further association."

George straightened her spine. "I'm afraid that is impossible. Grandfather has specifically asked that I educate Mr. Whittaker as to our methods of farming and the keeping of the estates."

"Your grandfather's stewards can do that. Just because you call yourself George, you are not a man and shall not do men's work."

"So, I am to disregard Grandfather's wishes?"

"The fifth commandment is to obey your father. Not your grandfather."

"Honor thy father and thy mother. It does not say to obey them, especially when they ask the impossible." Hopefully father didn't know children were told to obey their parents in the New Testament.

"Do not quibble with me, girl. Your mother spoiled you much too much as a child. Well, I will have none of it. You must give up these mannish ways." He pulled out a paper and inked his pen. "I know just the thing for you. A winter with the most prudish of all women. She will not allow you to traipse around in men's clothing."

It was on the tip of her tongue to tell her father she already gave up the practice, but he continued.

"My sister writes that she needs help. As if I have extra money to send her with your coming out. I shall send you to her. You will figure out why she cannot manage her expenses. I've rented much of it out so she does not have to labor. At least then this self-education you have given yourself will be of some use. Then you will not need to worry about defying the sainted earl by not helping the colonist. You will then meet us in Town for the Season. Five months away from your sisters will be good for all of you. My sister will not put up with your willful nature. Inform your maid to pack your bags. You will leave for Yorkshire on tomorrow's post."

"Father—"

"My word is final. Your grandfather has no say in how I raise my children. He may have barred my friend from this house, but he cannot declare where you live."

Sending her to Yorkshire was a way to prove he didn't need to kneel to grandfather's wishes. Did father suspect her feelings for Johnathan? Where had Father been to know about the dances? Neither she nor Jane saw him.

"Now go. You have much to do. And do not leave Jane in a state of weeping. You know I cannot abide tears."

George stood on shaky legs and exited the study as quickly as possible. Instead of going to find her sisters, she headed for the nearest door.

Outside.

Alone.

Directly to Mother's rose garden and her favorite bench, where she crumpled.

"Oh, Mother, Mother, why did you have to leave us?" Tears came then. George wished she was better at carrying a handkerchief like Jane, for there was none to be found. She gathered her tears with her sleeves. She did not know why Father did not get along with his sister, although she suspected whatever the reason her aunt was in the right. Perhaps she would fare well there. She knew so little of the woman, other than she was a widow with a son.

Yorkshire. It was colder there. That fact was the extent of her knowledge. All she recalled from her single childhood visit was the endless carriage ride lasting for days. Weeks? Though Mother did her best to entertain them.

She dried her eyes and tried to think logically. Grandfather could not intercede. He would try, but it would come to naught, for eventually Grandfather would leave, and Father would take it out on her and possibly her sisters. Her refusal could come back on Jane. More tears came. Georgiana wiped her tears on her damp sleeve.

"I believe this will work better." Johnathan stood before her offering a neatly folded handkerchief.

"Where did you come from?" Georgiana dabbed her cheeks with his proffered cloth.

"I hope I'm not interrupting. I was returning from a stroll when I saw you." More of a hike. After visiting the hounds, Johnathan walked as far as the ruins of the old abbey, composing in his mind what he might say to Sir Lightwood to gain his approval for a courtship.

Georgiana dropped her hands to her lap, clutching his handkerchief in them. "Thank you. I never seem to have a handkerchief when I need one."

Johnathan pointed to the bench next to her. "May I?"

She nodded. "I suppose my face is all splotchy. I do not wish my sisters to know I've been crying. There will be tears enough when I tell them."

"Tell them what?"

"That I am being sent away to my aunt."

"Your father's sister?"

"The same, in Yorkshire."

"Whatever for?" Johnathan's mind raced. Could Sir Lightwood possibly know of his intentions already?

"Father is displeased with my behavior last night."

"Why? You acted with perfect propriety."

"It is simple enough. He gave me simple instructions to win Mr. Dalrymple's affections. As he is rumored to have eight thousand a year—which, in case you did not know, is quite a bit."

"Is your father trying to force you to marry for money?"

Georgiana let out a deep sigh. "He is trying, as he did with Phil. The Duke of Aylton ended up intervening after Phil climbed out of an upper-story window."

"Your sister climbed out of a window?"

"At an inn. There were spiders." Georgiana waved her hand dismissively. "My point is father may not force us into marriage, but that does not mean he will not try to manipulate things even if the Duke of Aylton threatened to send him to Australia."

"So let me understand. You did not flirt to your father's satisfaction with a man last night, so your father is sending you halfway across the country—or further—so that you cannot attract this man anymore?" Johnathan disagreed with Sir Lightwood. Georgiana had flirted far more than necessary. The fact that the flirtation was not done out of desire was small consolation indeed.

Georgiana absently played with the hem of the handkerchief he had loaned her. "It is more than that. Father is upset because I danced the waltz with you. He is very irritable about your entire presence here."

"So my asking to court you will not be met with a positive answer." He spoke his thought aloud.

She lifted her eyes to his and gave him a half-smile. "I think it's better that you not discuss that with him now. Father will find a way to send me all the way to Sweden if he knew of your wishes."

"So you will go without protest?"

"It is the wisest course. I fear he will visit his anger upon my sisters should I refuse him. Too often, poor Jane bears the brunt of his ill humor. I must protect her."

Johnathan frowned. "A father should not— Pardon. I should keep my words to myself."

Georgiana studied him for a minute. "There's no need to keep things to yourself on my behalf. I am more than aware of my father's shortcomings."

"No father should be like that."

"And your father? What was he like?"

Johnathan closed his eyes for a minute, letting memories wash over him. "When not in extreme pain from the limb he lost, he was very kind, and my mother misses him with a ferocity that exceeds my explanation. Though he was unable to help us with all the farm work, he supervised but rarely yelled. There were times when my father often went into what my mother called a 'mood' on account of losing his leg in the Revolution. Unfortunately, his leg was his ultimate demise, as it never healed properly, and he was given to infections and fever. His memory is one of the stumbling blocks to what the earl asks of me, as my father was not particularly keen on the English—especially Redcoats."

"And your mother? What sort of woman is she?"

"My mother is not what one would term delicate. She has, when necessity urged, worked a plough to till the rocky ground, chopped trees, and butchered pigs."

"As English ladies, we must seem quite useless by comparison."

"Not at all. I have seen you rise to your own when needed." The fact she chose to leave showed more strength than cowardice.

"Tell me more about her?"

"She has a quiet voice, but one that will pierce you through to the center, and when she uses my full name, I can do nothing but obey her. Much of what I am, I am because of her tutelage."

"You have a second name?"

"Hector."

"Johnathan Hector Whittaker. That is much, isn't it?" A smile teased her face.

Not when she said it in that tone. "It is when I am in trouble."

"Do you miss Massachusetts?"

"Of course I do. I am surprised to find how similar England feels to it. The trees, the weather, the farms. Of course, there are not as many fine houses, or old ones, or castles, or anything of that sort at home. It is all quite new, small, and even a bit rough. I am unused to your type of society and servants. We have been well enough off without my father. My mother has been able to employ a cook and a maid. Of course, neither my sisters nor she has a lady's maid, so they help each other when they must. We are not the wealthiest in our little town, but we are able to feed everyone who lives with us and have new clothing whenever required."

"Thank you for telling me a bit about your life. Thinking of something else helps in times of trouble." She shuddered out a sigh. "I assume you miss your family very much."

"More than I can say. The thought of not returning to see my mother or my sisters, and even my brothers, is another difficulty in accepting the earl's offer."

Georgiana folded the handkerchief in her lap. "Thank you for talking to me. My spirits are much restored, but I am afraid I must inform my sisters of my departure before they realize my maid is—" Her hands flew to her cheeks. "No doubt Father has told my maid. Jane will be distressed if she finds her packing. I am sorry, I am not making much sense. If I had time, I would wash this." She held up the handkerchief. "My apologies for not returning it clean."

"Keep it." He offered his arm, knowing they might not have another quiet moment together. "Come, I'll escort you back and help you locate your sisters."

They were fortunate enough to find both sisters in the library with the earl. Sensing the need for private family time, Johnathan excused himself and returned outdoors. His feet led him to the cider press he first saw last week with Miss Georgiana. Being Sunday, there was little activity in the fields beyond the occasional lowing of a cow, and none at the press.

Thoughts of his family swirled through his mind. He could not picture his father sending off any of his sisters simply for failing to catch the right man's eye at a dance—or for dancing with the wrong one, for that matter.

This new development, with Georgiana being sent away, troubled him. He needed to at least ensure she came back to her family. She had not mentioned when she could return. Might she be back for the Season?

Perhaps then he could court her after the earl's plan was sorted. That was if she did not find someone else. She would be cast into a new world of people. She might not want to return.

SIXTEEN

The entire household was up well before dawn. Cook set out a breakfast including all of George's favorite foods hours before breakfast was normally served. While Jane's eyes remained moist most of the morning, she had yet to shed a tear. For the first time in years, George forced herself to eat, thus maintaining a guise of normalcy.

A discussion between the earl and her father, which started last night ruining the evening for all, spilled over into the morning. Raised voices echoed from her father's study. Two carriages sat in front of the house, both waiting to receive Georgiana's trunks. The carriage Grandfather brought with him and Father's which would only go as far as the village inn to meet the Post coach in an hour.

Six or more days on a coach with strangers and no chaperone did not terrify George as much as the prospect of being away from her sisters for the next five months. Could Jane abide without her? Or she without Jane. She always worried about the day they might be parted. Little had George suspected that the thought of not being able to confide in Jane each night would be the most daunting part of leaving.

Alex sat stiffly at the breakfast table, a sign that her hip, at the very least, was bothering her. She stirred another bit of sugar into her tea. Her third spoonful. It would be as sweet as candy soon. "I still have half a mind to write the Duke. He could stop this nonsense."

"Hush, sister, it will not do any good," George replied. "Father is not forcing me to marry someone. And if our Aunt is in need of help, at least I can do some good there. Father said I will be back for the Season."

"Perhaps." Alex sipped from her cup and made a face.

Jane whirled on Alex. "Do not say that! She must be back for the Season. I cannot do it without her, especially with you in Bath."

"Grandfather will be sure of my return," said George.

Alex pushed aside her tea. "If you do not come for the Season, I will write the Duke of Aylton. He is the only man I have met who can cow father."

George saw the Duke briefly once. The forbidding man stopped by to bring a gift and his apologies for not attending Phil's wedding. She could not understand why Alex would place trust in a man who had so little connection to the family. There was nothing to gain by the acquaintance, the duke needed neither a wife nor the earl's support.

Jane tilted her head. "Do you hear that?"

"Hear what?" asked Alex.

George set her fork down. "Silence."

Father and Grandfather must have come to some sort of agreement. The front door opened, followed by the quick footsteps of footmen.

Father burst into the breakfast room. "Are you ready yet?"

"I was just preparing to take my leave," George replied.

"Your grandfather insists upon sending his coach, although likely that means he will be here for another fortnight. I believed the post would have been good enough for you, but since I am not willing to spare someone to act as a chaperone, we are once again at the earl's mercy."

George hid her smile. Much better Grandfather's coach than the post. She may not have been concerned about strangers, but still it would be a relief to not be completely alone.

"There will be a chaperone?" asked Jane.

"Of course she will have a chaperone. The earl insists I pay for one even if she were to go by post," Father said. "Cook's widowed sister has agreed to accompany Georgiana. Though I do not see the need, since he is sending his coachman and two footmen. Georgiana will be more than adequately protected. So much expense. It will cost me thrice as much as the post. Funds I could have sent my sister." He stormed out the same way he came in.

Not that he was paying for the expense, nor that he would have sent money to his sister. According to Alex, there were no records of transfers of funds to their aunt, but the books only included records of finance for Kellmore Manor.

"At least that prayer has been answered," said Jane. "I was afraid for you to travel for days on top of a post chaise. And it will likely rain."

"I was not looking forward to it either." Although father would not have purchased one of the cheaper tickets would he? Even he should have seen the necessity of a gentlewoman traveling inside.

Cook entered the room with a large basket. "This should help ye on yer way. I made extra for the coachman, footmen, and my sister. Theirs is already aboard."

Proper or not, George leapt from her seat and embraced Cook. "I will miss you."

"None of that now. Jane helped me write out some of my best recipes. If you be miss'n us, perhaps yer aunt's cook can fix 'em." Her accent grew thick. Cook dabbed a tear with the corner of her apron.

Unable to speak, George hugged the woman again.

"Don' eat everythin' at once. Ye will get ill from the motion of the coach." Cook hurried out of the room, likely to hide her tears.

George returned to her breakfast. "When did you have time to write down the recipes?"

"I've been working on it all summer. When we leave, we will all want to eat some of our familiar favorites."

"Likely will not taste the same without Cook making it, but I love the thought."

The earl stepped into the breakfast room. "Godspeed, my child. I hope my bargain with your father proves not to be a mistake."

Alex looked up from a fresh cup of tea. "What do you mean?"

"Never you mind. All will be well."

"Thank you for saving me from traveling by post," George said.

"A granddaughter of mine is not going to ride by post half-way across the country. It is unthinkable." Grandfather made himself a plate from the sideboard. "I've ordered your trunk loaded. I am not sure which bothers your father most—the money for the chaperone or the fact that Mr. Whittaker and I will stay in residence until the coach returns."

Grandfather could order another coach from his estate, and it would be here no later than tomorrow morning. His staying was simply to vex Father, Georgiana was sure, but she would not say such a thing.

"Speaking of Mr. Whittaker," the earl continued, "I passed him in the corridor just now. He was off to the stables, but when I said you were leaving shortly, he said he would wait in the parlor for you. I believe he wishes to say goodbye. Jane,

I hate to put this upon you, but will you act as chaperone?"

Her sister agreed.

George needed another moment. Although her appetite had yet to return, food seemed the answer. "I find I am in need of one of Cook's excellent apple tarts."

Georgiana swiftly downed all of a whole new tart. Alex hid her mouth behind her hand to keep from laughing.

"You know you can take some of that with you," Alex said. "Cook will not be offended."

"But she has already made a basket."

"I recall you once claiming that it was impossible to have too many of her tarts."

"Then be a dear and wrap one for me. Maybe two," George said. "Are you ready, Jane?"

They hurried to the parlor room, glad not to find their father along the way.

Johnathan stood near a window. "I wanted to say goodbye, but I was afraid if I did so in front of your father, it would only make things worse."

Jane studied a painting near the door. George joined Johnathan at the window.

"Your instincts may be right," she said.

"May I have permission to write to you?" Johnathan asked.

"You wish to write to me?" George asked, surprised.

"Of course. We were just getting to know one another."

"Exchanging letters, um—" George watched her hands twist her skirt. "It is not proper when we do not have an understanding."

Johnathan leaned closer. "I intended to ask your father if I may court you. If he gave his permission would it be proper then?"

She raised her eyes to his face. Was he in earnest? Her breath caught. He was looking at her as if she was adored. No, wanted. No, that was not accurate either. There was not a description for what his eyes were doing as they begged for her to agree.

"You may write. Although, from what Father says, I do not know if my aunt will allow it."

"I shall be spending a great deal of time in London," Johnathan said. "Are you sure I will not see you before the spring?"

"It is unlikely. Father will not pay to have me back, and the roads can be quite hazardous in the winter—or so I understand."

Johnathan held out his hand. George set hers in it.

"Then until we meet again." He lifted her hand to his mouth and dropped a kiss on her knuckles, his eyes intently watching hers.

"Until we meet again." Her words were not as firm as she wished. Too breathless, too desperate.

He dropped her hand, bowed, and strode from the room. Leaving the warmth of her hand as the only reminder of the touch.

Jane was immediately at her side. "Did he kiss your hand?"

Unable to form words, George nodded.

"What else? Did he ask to write to you?"

"You're the eavesdropper. You know exactly what was said."

"Well, I do, but I wanted you to confirm it."

George turned from the window. "Yes. If you'll be kind enough to slip at least his first letter in with yours."

"How do you know I will write to you?"

"How can you possibly not? I will write to you at the first chance I get," George promised. "But not from inside the moving carriage."

"Then expect a letter no longer than a day or two after you arrive."

"You are the darlingest of sisters. I shall miss you."

Jane stepped back, out of reach. "Please, I do not wish to cry in front of Father. Do not let me start now."

"Very well. Let's go find Alex—and pilfer all the leftover tarts and egg bakes that Cook has made." Food would keep her from crying, at least for now.

The curtain hid Johnathan from view—or so he hoped—as he watched the scene below. It was as predictable as it was heart wrenching.

Sir Lightwood's farewell was brief. Though from the window it was difficult to tell if it was a farewell or the barking of orders as he handed over a missive to Georgiana. He returned inside long before the rest of the farewells were over.

A few servants hovered near edges, most notably the gardener, who snuck a box into the boot of the carriage. The oddity that the household staff seemed more distraught at Georgiana's departure than her father twisted Johnathan's heart. Grandfather said that the men of the peerage could be cold and unfeeling toward their families, yet nothing prepared him for the reality he witnessed over the past fortnight. A man who would bring his paramour to his home and attempt to install her in his deceased wife's room. A man who could dismiss his daughter because another was not interested in her. A man that, if Johnathan chose, he could prevent from gaining more power.

Never could Johnathan be that man. Lord Godderidge, from what little he saw while preparing for and holding the harvest fair, did not appear to be that man, so it was possible. As for the earl, he cared for his family now, but from their conversations, that might not have always been the case. Proof being in the fact his daughter married Sir Lightwood under some sort of duress. The other daughter had been cut off for some time for marrying a man deemed far below her.

At last a footman helped Georgiana into the carriage. While climbing in she turned on the step and looked up at his room. Was it his imagination, or did she give the barest of waves? He pressed his hand to the glass in case she had.

It was as likely as not that five months apart would accomplish exactly what her father sought. They had made no declaration of feeling and no more than a small depth of friendship. Writing her would help deepen that, only if she was allowed to receive his letters. For the aunt could stop them. And even then it would be difficult, as letters were not conversations, sometimes it was near impossible to discern a meaning without knowing if the other person smiled or frowned. He would not know if she was twisting her skirt because she was unsure how to respond or worried. One could hide many things in words or not express them at all.

What if his bold request was premature? Not all courtships ended in marriage, and she was still young. Perhaps her hesitation should have been heeded, and he asked amiss. English society followed so many rules, there needed to be a book. If only they had more time together.

Alexandra and Jane stood on the drive long after the carriage drove out of sight, holding each other. Johnathan waited until they retreated into the house to leave his place by the window. Already the house felt emptier. He went in search of his cousins. The least he could do for Georgiana was to see to their comfort.

SEVENTEEN

If one enjoyed silence, broken only by the click-click of knitting needles, there was little to complain about during the ride to Yorkshire. Grandfather's carriage was comfortable and well sprung. The late fall weather gave way to misting rain that did little to hinder travel. However, if one, like George, was given to the chatter and confidences of her sisters, the lack of conversation became unbearable only ten miles from home.

George had very little to entertain herself with. She had not, as Mrs. Brown pointed out, brought needlework, nor was she proficient enough to borrow a spare set of knitting needles to knit a scarf of her own. Although on the second and third days of travel she produced two lopsided scarves, only to later pull them apart. If she had thought to bring a book, it would have been impossible to read while facing backwards. Nausea plagued Mrs. Brown if she rode in the back facing seat so George took her seated position there.

For most of the journey, George contented herself with forming letters in her head, as an inkwell was completely out of the question. However, on the third night of her journey she was able to write a portion of the words composed in her mind. The large inn where they stayed boasted a ladies' parlor where George could sit and write without Mrs. Brown looking over her shoulder.

Dearest Jane—

Our journey has been uneventful. While I do not wish for highwaymen to accost us, it would have given me something of greater interest upon which to write about than Mrs. Brown's incessant knitting. I believe she has finished at least a shawl, two scarves, and enough stockings for half of the parish. She only speaks to chide me for not bringing along something to occupy my time. Can you imagine how ill my embroidery would look if I attempted it in a carriage? Still, she is correct. Although I am at a loss for anything I could have brought. My attempt at knitting was as terrible as you are imagining.

Each night, we have slept in the same bed. It is not the comfortable sleep we have shared our entire lives. Her snoring has kept me up, and she has extremely cold feet. It follows that I spend much of my days looking out the window or dozing as the countryside rolls by. I would have written sooner, however, Mrs. Brown insists on retiring immediately after we dine for the evening and has no patience for me to even have one candle.

I do not write this to complain of my situation, but to point out how much I miss you and my dear sisters. Mrs. Brown is far from the worst traveling companion I could have. She is committed in her care to look after me and even returned a meal to the kitchen saying the meat was bad. (The meat was a sickening blue-green color.) She has no cause to chase off any man who seems enamored of me, as you have read in some of your novels. However, I am certain she would if it became necessary.

It rained most of the day today, which made the carriage ride quite chilly. I must admit, I am jealous of the knitted scarves. Tomorrow we shall reach our Aunt Hale's. I am growing nervous. The landscape has changed markedly. I saw more sheep and cattle today than I normally see in weeks. I hoped to help with plans for planting, but I fear it will differ greatly from what I have learned. Could that be true when I am still in England? Our American cousin has farming methods very similar to ours. Perhaps I am worrying about nothing...

George wrote until the paper was full detailing a twisted tree, the livestock, and any other details she could recall from the many letters she had composed in her mind.

Since the hour was not yet late, and there were still mothers and daughters in the parlor, George started a second letter.

Mr. Whittaker,

I am writing this in anticipation of you writing me. I cannot send this first as it would break one of those societal rules of which we Englanders are so fond. I hope someone has adequately explained this to you lest you think me rude. Although it may be the same in the colonies. I doubt we should be writing at all as it could appear that

———————

George scratched out the last part of the sentence, as it must end in the word "engaged," something they were not. They were cousins, writing one another to learn more about the other. There was not the depth of feeling needed to be engaged.

As we travel north, it seems to me as if the days are shorter, as if fall is slipping into winter more quickly, but I cannot be sure. Perhaps it is that I check the time so often. The road north is well-traveled and in good repair. I have seen several castles from a distance, which I itch to explore, perhaps some other time. Farms have given way to pastures filled with livestock. A subject, despite my time spent with pigs, I am not adequately knowledgeable about. I hoped to be of some use to my aunt with my experience and knowledge of agriculture. However, given the difference in the land use, mostly pastures, I'm afraid I'll be of little use.

Of all the tedious letters George had ever written—which were few, even with a handful of good ones—this was by far the worst. None of the thoughts that filled her mind during the hours of admiring the countryside flowed from her pen. Yes, she thought of asking him what he knew of raising sheep and how the shearing of them would go. His reactions she could not imagine beyond his smile because she had no knowledge of her own to help her. The vast number of questions she had about America had also gone unanswered in her imagination. Asking questions about home construction, churches, (how did they differ from the Church of England?), and fashion (she had been extremely bored when she saw a farmer's wife and wondered) did not seem the questions she could pose now.

The coachman discovered a box Mr. Sprout, our gardener, packed for me. It is full of seed packets and cuttings wrapped in moss. I am unsure what to do with some of them as I do not know if I shall have them all planted before I go to Town for the Season.

It turns out that the Lightwood Manor is not on the coast of Yorkshire as I supposed, but on the edge of the moor. I remember so little about my visit and nothing of the sea, so I do not know where I got such an idea from. Mrs. Brown says the moors are lovely in the spring. They are a bit like the sea as they are such a vast area of dried grasses that one can see nothing else. I imagine the sea is the same way. I have never visited—

As the other ladies in the retiring room took their leave, George knew she must also seek out her room for the night. While Mrs. Brown's snoring echoed through the door to their room, George wished—not for the first time—for a bit of cotton to soften the noise.

The following morning proved damp and grey, much like George's spirits, especially since Mrs. Brown pulled off the blankets on her side during the night. George tucked the coach blanket around her legs and stared out into the grey morning. Soon, the city gave way to the countryside.

The lunch stop was unremarkable. The coaching inn offered bread and cheese, neither of which was fresh, nor stale. George regretted finishing Cook's delicacies in the first two days. If she had been wise, she would have saved them. But who could resist an apple tart?

They passed through little village after little village, finally, the coachman turned on a short lane and stopped at a Tudor-style home—much larger than a cottage, but easily less than half the size of Kellmore Manor. She should not have been surprised that Lightwood Manor's name was larger than the structure. Rain fell in a soft mist adding to the greyness of the house.

Leaving Mrs. Brown in the carriage, George, accompanied by a footman, approached the door. A boy of about seven or eight years answered the footman's knock.

"Is Mrs. Hale at home?" asked George.

The boy shut the door in their faces leaving George and the bewildered footman standing in the barely sheltered alcove.

A moment later, the door opened only far enough for a woman with her hair tucked under a mob cap to stare out at them. "May I help you?"

"I am Miss Georgiana Lightwood. I'm looking for my aunt, Mrs. Hale?"

"I am she." The woman's eyes narrowed as did the gap in the door.

Much less than the welcome she expected. It never occurred to George that she might not be admitted at all. "My father has sent me in answer to your request for help."

For a long moment her aunt pondered before shaking her head and stepping back to open the door wide. "Trust Felton for that. Come in, out of the rain, you and your party. It will not be said that I am inhospitable. Timothy, ask Nettie to put on the tea, please."

The entry was dark but clean. George removed her bonnet.

Her aunt held out her hand. "I am sorry, I have no butler to take your things." She turned to the footman. "There is a stable round back. You'll find it empty, as I keep no horses. It will provide shelter, but no fodder for your animals. Had I been expecting—"

The sentence faded as the footman took his leave. Mrs. Brown replaced him in the doorway. George introduced her traveling companion.

Aunt Hale ushered them into a tidy parlor. Lace doilies covered worn spots in the furnishings. The boy returned and stood next to aunt. "This is Timothy, your cousin."

George dropped a curtsy to the boy who would inherit her father's title. "Pleased to meet you. I am Georgiana, although my sisters call me George."

Timothy's brow wrinkled. "What should I call you then?"

"Whatever suits you." George answered as she took the seat her aunt offered.

A thin woman with a long nose appeared with a tea tray that offered only tea and thinly sliced toast.

Aunt Hale poured out four cups of tea handing one to Timothy. "Take a bit of bread and go to the kitchen while

I speak with your cousin."

After Timothy left, Aunt Hale set her cup down. "I am afraid your trip is for not. Felton misunderstood my request. I do not need another mouth to feed. How dare he send you in his finest carriage to mock me when he knows I am desperate for funds?"

The scalding anger was hotter than the tea.

George spoke in the most soothing voice she could. "The carriage belongs to my grandfather, the Earl of Whitstone. Father was determined to send me by postal coach. No doubt he would have paid for a ticket on top rather than inside and would not have sent a companion. My grandfather stepped in to spare me the censure such a trip would entail."

Aunt Hale's eyes softened, but her face remained pinched. "How long are you to be here?"

"Father says he wishes me to help you until the Season starts. I have a letter." George pulled the letter from her reticule and handed it to her aunt.

Her aunt stepped over to the window to get better light for reading. There were no candles burning in the room, nor was there a fire in the fireplace. Whatever had Father been thinking? Was he aware of how humbly his sister lived, how little she subsisted on? What ever financial woes Alex and Phil dealt with were nothing to Aunt Hale's. Where were the rents that the barony provided? Where was the food?

Georgiana sipped her tea, realizing at once that it was not a proper English tea at all, but made of some sort of berry, which was not at all unpleasant.

"Felton claims he sent you with twenty pounds?"

George took the money from her reticule and handed it to her adding an additional five. "There is also this that I did not need to spend on my journey, thanks to my grandfather."

Aunt handed back the five pounds. "I will not take the money your grandfather gave you."

George refused it. "My father's insistence in sending me to you has caused you a burden. This will not lighten it much, but I believe it is your due."

The money disappeared into a hidden pocket. Aunt Hale turned to Mrs. Brown. "I am afraid I cannot lodge you, the coachman, nor the footmen for the night. I believe it is possible to reach Leeds before the sun sets. I would advise that you do so. I apologize for not being able to offer any hospitality."

"I will let them know right away." Mrs. Brown stood, arriving at the door just as the footmen entered with George's trunk, bag, and the box of seeds.

"Do you have directions on where we should set this?" asked the taller footman.

"Yes. If you follow me, please." Aunt led them up a creaky staircase and down a corridor. The door that her aunt opened squeaked with misuse. Dust covers draped every inch of furniture. "I suppose this will be best."

The men set her trunk down on the edge of an old carpet with a thunk. A puff of dust swirled around the edge of the trunk.

The most senior of the footmen bowed to her aunt. "We shall take our leave directly."

Mrs. Brown pulled a knit shawl from her bag. "You nearly forgot this."

Before George could properly thank her, the chaperone left.

Alone with her aunt, Georgiana looked around the room.

Aunt walked over to the window. "It is not much, but at least, last I checked, the fireplace worked. I would not want you to get terribly cold. I have no maid other than the cook. Are you capable of cleaning after yourself?"

"Yes, quite." Georgiana hoped her face did not register all

the worry she felt. "I did not mean to be a burden to you. I had no idea—"

"Of course you did not." Her aunt sighed and lifted a dust cover from a dresser. "Felton has not come for some years. He barely appeared for his own mother's funeral. So I should not be astonished."

George folded the cover on the bed.

"We eat an early dinner and retire with the sun. I hope you will not require many candles."

"I will be most frugal. My sisters and I grew accustomed to economizing since our mother's death." Not to this extent, as Grandfather eventually stepped in and paid the servants directly.

"Yes, my condolences to you. I would have come. In fact, I expected to come, especially after Felton—well, especially." Aunt pulled the dust cover from a chair near the window. "I will let you get cleaned up, and I must return to what I was doing. If a door is closed, the room is likely closed off like this, and I ask you to leave it as such."

"Yes, Aunt Hale."

"If you are to live here, calling me 'Aunt Hale' all the time is going to get tiresome. My name is Elaine."

"I am called George or Georgiana."

"You still keep the names my brother used when you were young?"

"You know about them?" For once, she might not have to explain.

"Do you remember accompanying your father here when you were little?" Elaine smiled at George's nod, "Your grandmother was scandalized at the thought of her granddaughters calling each other by boy names, much more by your father often doing the same."

"He stopped the practices when our brother was born. We were too accustomed to our names to change."

"I must know, does your use of the male version annoy Felton?"

George bit her lip.

"I see it does." Elaine laughed. "I shall call you George then. We shall adjust to this situation the best we can. It is not your fault my brother is a dolt. Help me with this cover on the bed. This room may be a wee bit dusty but it is free of rodents. I keep a cat expressly for that. I imagine you'll see Atlanta soon."

After the room was put to rights, George opened her bag. The letters sat on top. She was determined to finish them tonight and send them by post in the morning. If only she thought to send the partially finished letters when the coach left.

EIGHTEEN

The earl's coach returned at dusk on Sunday. A full day before expected. Jane flew down the stairway passing Johnathan where he stood in the entry on his way to inquire on behalf of the earl as to the coach's early return.

Dodging the butler, Jane threw open the door.

"Stop, miss!" The butler's cry was not heeded.

Johnathan hurried after his cousin. Chasing a coach at twilight was not advisable. He caught up with her in the side yard where the driver brought the horses to a stop.

"You're back early. Is George—" Jane's question ended when one footman shook his head before opening the door for Mrs. Brown.

Mrs. Brown stepped down with her yarn basket. "Miss Jane. My, what a welcome. Your sister is safely delivered and was well when I left her."

"Did she send a letter?"

"A letter? No, she's scarcely been gone a week. What could she have to write? It was a pleasant, quiet journey with no disruptions. And I finished scarves and gloves enough for all of my grandchildren for winter."

Jane's face fell. "Thank you for your report, Mrs. Brown. I'm sure your family will be delighted to have you back so soon. I shall not keep you."

Johnathan offered his arm. "May I escort you back?"

Jane took it. "I was so sure she would have sent at least a note."

"They returned a day before expected. Perhaps there is another reason. If you would like, I could make an inquiry of the coachman?"

"Would you?" Jane's eyes reflected her newfound hope.

After leaving Jane in the care of Alexandra, Johnathan sought out the coachman and footmen. The conversation started off with some difficulty, as none of the three men were inclined to tell tales. Only after Johnathan implied he was to relay the information to the earl was he given the information that Georgiana's aunt was not only uninformed of Georgiana's arrival but lived in a state of gentile poverty and had been unable to stable the horses or provide for the visitors for the night. This was indeed news for the earl.

Upon returning to the house, he discovered the earl retired, putting Johnathan in the awkward position of bearing the news to his cousins or concealing it until morning.

Jane waited in the corridor, giving him little choice but to disclose what he knew. "What news?"

"Come let us find Alexandra, and I'll tell all."

Jane led him to the small parlor upstairs which the sisters called the sewing room. To Johnathan's eye there was little difference in the name as Alexandra and Jane were given to stitching in whatever room they might be in.

"Johnathan has news." Jane sat next to her sister.

"Not much, I am afraid. Georgiana was left with your aunt as expected." He picked his words carefully. "Since your aunt does not keep a stable, it was better that the coachman return to Leeds the very day they left your sister since there were no accommodations for the horses."

Alexandra set her stitching in her lap. "Surely there is a stable there."

"I gather it has been long empty of animals."

"No horses? Not even a pony?" Jane's brow furrowed. "That cannot be. I clearly remember them.

"That was many years ago." Alexandra patted her sister's hand. "I wish I could say that I would have thought father more responsible than to leave his sister without conveyance. It is still his barony. I know he receives reports and rents, though I have never seen those books."

"Perhaps Mrs. Brown will tell Cook more news." Jane stood.

"Sit sister, we will ask in the morning. Cook retires early and will not welcome the intrusion." Alexandra turned to Johnathan. "That is the whole of it then?"

"The coachman is not one to pass tales. I pressed him for what little he told me. And that he only gave because I made him believe I was asking for the earl."

"Leave a note with Grandfather's valet, then your news will reach him first and you will not have lied." Jane's matter of fact comment caught Johnathan off guard. Her reasonable solution to his small dissection allowed him to move to the palest grey side of honesty.

Johnathan excused himself and went directly to his room to write the note. When he finished he started another letter to Georgiana, having discarded his last in the embers of his fireplace.

Miss Georgiana,

We were surprised by the early return of the earl's coach. After speaking to the coachman, I understand the reasoning for it. I find myself concerned for your welfare and welcome. Although it was suspected that your aunt lived in some reduced circumstances, the report we have received is much worse than I would have assumed. While your sisters seem to worry for you, particularly Jane, I have little doubt that you will make the best of whatever lot you are thrown into.

Harvest is finished. I have been helping and learning where I can.

Lord and Lady Godderidge asked us to dine this week. Their daughter-in-law was not pleased. Although she does not seem as hostile toward me as the day we first met. Miss Godderidge was disappointed that you were not in attendance until we played cards as we won against Alexandra and Jane.

Our evenings are quieter in your absence and I miss our conversations. You must excuse me for my brief letter, my mother says I am the poorest letter writer of all her children.

Yours,

Johnathan Whittaker

The letter was not half as long as it was in his head. He gave no specifics of the harvest or told of the cat who attacked his boots every time he entered the hay barn. He negated to detail the game of cards either. Questions about Miss Godderidge's manner would not be welcome. Had she been flirting with him or was she naturally so affable? That was a quandary. He had no desire to lead Miss Godderidge on a merry chase when he was quite sure he preferred Georgiana. However, Miss Godderidge was more of age and possessed all the qualities that an Earl's wife would require. She was nice enough and if he could not convince his distant cousin to wed, he did not want to close the chance on Miss Godderidge.

That conversation would not be good to have with anyone. He reached to crumple it up and sighed.

His letters were unlikely to get better. Since George could

not write him first, it was better to send something short so it could be included with Jane's thick missive in the morning post and heed Georgiana's warning about his letter being dismissed by her aunt.

NINETEEN

Grey clouds hid the sun from view, as they had for most of the month since George arrived at Lightwood Manor. As far as she could tell, the clouds' only purpose was to prevent the warmth of the sun from reaching the ground.

"Do you think it will rain?" said George as she cracked open her egg.

Elaine did not bother looking out the window. "This time of year, it's just as likely not to rain. If you walk to the village, it will rain—likely a downpour. If you stay at home, not a drop will fall."

"I'm afraid I've been putting this off as long as I can." George tapped the letters she finished last night. "Nettie has several items for me to purchase."

"You best be off, then. I have a letter for your father. I trust you can send it?" Elaine implied the real question—did George have enough to spend for postage on another letter?

"Let me put it in the same packet as the ones to my sisters, as I have yet to seal it. Then I can post them together. That would save a few pence on the postage."

"Are my frugal ways rubbing off on you?" Elaine's voice held a bit of teasing in it.

Her aunt had been surprised to discover that George was not only accustomed to frugality, but quite adept at living simply.

"May I go too?" asked Timothy.

George shared a glance with Elaine before answering. "I suppose we can do our lessons as well walking as we can sitting at a table."

"Must I do lessons?" he asked, frowning.

"Our lessons will be a bit of a different type. But yes, it is important for you to learn. And it will be a good way to pass the time." The near three miles to the little town required distraction.

Timothy lowered his head and shoveled his porridge into his mouth.

Elaine smiled a grateful smile over his head.

Other than the seedlings George planted upon her arrival, she could not help with the garden—at least not immediately—due to the cold, damp weather. To be useful, she took over much of the burden of Timothy's lessons. Next year, he would be off to the Richmond School, providing Father paid the tuition. George was sure it would be easy to shame her father into doing so. The future baronet's education had been left to his mother rather than a tutor. For much longer than customary. As father had no sons, society expected him to foster the heir to the barony.

George's Latin was not nearly as good as Jane's, so she avoided that subject, sticking with math, history, and horticulture. Elaine offered her son lessons in English and grammar.

"We shall leave as soon as we have both finished breakfast." George eyed the salt cellar. She much preferred salt on her eggs, but like other commodities in the house, it was running low. She dipped the end of the cellar spoon in, taking only a few granules—she was sure she could count them on both hands—and shifted them over her egg.

Elaine clucked her tongue. "I did not think I would ever see the day when I would be counting salt granules."

"I believe salt is on Nettie's list for today."

"Be sure you buy things in the order I've given. There are things we can do without, if we must."

Timothy finished his meal and scampered out of the room without taking his leave.

Elaine sighed. "I suppose I shall have to add lessons in manners. He can hardly show up at school like that."

"My understanding is they will fix him well enough if he does, but it is better that we instill in him at least a few," said George.

"Do you hear often from your sister at school?"

"Rose? No. She abhors writing. She sends letters to Alex, which Jane copies and sends to both Phil and myself. They are getting much better. Reading and arithmetic were always so difficult for her, though she could recite any poem or essay given her."

"I could remember so much more when I was young." Elaine ate the last crumbs of her toast.

George finished her egg. "How much longer do you think the hens will continue laying?"

Elaine shrugged. "I'm not sure. They've never laid this far into the winter before. Your idea of moving the coop into the empty barn to keep them warmer seems to have helped them."

"I'm glad I could be of some little use." George bit her tongue before making any more of a self-deprecating comment. Elaine did not appreciate them, and they had made their peace with her father's actions. At least the little money George brought was of some help.

The slap, slap, slap of Timothy's shoes on the tiles in the corridor announced his return.

"I am ready."

"Not without a scarf, you are not." Elaine pointed her son back out of the room.

George hurried from the room to get her coat, which she learned was less than adequate against the cold winds of Yorkshire.

As they walked, George quizzed Timothy on mathematics problems. A rider in the distance prompted one. "A boy can walk a mile in twenty minutes. A horse can walk a mile in ten. If a rider and a boy leave for a village two miles away how much sooner will the rider get to the village?"

"Do either of them run?"

"No."

The rider reached them and slowed, he touched the brim of his hat. "Master Hall, Mrs.—oh I am mistaken."

Timothy stood tall. "Lord Banbridge, this is my cousin George."

Lord Banbridge's eyebrows rose as he assessed George head to toe."

"More accurately, I am Miss Georgiana Lightwood." George made the smallest of curtsies.

Timothy pursed his lips. "I did not do the introduction correctly, did I?"

"Well enough young man." Lord Banbridge dismounted. "Pleased to meet you. I assume your father is Sir Felton Lightwood?"

"Yes."

Timothy held up his basket. "We are going to the grocers and to post letters."

Lord Banbridge focused all his attention on the boy. "A very good place to go. Is your mother well?"

"Yes." Timothy turned to George and whispered. "Am

I supposed to ask about his family now?"

George nodded.

"Is Patrick well? Does he like school?"

"He writes that he is well. He is coming home this Friday for a few days before I must go to Town. Shall I tell him you asked?"

"Please do. Does he do mathematics?"

"Yes."

"Geor— I mean Miss Georgiana, was just asking me about how much quicker a horse could get to the village than a boy walking. Would you mind going and telling me how much time passes before I get there?"

George laughed. "Timothy, that will not work as we are already nearer the village than the two miles and Lord Banbridge was heading in the opposite direction."

"I'm afraid Miss Georgiana is correct. You will have to work out your problem on your own." Lord Bainbridge's horse danced to the side. "I must be off. My horse is still in want of a run. I hope to see you again soon."

George waited for Timothy to bid farewell to Lord Banbridge as he mounted his horse. Considering how friendly of terms her young cousin was with the man, it seemed odd that she had not heard of him before. Her aunt was a baronet's daughter, and he was a man of some rank, there should have been some mention of the family. His son must be the friend Timothy spoke of on several occasions. That would make Lord Banbridge a widower.

"Three minutes," said Timothy.

"What?" George's mind raced trying to make sense of his statement.

"The rider beats the boy by three minutes."

"I think you are only guessing."

They continued walking to the village, working through the problem until Timothy found the correct answer.

The village shared much in common with the one George had frequented most of her life. It was centered around a church, a long hall of some sort, an inn, and a few shops, with houses clustered here and there. Unlike her first visit three weeks ago, George did not need to ask Timothy for directions.

The post was collected at one side of the apothecary. They headed there first. Two large letters, franked by her grandfather, awaited her—one in Jane's handwriting. The other claimed to be from the earl, but she knew the writing to be Johnathan's. She stuffed both missives into her reticule and headed to the grocer's.

"Do we have a very long list today?" Timothy asked.

"Not overly. We should be able to carry it in my basket."

"Does that mean I'm going to have to carry it too?"

"It would be very gentlemanly if you tried—at least for a while."

"It would be much better if I had some sort of sack rather than carrying a basket."

"We shall have to see about that. Perhaps we can find something in the attic."

"My father carried a sack when he went to sea." Timothy rarely spoke of his father, so this conversation was surprising.

"Do you have it, do you think?"

"No, they did not bring it back when he died. Just a letter. Everything was lost at sea."

George never thought that Mr. Hale might not be buried in the church's cemetery. "Do you miss him very much?"

"I do not remember him much at all. I remember the last time he left, which is why I know he had a sack."

"Well, if we do not find one, perhaps we'll find something we can make one from."

"Really? You would do that for me?"

The bell clanged overhead as they entered the grocer's. "Of course I would."

George went to the counter and turned over her list.

"All of this, miss?" asked the clerk.

"Top items, starting down, please stop when the total equals a crown."

The clerk raised his brows. "So it shall not be on credit?"

"No. Mrs. Hale wishes it to be paid in full."

"Very well."

The clerk gathered the items. It seemed less than what it should be, to George's mind. But it always seemed that way, even when she shopped with Phil, who was extremely good at bargaining.

The clerk finished the order and pulled out a butterscotch.

"I do not believe that is on the list."

"My treat. Young Master Timothy looks like he would not be worse off for it," he said with a wink.

"Thank you, sir," Timothy tucked the candy into his pocket, holding open the door for George as they left.

"Now, to see if the butcher has any good cuts."

George inspected the pieces of meat, suspecting that more than one was not as fresh as she wished. "Ah, that there—I will take the lamb, please."

"Would you like me to cut it?"

"No."

George was not going to take any chance that the piece of meat she saw would be exchanged for another of lesser quality—a trick Phil learned after the less than scrupulous, now no longer in business, butcher switched out their pork loin for one too far gone to eat. Since she did not know this man well enough yet, she would not trust their precious money to chance.

The butcher wrapped the lamb shank in paper under George's watchful eye.

They exited the shop to discover a fine mist falling.

"Oh," whined Timothy, "I knew it would rain."

"We have our warm wraps and our best boots. We should hurry home before the storm grows."

"It always gets worse and we will be soaked through." Timothy was not wrong in his statement.

"If we try to wait it out, it could be quite some time."

At the end of the street a carriage stopped before them.

The door opened, and Lord Banbridge leaned out. "In answer to your question, Timothy—a man on horseback can make it home, get his carriage, and return to town before a lady and her young cousin can complete their shopping. Would you like a ride, Miss Lightwood?"

Timothy climbed into the carriage before George could answer.

"It seems Timothy has decided for us. Thank you."

A footman took George's basket from her, set it on the floor of the carriage and helped her inside.

"I hope you do not think it was too presumptuous of me to stop. I had an errand in town, which I also completed—so add that into your mathematics, Timothy."

"How am I supposed to do math for that?"

"It would be a very interesting equation. We will have to work it out when we return home," said George.

"So you have been to town twice today?" asked George. What was this man's reasoning for why he had come? He had a motherless son, he must be in want of a wife. With her next breath, George prayed she was wrong, almost missing Lord Banbridge's answer.

"No. When you saw me before, I was returning from another matter."

The raindrops plunked on the roof of the carriage.

"It is raining harder," said Timothy, drawing George away from her pondering.

"Very true. You warned me," said George.

"Mother said it would rain if we walked to the village."

"Your mother is very wise," said Lord Banbridge. "I have not seen her often—other than at church. She has not come to a single assembly this year."

"There are assemblies?" asked George.

"Why, yes. I keep hoping for Mrs. Hale to attend."

Perhaps her aunt was the reason for this kindness. He was a widower, wasn't he?

"Perhaps my aunt feels it is better not to leave Timothy to attend them," George offered.

"I have an idea, what if all of you come to luncheon on Friday afternoon? Patrick will be down from school." Lord Banbridge's rushed request was at odds with his calm demeanor. If George had to guess it was this very question which prompted him to bring his carriage to town.

"May we?" Timothy bounced in his seat.

George could not answer him as it was not her place. "I cannot answer on Mrs. Hale's behalf, but I will relay the invitation."

"I would extend it myself, but she does not seem to want me inside to visit."

Timothy talked around the butterscotch he put in his mouth. "Mother does not like visitors."

They stopped in front of Lightwood Manor. A footman opened the door and helped George out into the heavy falling rain and delivered the basket to the door stoop.

With Timothy's help, George emptied her basket on the kitchen work table. "Never looks like enough, does it?"

"But you purchased good quality flour—not a single bug in it."

Elaine unwrapped the packet of lamb. "And this meat! How did you convince the butcher to give you that?"

"I used a trick Phil taught me. You choose the best cut and do not let the butcher cut it again. We met Lord Banbridge. He is a neighbor?"

"Yes, he rents most of the land." Elaine turned away, though she seemed slightly interested.

"And then again on our way back—we ran into him again with his carriage."

"Ah, that is how you returned so quickly—and so dry."

"He's invited us to luncheon on Friday."

Elaine paused for a very long moment. "We cannot go."

Timothy opened his mouth, but George shook her head at him wishing him silent.

"That will be somewhat difficult, considering he told Timothy that Patrick would be home for a few days."

Elaine bit her lip and looked at her son. "I suppose I must accept, then. The boys have not seen each other since Patrick started at Richmond, and Timothy misses him so."

"So… you will go?"

"Yes."

Timothy squealed. Elaine shewed him out of the room.

"May I ask…?" How far could George quiz her aunt?

"There is nothing to tell. Lord Banbridge is only a neighbor."

"A widower?"

"Yes—His wife died in childbirth with Patrick's younger sister. I believe she is two or three now."

"And he has set his cap for you?"

"I said I did not want to discuss him."

George held the rest of her questions inside. It would not do to ask further when no answers would be given. She would simply have to observe.

TWENTY

ost of the leaves had fallen from the trees, allowing a view of the crisp morning sunrise through twisting branches. Johnathan crested a hill that overlooked The Willows and dismounted. Time alone became a precious commodity for Johnathan. His early morning rides, though shorter than he wished, were precious. He pulled George's letter from his pocket. It arrived yesterday afternoon, but between the tutor's lessons on British history and customs, and the earl's instructions, he had little time to read it. He decided, rather than read it before bed, when his mind was heavy and slow, he would read it in the morning when he could be alone with his thoughts.

Dear Cousin,

I feel quite settled in. At the same time, I feel as if I am a stranger here. My aunt, her son, and I walk everywhere we go, which is only inconvenient on the Sabbath, as we are expected to be at church without mud on the hems of our dresses. We do not stay after to socialize.

I have been helping my aunt by cleaning the house, including the shuttered rooms. Not only are the rooms shuttered from the inside, but also from the outside. The glass has been pulled from several windows, and they have been boarded up. No doubt, my father's way of saving money. Almost every window that does not face the street has been boarded thus.

I do not think that this is what Parliament intended to happen when they created the glass tax, which by my way of thinking, is quite ludicrous. If they must, they should tax the windows when one buys them—not every year for them just being there. I am unlikely to ever have a say in such matters, but I may have an opinion.

There is a distinct lack of trees in the moors, which I suppose is what makes them moors. I am not precisely sure. I shall have to write and ask Jane as to their definition. The heather, like leaves on trees, turned orange before turning brown. Winter is close enough now that there is very little color left at all, but I can see for miles— especially from the remaining window of my bedroom on the second floor. I wonder which would cost father more, the glass tax or the extra candles needed to make a room useful? Since he is not the one purchasing the candles, I should never know. We are very stingy with them.

I have taken on the responsibility of teaching Timothy mathe- matics and history. Admittedly, he is somewhat easier to teach than Rose was. He is eager to learn, which makes all the difference. He has confided that he wishes to go to Oxford rather than Cambridge. I can only hope my father will pay for such an education. I fear, when Timothy becomes baronet, he will have much to rectify—provid- ing my father leaves anything behind other than what he is required to by the Crown.

My knitting is improving. Wool is in abundance in the North Country. In the evenings before we retire—for we do retire very early here, to conserve both firewood and candles— Elaine and I knit while

Timothy practices reading for us. Sometimes I knit just to keep my fingers warm.

My aunt receives no callers, though people seemed polite enough on Sunday. I think somehow that this is her choice—to turn them away rather than let them see the poverty in which she lives.

I do not think money should define a person. Truly terrible people have amassed prestigious wealth, and that does not make them good. Nor does lack of money keep a beggar from being mean. Some claim money would change a person. I'm not sure I believe it. Take you, for example. I hope you will be the same person when you become an earl as you have shown in all respects your goodness. Although my grandfather's wealth is vast, I have yet to see a trace of it changing you. I pray for your sake it does not.

Obviously, I have too much time to ponder. This is what going to bed so early each night does. More than ten hours in my bed each night gives me far too much time to think, and without Jane or Sir Galahad to keep me company I find my mind wandering down random paths. Sometimes to The Willows, wondering about you.

As always, yours,
Georgiana

Postscript: I nearly wrote "George"—but for you, I will be Georgiana, because I know you prefer it.

Johnathan returned his horse to the stables. At least he was doing one thing properly. No one corrected his riding. His handwriting, on the other hand, was an altogether different matter. Just yesterday, his tutor commented that he had not seen worse chicken scratch from a child over ten in his life. And now penmanship was to be added to the pursuits he must undertake—the things he must study—on his way to an Earldom.

He was not sure why penmanship mattered, as the earl's secretary took care of most of his correspondence, and the earl, from what he could see, did very little other than sign his name properly. And the writing his tutor saw was personal notes—it was not as if it was a letter. All of his correspondence was written in his neatest hand. Georgiana had not complained, nor his family. Of course, he only received one letter from America, as it took so long for mail to go by sea, if it ever made it.

Some of his studies seemed like a lot of fuss and bother. Was the correct fork that important? If anyone else were becoming an Earl, they would not have to attend studies. Of course, as the tutor pointed out more than once, he would have gotten a proper education at Oxford, or perhaps even Cambridge. Even if Johnathan graduated from Harvard, it would not have been enough.

A drop of rain fell from the sky as Johnathan made his way back to the mansion. At least he would not be giving up a lovely day for his studies. Those were the most difficult.

Wrapped in a blanket next to the dying fire, George pulled out the letters she retrieved earlier that day. The thickest one was from Jane.

Dearest George,

I'm getting used to sleeping alone in this big bed. Sir Galahad has taken to sleeping on your pillow. I do not like this, because when his tail wags at night, he hits me in the head. I am most afraid that Father will come home and find him. However, I now can sleep several hours at a time.

Speaking of Father—he has only come once since you left. Long enough to clean out the household accounts again. I wish he would stop gambling—but we both know that wish is not likely to come true.

We are well. The house is very quiet with only Alex and I here. I fear that I do not wish for the silence as I once thought I did. Alex says she will stay until I leave for town for the Season then she will travel to Bath so I will not be alone. If the weather holds, Phil and Michael will come during the parliamentary break. Will father allow you to come for Christmas? I dearly wish it, but I know he will not spare the expense.

Isabel has gone to Town with her parents. Her father is passionate about the Apothecary bill as is Grandfather...

Jane's letter continued on detailing everyday life. So much so that the only new piece of information in Alex's were two recipes she copied from Cook using potatoes. One of the few food items Aunt Elaine could easily grow.

George poked the fire hoping for more light before breaking the seal on the other letter. As she hoped, it was from Johnathan. She reached for the handkerchief she kept under her pillow. It was all she had of him.

Georgiana,

I believe your grandfather is trying, or more precisely, the tutors he employed are trying to bore the American out of me. He even hired a tutor to help me work on my English to give it that little bit of French accent that seems so popular. My speech, it seems, is too close to that of the farmers and laborers. I am doing my best to adopt the more formal accent of the peerage, but I do not think it will hide my American roots.

We depart for London in two days. Your grandfather has been marshaling assistance in my petition, or is it his petition? I am not sure. It has my name on it so I assume it is officially mine to be named as heir at every point. Apparently, we must meet with most of the lords, earls, viscounts, dukes and everyone else who can claim or persuade a vote in person. I have also learned that

I must meet all their daughters, granddaughters, nieces, near and far relations and all the while be utterly charming. I am not excited by the prospect. I do not find that I have the personality to flirt and flit with all I meet unless my heart is involved. Which it cannot be.

George paused and reread the line. Was he trying to tell her something? She was glad that he did not pass around his flirtations lightly. Again she read the paragraph, this time a dread filled her. How could she possibly be the daughter of a disgraced baronet of little consequence, compete with the sophisticated and educated daughters with important connections, fine complexions, and full dowries?

She read on hoping to find answers.

May I say, your grandfather's cook is not nearly as good as yours. I have been missing the apple and egg concoction she makes for my breakfast each day.

I am learning British history, monarchs and kings and such. It is a brutal history, but in many ways, it's also the history of my country, because we share common roots. I liked the Magna Carta. At home I learned it was one of the foundations for the Constitution. I do not know if you knew that. Of course you do.

I enjoy my rides each morning. I am told that I can still ride when we go to Town in one of the parks. I do not think it will be the same. I am certain I shall have less time for myself there than I do here. Still, I will save your letters for those few precious moments of privacy.

Yours,
Johnathan.

The last part was hopeful, was it not? He wanted to read her letters without interruption or witnesses just as she did. With a sigh, she folded the letters. She stored them in her trunk, carefully tucking Johnathan's recent letter with his others inside of his handkerchief. As of yet, Aunt Elaine was not aware that some of the letters that came each week were not from her sisters. George only mentioned Johnathan in relation to her grandfather's scheme, since if he was successful in changing the earldom, it would have repercussions on her Aunt as Father would lose the privilege of living at Kellmore upon grandfather's death.

Wind rattled her windows, and a draft swirled around George finally forcing her into bed seeking for warmth in the chilled room.

TWENTY-ONE

Johnathan grossly underestimated the duration and frequency he would be allowed to be alone once in Town. He spent the better part of his first day being measured and pinned by the tailor. Women were not the only ones who took fashion seriously. Gentlemen, especially those whose titles were not enough to impress, spent vast amounts of money and time preening and puffing themselves up like the peacocks that graced the royal lawns.

Not one single night since they arrived had been a quiet one. Unless he counted the nights when Lady Philippa and her husband came with various dear friends and acquaintances for a quiet meal and cards. Most often they brought the Duke of Aylton with them.

Tonight was no different. The Duke sat in the corner, not drinking the port that was poured for him. He never did. Johnathan wondered at the reasoning behind offering his grace a drink night after night, only to have it left untouched. Apparently it was "proper" so it was done. Which of the servants ended up with the drink when they cleared the room later?

Johnathan took his glass and went to sit by the Duke who was not nearly as surly as he first appeared. "How was your day? Anything interesting in Parliament?"

"The Apothecary Bill. I never thought of the need for some sort of licensing for those giving medical care, but the more I hear the more I believe it makes sense. So much more interesting than the divorces that were on today's docket. I am not sure if I pity or envy those involved."

From what little he knew, the duke would not be opposed to his own divorce, granted only if it would not cause a scandal. Indiscretion was often a word heard in the same sentence as the duchess's name. "It seems a sorry and complicated matter."

"What of you? Have you found a woman of your choice? I've seen them swarming around you."

"I have found a woman I wish to court. But her father is not as agreeable."

"Tell me which is worse, a father who is not in favor of your match or one who is overzealous for it?"

"I do not know. I was tossed over for another last year. I thought my heart was broken, but I believe I found one with the power to completely shatter my heart if she wished me gone."

"I have not noticed you showing particular interest in anyone." The duke raised his full glass. "You see, I am a great watcher of people."

"The woman of my choice is not in Town yet."

"One of Philippa's sisters?"

Johnathan nodded.

"Miss Alexandra?"

"No, Miss Georgiana."

"The one who likes to garden and work in the fields?"

"The same."

"Does she return your regard?"

"I believe so."

A rare smile broke the duke's stern expression. "I believe she is having her Season this spring. I shall watch with much interest and stand by to help interfere if necessary. Sir Lightwood is—what he is. I have a great love for Philippa as she has been the best person in my cousin's life. And I will do all in my power to help her and her sisters."

The other men stood in readiness to join the ladies. The Duke and Johnathan followed.

Lady Philippa, her husband Viscount Endelton, his sister, Mrs. Deborah Godderidge, who was also Lady Godderidge's daughter-in-law, sat in the corner with Miss Isabel Godderidge. It was the second time this week that he had been thrown together with Miss Isabel, and he was not sure what to make of it.

"Cards?" asked Lady Philippa as she moved them from the box on the shelf.

"Only if you do not cheat," said her husband.

The room erupted in good natured laughter.

"I do not cheat, and you know it. You'll give my new cousin the wrong idea."

"She does not cheat. And you should stop saying so." This grumble came from the duke. "She is as honest as the day is long. A rarity in some circles."

"Richard, you know it is in jest. As it was a card game with one of those less than scrupulous ladies, one you put on my list if I recall, that first brought my dear Phil to my attention."

The duke frowned. Yet there was something good natured about it. "I will never hear the end of that infernal list, and I was not even the one with that harebrained scheme."

"Are you calling me harebrained? For that you shall have to be my partner, and I will play terribly ill. While we convince Mr. Whittaker that the only true advantage a duke has is his ability to be unsociable and still have the entire ton vie for him to attend their function." Mrs. Godderidge sat across from the Duke. Forcing him into a hand of cards.

"dread filled her, then Mr. Whittaker must be at my table. He is the only one of you that does not torture me."

"Only because he does not know you. By the time he is the next earl he shall bother you as much as the rest of us do." Michael's comment set the jovial tone for the rest of the evening. Which Johnathan found quite enjoyable.

Near the end, or what brought the evening to an end was Philippa rushing from the room, her hand covering her mouth. What happened next everyone in the room heard and politely pretended not to notice. Johnathan took advantage of the disruption to their party to retire to his room and read the letter that was delivered earlier in the afternoon from Yorkshire.

Johnathan,

I fear there is little news to write. One grey day blends into another. And to be honest, I have used all of my cheerfulness on letters to my sisters. I am afraid I will never quite be warmed through again. The days continue to be grey and even those without rain are damp.

There has been one interesting development which I could not write lest it get back to my father. I believe my aunt to be in love with a neighbor and widower. She will not speak of him without becoming flustered. We are to have luncheon there tomorrow. I am looking forward to seeing them interact. Of course by the time you receive this Lord Banbridge will be in Town as he leaves two days hence. I will write tomorrow night. I misjudged the amount of light I had, it is far too dim to continue.—

I believe it is as I hoped. Lord Banbridge seems to be much taken by my aunt. Yet she is very hesitant to acknowledge him. They have been acquainted since childhood, as Lord Banbridge is some years older than my aunt but younger than my father. I hope for aunt's sake that something comes of this attraction. It has occurred to me that if your petition is successful, father will have to return to his holdings here in Yorkshire. Which will likely be a great burden to my aunt. While she endures the imposed poverty well, she and Timothy are happy. I cannot imagine that it will be so once my father is in residence.

Yet another person who the petition would inconvenience. Mrs. Hale did not deserve to wait on her own brother, for although Georgiana did not write such in her letter, he read enough to know how it would be. Was there a way he could prevent the pain his earldom would cause Mrs. Hale? But what pain would he cause Georgiana and her sisters, not to mention the earl's tenants, if he did not go through with this plan to become the heir?

Do you like London? I imagine you have met so many people. I hope you are enjoying all the sights. Have you met the Duke of Aylton yet? Both Phil and Alex speak highly of him. His cousin is Phil's husband so you should be able to make the Duke's acquaintance. I hope you have much to tell me in your next letter.

As always,
George

George not Georgiana. At least if their correspondence was discovered, only someone close to the family could immediately discover the impropriety of their written relationship. Not that their letters held enough depth of feeling that if read they would appear improper. Oh how he wished her by his side. She was a more pleasant card companion than Miss Isabel. It was so difficult to speak with Miss Godderidge.

As he did not want his words or actions to be perceived as flirting. It would be much more fun to tease Georgiana. But he could hardly do that in a letter. It could be mistaken as something else entirely. If only he could write how much he missed her wit, banter, and mostly her warm smile.

"Eat up! Eat up, boy! We've got lots to do ahead. My solicitor is expecting us."

Johnathan moved the eggs from one side of his plate to the other. Was he really doing this? If he could save Georgiana and her sisters from their father, it would be worth it. He knew that. But why did he still feel such reluctance? The King... Having to pledge allegiance to a King... A man, by all accounts—or rumor—was mad. His son, the Prince Regent, was by no account a man of high moral standards. The power of these men is what his father fought for independence from. What would Father—

The earl interrupted Johnathan's thoughts. "After the solicitor, we'll stop by my club this afternoon. I have a friend or two who have agreed to help sponsor you until we have this all sorted and you can have your own membership to White's."

The earl bubbled with excitement, his enthusiasm grew each passing day. Several men they met commented on how he seemed much improved with health. Perhaps the earl could live to a hundred like Johnathan's grandfather. Time could solve the problem if he outlived his son-in-law. And in twenty years, all of Georgiana's sisters should be safe.

Even if this grand scheme did not work out, perhaps Johnathan's presence would be enough to help the earl live as long as his grandfather. Longevity was common in some families, was it not? The thought was enough to give Johnathan his appetite back, and he shoveled the remaining food into his mouth.

All too soon, Johnathan found himself in the earl's carriage, rumbling through wet cobblestone streets. The rain maintained the low drizzle that reminded him of Georgiana's letters. The carriage stopped, and they were led to a small office that, while perfectly clean, maintained an air of dustiness. Perhaps the drab browns and greys, and the multitude of books along the far wall, contributed to such a feeling.

"Your Lordship," a balding man greeted the earl and bowed slightly. "Now, this is your grandnephew, is it?"

"Not precisely," said the earl, "but close enough."

"Well, do come in. I have much to show you."

"Are there any problems?" asked the earl.

Instead of answering the question, the solicitor gestured towards the chair. "Would you like tea? I can send my man out for cakes, if you wish."

The earl leaned forward, inspecting the papers on the table. "No, we've just finished eating a large breakfast. What have you found?"

"What you are attempting is highly unusual, even under the best of circumstances. I have reviewed all the papers you sent me and suggest that we send a man to Boston immediately to verify if this Mr. Whittaker is indeed Lord Nathanial Ryeland. It would be most embarrassing to find that this young man was an imposter."

Johnathan's back stiffened. He was not an imposter. This was not his idea. And why would his grandfather tell such a story if it was not true?

The earl must have thought the same thing as he cleared his throat. "Johnathan Whittaker is no more an imposter than I am. In fact, he has only agreed to this action under some duress. It was not his plan at all, but mine."

"And you are sure the man you have been writing to in the colonies is indeed the original heir?"

"You have the papers before you, man. Can you not see that? We have been in correspondence for some time."

"Still," insisted the solicitor, "we should send somebody to verify his identity. These papers could be forged."

"You know they are not!" The earl stood and thumped his cane.

The solicitor held up his hands. "What I know, and what questions you will be asked when you defend this petition in Parliament are entirely different. We must cover and anticipate every question. It would help greatly if there were something other than papers. A seal, a signet... Anything."

The earl retook his seat. "I have the portrait, found in the attic. It has been verified to be my father's cousin."

"So you have said. But a portrait that shows some resemblance between the two men is hardly proof." The solicitor turned to Johnathan. "When your grandfather ran off to the colonies, did he take anything that would prove who he was?"

How was Johnathan supposed to know that? No one in the family knew about Grandfather's past. According to him he never even told all of his successive wives. In fact the only person living who could verify hearing the story was a shoemaker who had once been a minister who lived in East Stoughton. A vague memory of the minister leading their congregation when he was ten or so was not enough to help. "My Grandfather has a set of miniatures, including one that he said was his mother. That is how I recognized my great-grandmother's portrait so quickly in the portrait gallery."

"Did he have anything of his father's? A signet ring perhaps?"

Only the miniatures in the drawer. Johnathan could not

recall his grandfather wearing a ring. "I have never seen such. Grandfather was not on good terms with his father when he left England. You have all that I have seen and the packet of letters I brought. That Grandfather was sent the death notice of his father and kept it should account for something, should it not?"

"Yes, yes, all that is much in our favor. Unfortunately, there are few men alive who would recognize your grandfather, being in his nineties. And you, your Lordship, were only what? Two years old when he left?"

"Something like that."

"I suppose he fought on the side of the colonies during that unfortunate war?" There was a certain sneer with that comment that Johnathan was coming to recognize as not so much a personal vendetta but a national feeling. The English did not like losing. The fact that this current war was destined to end in a draw did not sit well with either side.

"He took up arms in what we call the French and Indian War. He did not fight in the Revolution, although my father did, as well as my uncles."

The solicitor thinned his lips. "I must know this before we go on. Are you willing to swear fidelity to our King and give up all your American ways?"

The last two words were said with such disdain that Johnathan wanted to answer "no." He took a deep breath before answering. "If this petition is granted, I will swear fidelity to the King."

"You are eager to be an Earl?" The solicitor raised an eyebrow.

"Not particularly. But I have become much invested in seeing that Felton Lightwood does not inherit the Earldom. It would not be good for his family, or for the tenants, or for those who rely on the Earldom."

"I understand several of the granddaughters are unmarried. You realize you could take care of at least one of them with much less bother."

"That would only be one, which would leave three. And with their sister already married to Viscount Endelton, I doubt they would want to return to the colonies with me."

"Is that what you intend to do?"

What choice would he have? His knowledge of farming would not go far to support Georgiana here where he was unable to own his own land. "I have no way of making a livelihood in England unless I am the earl. I can see no option but to return to Massachusetts. At least there, I have land and can provide for a wife."

The earl cleared his throat. "A reserve plan that we shall not need. Now, what else must we do?"

"As I said, the first thing we must do is send a man to Boston. There is a ship leaving in three days. If he leaves on it and is quick about his work, he should be back before Easter."

The earl steepled his fingers. "You should send two men."

The solicitor looked up from the paper he perused. "Why?"

"Two witnesses. Also, if some ill were to befall one of them, the other would survive."

Johnathan leaned forward. "You should send them on two different ships."

"Why?" asked the earl.

"While there are ambassadors in the United Netherlands for peace talks, hoping to end America's current disagreement with England—there are still raids and blockades. And they should not be sent from England at all. Send them from Amsterdam, the same way I came in."

"That is a good idea," said the solicitor. "I had not thought of it. I was hoping by the time they arrived, we would have peace."

"I believe we all wish for that, do we not?" asked Johnathan.

"As you see, he has wisdom beyond his years," said the earl. "As we have learned from past wars, it will take time for the news of the treaty to reach the Americas, and even more time to reach any privateers who might stop British ships."

"Very good point. I shall send a man, ahem excuse me, two men, as soon as possible. I have engaged the services of Mr. Fawkes, a renowned genealogist and expert on the peerage. He has asked that you meet with him on Thursday." The solicitor made a note in his agenda.

"Why a genealogist?" asked Johnathan.

"The current heir is Sir Lightwood, whose own claim to the earldom is, according the information given to me, is convoluted at best. While your lineage is straightforward, there is a possibility of a closer heir than Sir Lightwood. We do not need any surprise challenges to your petition." The solicitor handed Johnathan a card with the genealogist's address as he ushered them out of the office.

TWENTY-TWO

The unfamiliar writing on the unfranked letter gave George pause. Did she wish to pay the postage on a letter from an unknown sender? Curiosity won and she picked out the necessary coins from her reticule. The post from her grandfather, most likely Johnathan, Jane, and Phil were all properly directed. This last thin missive that either the sender had no means to pay for the postage or no desire to. The fine hand led George to believe it was the later as the writer was obviously educated.

She walked to town alone today owing the fact that Timothy showed signs of a cold and the day was blustery. George tucked all the letters, including one from her father addressed to her aunt, also unfranked, into her reticule and cinched it tightly shut before finishing the little shopping required.

As soon as she stepped from the shelter of the building the wind commenced a game of tugging at her securely tied bonnet requiring George to keep one hand on her head and the other firmly on her basket. Walking to town was pure folly. Without the benefit of trees there was little to break the force of wind off of the moor. Aunt Elaine was right, she should have waited until tomorrow for better weather, but she wanted her letters too badly. There was little to do but forge ahead.

At the crossroads, a well-used carriage, not unlike her father's, stopped. A man not much older than her opened the door. "Miss, is this the road to Limewood?"

George eyed the coach. The occupant was slightly shabbier than the driver. Having never heard of Limewood in her life, she pointed to the village without saying a word. Someone there would be able to answer the question. George hurried across the road and heard the coachman urge the horses forward. Only to her dismay the coach did not turn the direction intended but pulled up beside her and slowed.

She was alone with little cover. While this might have been thrilling in a novel, the thumping heart in her chest was all too real.

The man opened the window. "Let me give ye a ride."

George weighed her options. She could run into the moor in hopes that he would not follow. Lord Banbridge's manor was less than a quarter mile ahead, although he was in London, his staff would likely shelter her, but a quarter of a mile walking next to the coach seemed like an invitation to trouble. That left one option.

George turned and hurried back toward the crossroads. Just beyond the right fork was a small house of a farmer or shepherd or such. Since the coach would have to turn around and the wind was now at her back, she might have a chance.

She could make out the chimney and its promising puffs of smoke. At the frustrated shout of the driver, George left the road running as fast as her skirt and the wind would allow in the most direct path to the house. A yell behind her propelled her faster toward the friendly chimney.

A rabbit darted out of her path as another shout came from

behind her. Or was that her own scream? Had the basket not been her aunt's very best one, George would have abandoned it. The chimney was closer now and she could make out the entire form of the house and its accompanying stable.

Cries behind her were louder as the man was surely closer. No man with good intentions would pursue a lady through the moor.

Lungs burning, George kept running. A man exited the stable near the house with the chimney carrying a bucket.

George tried to yell, but her lungs were burning, and no sound came out. Still the man turned her direction, his face registering surprise. She slowed her steps, confident that the man chasing her would stop.

"What—" the wind caught the farmer's voice and whipped his grey hair around as George slowed to a stop feet from him.

"Miss!" shouted the man chasing her.

Still? George whirled to face her assailant, confident that he would not inflict harm on her in front of a witness.

The man held up her reticule. "You. Dropped. This." He bent over, struggling to catch his breath.

George wished she could do the same, instead she held on to a fence post for support.

"I did not mean to scare ye." The man stepped closer, holding out her bag.

George took it with a grateful nod.

The coach that she ran from pulled into the yard.

The man turned to the farmer. "I'm looking for Limewood. Can you direct me?"

"Never heard of a Limewood."

The man pulled a paper from his pocket and showed it to the farmer, who shook his head. He then held it close enough for George to read it. The paper was dappled with water stains blaring the writing in a feminine hand. It was a letter addressed to a Mr. F. Hale.

"Who is this letter from?"

"My late brother's wife."

"And you are?"

"Mr. Fredrick Hale, at your service." He bowed.

"What is your sister-in-law's given name?"

"Elaine."

Her aunt mentioned that Mr. Hale had younger brothers.

"Do you know her? I returned home from Canada to find this letter waiting for me—"

The wind ripped the letter from his hand and into George's dress. She grabbed it, crumpling the letter further. "May I read it?"

Mr. Hale looked at the farmer. "May she stand in the shelter of your barn?"

The man led them to the door. The wind immediately lost its fight and George's skirts fell into their proper place. She took the offered letter and unfolded it, looking for the signature. It was indeed her aunt's.

If the solicitor's office managed to be clean but dusty, the genealogist's office was dusty yet clean. Several slightly harried clerks bent over desks covered with odd papers and books. Mr. Fawkes offered more than one bow to the earl as he led him back into an office where a large, dark wood desk was piled high with folders and papers.

Mr. Fawkes set his hand on a stack five inches high. "This is what I have gathered so far. I have never seen a family tree with so many loose ends."

The earl sat in the nicest chair, and Johnathan followed in the other. The genealogist adjusted his spectacles and opened up the folder containing the first set of files.

"Now, this is what you sent me regarding your current line and the entailment that leads to Sir Lightwood. Unfortunately, I do not believe it is correct. Nor is it the line of succession."

"What?" exclaimed the earl.

Mr. Fawkes tapped a line on a chart full of names. "You see here, this line. The Lightwood Barony's connection goes back to the Second Earl of Whitstone. That is four generations that must be checked. I highly doubt that only one child was born for each of that many generations."

"And up here is all a muddle. While your father took the title…" Dizzying words continued out of Mr. Fawkes's mouth as he explained two other anomalies, which made him curious. "The man now known as Mr. Nathan Whittaker of Massachusetts is the only son of the Fourth Earl and his second wife."

"Yes, the first and all their children died of a terrible illness. Everyone knows that," said the earl.

"The parish records do not confirm that children passed. However, they are not in good order."

"So what does this mean for our petition?" the earl waved at all the papers.

"Nothing at the moment. Because it is an unconfirmed conjecture. I need more documentation or, better yet, witness accounts, journals and such. Until then, you continue as though your information is correct."

He opened another folder. "Now, this is somewhat problematic. The son of the fourth Earl of Whitstone now known as Nathaniel Whittaker, an American and Johnathan's grandfather did not officially abdicate. He simply left, and the title was bestowed on your father without proper process."

The earl took the papers and read them. "My father was not legitimately an earl? What of me?"

"If Mr. Nathaniel Whittaker wrote a declaration of his allegiance to the King or the colonies, then things would be much cleaner." Mr. Fawkes pinned Johnathan with a glare. "Did he in any way help with the Revolution?"

"He lost two sons to it. My own father eventually succumbed to losing a limb. I do not know financially how much he contributed. But he was with the Yankees."

"Hmm, that will not help you at all. And this is another problem: the man born as Nathaniel Ryeland, now Whittaker, refused to return to England upon his father's death in 1771. He was still a British citizen at the time. The earldom should have never passed to the man recognized as the Fifth Earl and hence to you as the Sixth Earl without a petition to Parliament. From the letters you provided, it is obvious that the dowager Countess of Whitstone, Lady Eugenia Ryeland, was aware that her son was alive and in the American Colonies and very much a subject of the crown."

"So I should not be an earl?"

Mr. Fawkes looked John Ryeland, the Sixth Earl of Whitstone, in the eye and spoke the words only he could say. "Quite possibly not."

Silence filled the room.

Mr. Fawkes opened yet another folder. "However. This correspondence from the King to your father is proof that he acknowledged the earldom as it was bestowed. Which is highly in your favor and I doubt Parliament will strip you of the title."

Another file was opened. "Mr. Whittaker, you have no living uncles, correct?"

"My Uncle Francis lives in Hingham," Johnathan paused, "Massachusetts, not England."

"Is he older or younger than your father?"

"Younger."

Mr. Fawkes slid a paper in front of Johnathan. "I understand your grandfather had four consecutive wives. If you can write down everything you know about your relations, it would be helpful. The information provided to me left many potential holes."

Johnathan looked over the paper. The first wife died in childbirth with her child. Nothing to add there. The second and all of their children passed from illness before the oldest was ten. The third was his grandmother and the last was Widow Black and she had grown children of her own. As for his uncles, aunts, and cousins everything appeared to be in order. "I have nothing to add. That is my family as I know it."

Mr. Fawkes frowned at the paper. "It is missing proper dates. There must be proper records kept."

Johnathan rubbed his chin. "There might be church records and such."

"I presume I cannot expect more from the colonies." A king could not have spoken with more condemnation than did the genealogist.

"My solicitor is sending men to my cousin in Massachusetts to confirm information. If you need clarification, I suggest you send a request to him immediately." The earl stood, ending the conversation. "If you learn more please contact me through my solicitor."

The oddest feeling that the earl was somehow snubbing Mr. Fawkes for his haughtiness toward him pleased Johnathan. A warm pride filled him. The earl's protectiveness had grown to include him.

TWENTY-THREE

Johnathan sighed as Georgiana continued to extoll Mr. Hale's virtues. Considering how frightened she was upon their first meeting, his cousin had more than warmed to the man. Part of that no doubt was the fact that he brought some much-needed funds to Mrs. Hale that were inadvertently sent to Mr. Frederick upon his brother's death. Funds that could be spent on Timothy's schooling. Although Georgiana did not specify the amount of the inheritance, it eased his mind somewhat as to the future of Sir Lightwood's sister knowing that she had other relations who might care for her.

Georgiana's letter continued for another page.

Mr. Hale has been a great boon to us and he has commenced many of the essential repairs that are beyond our skills. When he is not talking of Canada or the war I find him extremely delightful He says he can only stay for a fortnight much to the disappointment of all.

The letter finished with Georgiana's signature without any endearment. Her earlier letters showed what he thought was an increase of affection for him. What caused the change? He had little time to dwell on it as he had been invited to another ball. Thankfully, Miss Isabel would be there to save him from the attentions of Miss Simesson. Even Philippa did not like her, and that was saying something as she seemed to enjoy most people's company.

Johnathan was unclear as to what Miss Simesson had done in the past, only that it was enough to have the others warn him of her. She seemed no different than the many other daughters of untitled gentlemen he met, desperate. Fortunately, Isabel's presence could dissuade the eager Miss Simesson.

For the second night in a row George woke from a dream to find herself in tears. She never cried. Well almost never. She cried when her mother died. That was different. This was a dream.

A wedding at the chapel on her grandfather's estate where Phil married Michael at the end of Summer. Like Phil's wedding all her sisters were there, and Lord and Lady Godderidge. Only this time it was not Michael standing near the priest, it was Johnathan. The bride had yet to enter the room. But it was not George, because she was tied to the pew next to Jane who kept patting her hand. Then as the bride entered, George woke so full of loss that tears fell.

Why should she care so deeply. A few conversations, a half dozen letters exchanged. Yes, he asked her if they could court, and the memory of her hand in his still warmed her.

That contemptible letter she received several days ago, penned by one who has not the fortitude of character to reveal their identity, was invading her sleep.

She would have shown it to her aunt if not for Mr. Hale's arrival which had made any mention of Johnathan an invitation for discord. Not only was he an American, but they were corresponding in secret. No good could come of mentioning him now.

If only Jane and Alex were here to confide in. However, they knew little of her growing feelings for their American cousin, and she most certainly had not mentioned her attraction in letters to Johnathan, lest father read them.

Even laying in the darkened room George could see the words of the letter clearly in her mind.

Miss Georgiana Lightwood,

Permit me to acquaint you with intelligence lately circulated throughout the assembly rooms: that you stand foremost in Mr. Johnathan Whittaker's estimation as a future bride. With the full blessing of your Grandfather, whom Mr. Whittaker shall one day replace. One would suppose that a lady of sense would hasten to Town to safeguard such a promising connection from the artful designs of Miss Godderidge, whose attentions to the gentleman have not gone unnoticed.

Mr. Whittaker, as you must be sensible, is the most distinguished bachelor of our circle this Season, with his fortune and connections rendering him universally sought after.

I must confess that I cannot reconcile myself to the prospect of seeing Miss Godderidge secure such a prize. But neither, I am determined, shall you.

I advise you to maintain your residence in Yorkshire.

Yours, with perfect candor,
The future wife of an Earl

How the writer came to know of her living arrangements or of any interest Johnathan might have in her was a mystery that now invaded George's dreams. While Isabel might know from her sisters or perhaps Grandfather mentioned his wishes for nuptials, it was unlikely that either would be generally known. Isabel had never been much for gossip. However, she showed particular interest in Johnathan at the harvest fair, had she not? And Isabel possessed no intelligence of George's feelings toward her cousin due to George carefully concealing her feelings. But to have Johnathan openly flirt with Isabel?

George punched her pillow both out of frustration and in an effort to make it more comfortable. Writing her last letter to Johnathan was more difficult. She had not counted on the voracity of the London marriage mart during the Little Season.

Johnathan's letter was not much better as he complained of aching feet from dancing and mentioned more than a dozen women whose father's approval he was seeking. There were still two weeks until the end of the Little Season and the parliamentary break. Although given the difficulty with the genealogist, Johnathan might have to stay in London. Not that it mattered. Everyone would be together to celebrate Christmas and the New Year, except her.

Cease this George! Wallowing is not your nature. There is plenty to do in the day and Timothy and Elaine need not be the victims of your melancholy.

The lecture helped a little. In the morning she would burn the anonymous letter and end her pain.

TWENTY-FOUR

With the start of the parliamentary break, London society slowed to a stop. Johnathan looked out his window onto the square. Almost every townhouse was shuttered, as their occupants fled to the country to be with family and friends. Only a portion of the men—Lords, Earls, Barons, and whatever else—brought their families with them for the November session as most wished to be home.

Johnathan's daily routine remained the same. If anything, it became busier, as the earl secured a copy of the minutes of the House of Lords from the last two parliamentary sessions. Johnathan spent at least two hours a day familiarizing himself with all that had gone on, in addition to his other lessons.

To his relief, the balls seemed to have ended. A footman tapped on the door and delivered a thin letter. The name on the front was not, thankfully, anyone he met in Town. He broke the seal, eager to read Georgiana's news.

By the end of the letter, he was filled with disappointment, as it contained almost nothing of substance. Mr. Hale left—to the disappointment of all, including, apparently, Georgiana. The weather had grown colder. But not once did Georgiana share her own thoughts or feelings. A news sheet would have contained more detail.

What was wrong with Georgiana? Had Mr. Hale wooed her? Time could not pass swiftly enough until he and Georgiana would be together again.

Unsettled, George walked into the moor where no one would hear her yelling her frustration to the sky. Father refused to relent and would not have her home at all before the beginning of the Season. According to Alex's letter, Jane was so upset by the news that she refused to come out of her room for two days. The cost of sending a package, even only knit woolen mittens, was too prohibitive for George to send her sisters as a gift. Phil and Michael intended, weather permitting, to visit Kellmore from Christmas to Twelfth Night. Although, if Johnathan's suspicions about Phil being with child were correct, that plan might necessarily fail. Adding to her pain, snow began to fall. Not the soft fluffy flakes of magical winter days but harsh mini shards of ice that fell like daggers launched by a malevolent spirit. By the time she reached the kitchen door, miniature ice shards had cut every exposed bit of skin.

Elaine turned at the sound of the door, her hand on her heart. "Thank heavens. I thought you lost. Though I hoped you had sought shelter."

George lifted the scarf from her head. Frozen as it was, it retained its shape as well as a summer bonnet. "There was no shelter, not even a tree. Fortunately, I am no stranger to running."

"Get out of your clothes before you catch a cold." Elaine did not need to expound on the fact there was no money to be spent on a doctor. "I've heated you a bath in the still room."

The bath, poured much deeper and warmer than the weekly baths they drew for each other, made her fingers and toes burn. At least she would have them all. The water began to cool, and not wanting to waste it, George rinsed her hair. She emerged to find Elaine sitting at the table with the household books.

"Thank you for the bath. Would you like me to dump the water or refresh it?"

Elaine closed the ledger. "I'll refresh it. I could use a soak as well."

Alone in the kitchen, Georgiana reread the letter that sent her to the moor in the first place. Johnathan's letter was nothing more than a list of dates and tasks. The last paragraph was what galled her:

> *Georgiana, you seem not yourself. Your past letters have been as cold and singular as you described the Yorkshire countryside. Are you unhappy?*

Unhappy? Of course she was unhappy. She was denied the association of her entire family, and the man who supposedly wanted to court her was dancing with every female in London—and telling her about it. As much as she tried not to be jealous, she found it nearly impossible. For while her sister, Isabel, and all the other ladies seemed to have carefree days, she was knitting socks and hoping that a twice-boiled bone would create enough broth for a decent stew.

And for all his complaining about studying, at least Johnathan was warm all night.

And there it was. She was complaining about her lot again.

TWENTY-FIVE

A knock sounded on the door. It was much too early for Lord Banbridge's driver to come. Perhaps the beginnings of a storm sent the coach early.

George hurried to her aunt's door before Elaine could be disturbed, as she had only just gone to her room to change. A man in a heavy blue wool coat, his face mostly concealed under a scarf, stood in the lightly falling snow. It was not until George's eyes connected with Johnathan's that she recognized him.

"Johnathan! What are you doing here?" She held the door wide and beckoned him in.

He pulled the scarf off. "I have come on an errand, but I need to see to my horse."

George bit her lip. "We have a stable, but there's no provisions. We are to leave for Lord Banbridge's within the hour. Perhaps he could keep him for you."

"Lord Fitzwilliam Banbridge?"

How did he know the Lord's Christian name? She was sure she never wrote it, since she only knew of it from Elaine.

"Yes. Do you know him? Or only from my letters?"

"We met in Town. I hoped to reside the night at his home. I did not know he was hosting a party."

"Oh, he is not. He asks us to dine with him twice a week so Timothy and Patrick may see each other." At least that was the excuse Lord Banbridge used. "I see you've gotten used to calling London 'Town' the way we do."

It was more than just that—the accent that laced his words when he first arrived only months ago mostly faded. George pushed down the feeling of loss. This was what he was meant to be.

Johnathan chuckled. "I suppose I have. Are any blankets in the stable? I should at least care for my horse as much as I can until we are ready to leave."

George reached for her shawl, but Johnathan laid his hand on her forearm to stop her. "Stay inside."

Warmth spread up her arm, a warmth she'd missed so very much. "I believe there are some in the tack room. I'm sorry there's no food—"

"I will find it. I would appreciate some water."

"I'll fetch it, then, and bring it to you in the stable."

"You should not go out."

"Nonsense. I'll come from the kitchen. It's much closer."

Elaine appeared at the top of the stairway. "Is the carriage early?"

"No. Aunt Elaine, this is Mr. Johnathan Whittaker, my cousin."

"We were not expecting you, sir."

"No. I'm afraid it was a last-minute decision, and I would have outrun any express."

"We are expected at a neighbor's within the hour."

"As I've been told. I met Lord Banbridge last month. He extended a general invitation, should I ever be in the area. I hope that he will not be too put out if I arrive with you."

Aunt Elaine looked at George. "One can only ask. Well, then, welcome, Mr. Whittaker. I have heard only a little of you. Do come in and wait."

"I was going to take care of my horse the best I could until we remove ourselves to Lord Banbridge's.

"Very well."

George shut the door behind Mr. Whittaker and turned to her aunt.

"I told him I would bring water for the horse.

"Had you any notion of him coming?"

"None at all."

"Very well. Go and fetch the water." Aunt Elaine waved her off and returned to her chamber.

George found Johnathan in the stable, still bundled, rubbing down a horse she did not recognize. "Is he yours?"

"Yes. He is. Although I'm afraid I have terribly abused him on this journey."

She set the bucket of water near a trough. "You did not run him the whole way, did you?"

"No, although we did keep up a good trot to keep us both warm." Johnathan took the pail and moved it where the horse could reach it. "I hope your aunt or her cook do not mind that I did not transfer the water, I am not sure that the trough will not leak."

"It was not on our repair list. As the chickens do not need it." As if they knew they were being discussed, soft warbles came from the coop on the other side of the barn.

"I see you kept the coop in the barn."

"No reason to move it." This was not the time for chit chat so George chose the direct approach. "Why are you here?"

"You were not able to return to Kellmore, and your sisters were quite disappointed." He pointed to a bag. "I have come bearing gifts. Jane was beside herself with her worry about you not having more than a letter as your father refused to send a parcel."

George started towards the large pack.

Johnathan tugged her back by the elbow. "Not yet. Absolutely no peeking."

"I hate waiting."

It was Johnathan's turn to laugh. "So your sisters tell me on a regular basis."

"I have told you the very same myself."

"What I do not understand is how you can enjoy farming so much when farming is a waiting game."

"It is different with plants. They change every day. It is not like looking at a rock—at least you can see progress." Again with things they already noted in letters. More than one of which read like a farming almanac. "Will you return to Kellmore straight away?"

"If Lord Banbridge will extend a day or two of hospitality, I hope to stay until Thursday. Then I must return as I promised to be there for Christmas. Unfortunately, he has only a few hours' warning as I sent the message late last night from the inn. If today is not convenient for him, I will stay at the coaching inn and return tomorrow. I would not presume to stay with you. I have learned that gossip among the ton is spread in Napoleonic proportions."

"Ah, another thing you've gotten used to about our society."

"Sadly, yes."

"You must know that they have paired Isabel and you together—or so I have heard." George bit her tongue to keep from asking whether he had feelings for Isabel, and if the rumors she heard were true. She hoped they were not. He was here, after all—not with the Godderidges or some unnamed family.

"We have attended many functions at the same time. And owing to her family's connections with your sister's husband, we are often in the same circle. However, there is nothing between us beyond a mutual desire to avoid certain parties."

"What parties?"

"Fortune hunters, mostly. My future title and Miss Godderidge's dowry are both great enticements."

"Are you enticed?"

He set the bucket down and reached for her hand. "I meant what I said the day you left. I wish to know you better. Unfortunately, letter writing is not all I hoped it would be."

George looked up into the light reflecting in his eyes. She could stare at them very happily all day. "It is difficult to write of things of the heart. I find it so with my sisters as well. For one cannot know how one's words will be taken—or who might see them. I admit I often sign George mostly out of fear of discovery."

"I assure you, I receive your letters and read each one privately."

"As do I. We shall hope that at least in the next few days, we will have time to converse."

"Do you think it possible?"

"I believe my aunt has developed a tendre for Lord Banbridge—and he for her. Your addition will even out our numbers, so to speak," she said, smiling. "And allow for better conversation—and a bit of privacy for both of us."

"I quite like that idea."

"Come inside. Let's get you warm and presentable before Lord Banbridge's carriage arrives."

"I shall still have to ride my horse."

She looked at the animal. "He will be much more comfortable in Lord Banbridge's stables."

He offered his arm.

"Will you be bringing your bag inside?"

"No, I think it's best to keep you separated from it—as you

pointed out, you hate waiting. And your sisters asked me to make sure you wait until Christmas morning."

"I feel so bad. I've sent them nothing but a letter."

"They understand your circumstances."

"But I've made them many gloves. I've been knitting day and night. Do you think they will like them?"

"I would be delighted to wear gloves made by you or a scarf." His adam's apple moved more than usual. "I would like something of yours around me and holding my hands."

George felt heat flood her face and turned to hurry back to the warmth of the kitchen. She was not prepared to return his flirtation.

A footman showed Johnathan to a room that, according to Lord Banbridge, had been "hastily prepared." A warm fire greeted him, along with hot water, as if the room was ready for guests at all times. Johnathan changed his shirt for another in his bag. Traveling by horseback, he brought only a single change of clothes. He laid out his travel-worn shirt and hoped that he might impose upon Lord Banbridge's servants to clean it.

He found Georgiana and Mrs. Hale in the parlor with Lord Banbridge. Young Timothy disappeared into the bowels of the house the moment they arrived.

A footman announced the luncheon was ready. Lord Banbridge extended his arm for Mrs. Hale. Johnathan did the same for Georgiana.

The conversation flowed easily throughout the meal. Lord Banbridge asked many questions about life in the colonies and if he knew how negotiations fared in Ghent.

Instead of the women leaving and the men being left alone

to talk, as happened after most formal dinners, they all went to the parlor together.

"I wished to have a game of whist this past month, but since neither of our sons are ready to be partners, we have not played a good game. What do you say, Johnathan?"

"I like that idea very much."

"Ladies, would you prefer to partner with us or each other?"

Georgiana looked at her aunt.

Mrs. Hale looked down at her hands before meeting Lord Banbridge's gaze. "I believe I would like to be your partner, my lord."

The joy in Lord Banbridge's expression was not easily hidden.

The game was full of laughter and those little foibles that make it memorable. The clock struck five, indicating that the afternoon had well passed.

"Do you mind if I have the children join us?" asked Lord Banbridge.

Of course, nobody objected and the children were sent for.

Timothy bounded into the room. "Mother, we have been making paper boats."

"Really?"

A more sedate young man entered, followed by a young girl carried in a nursemaid's arms.

"Papa!" She held out her arms to be transferred to her father. The nursemaid curtsied and left.

"Mr. Whittaker, allow me to introduce you to my children. Master Patrick," the boy bowed. "And Anne Charlotte." The girl turned her head into her father's shoulder, peeking out from under long lashes.

"Pleased to meet you both."

"Is this the man from America?" asked Patrick.

"Yes, I am the man from America." Johnathan answered for his father.

"Have you ever been scalped?"

"I'm afraid the tales of America's native inhabitants are greatly exaggerated." Johnathan easily delivered the rehearsed line he used over the last month when equally inane questions were asked.

Patrick's smile faded and the sparkle in his eyes dimmed. "Oh. I suppose then they do not run about without any clothes on?"

"I believe they're well dressed," said Johnathan. "To be honest, I have only met three or four natives in my entire life. Once when I was about your age."

"Really? They're not everywhere?"

"No."

"Then I shall have nothing to tell my classmates."

"Oh, you can still tell them you've met an American. I much prefer coffee to tea, and I chop my own wood." Questions at his first balls in London taught him that information about personal labor was not well received by ladies of the ton, which meant it might shock a young boy as well.

Both boys gasped at that, and little Anne Charlotte giggled.

"You chop wood?" Timothy's shock was evident. "Are you not a gentleman?"

"Why would it not be proper to learn how to do hard work?" asked Lord Banbridge, crouching down until he was eye to eye with the boys. "A man's title comes about quite by happenstance because of his birth. A man's character comes about because he has cultivated it. Learning to work, whether it is with difficult sums or chopping wood, helps a man build character. Mr. Whittaker has built such a character, and he is unfailingly honest. He could have told you a story such as those you have read in your books about the American natives, but he did not. I hope someday you are both such men as Mr. Whittaker."

"I'm afraid, sir, you give me too much praise. I have my follies, as we all do."

Lord Banbridge stood. "I only wish my son not to judge a man only by his title, when there are so many other traits that make a man good."

"I think I understand, Father," Patrick said, turning to Johnathan. "It is not so shocking that you learned to chop wood. It's just shocking that you admit it."

Everyone in the room laughed.

A tea cart came in, and tea and sandwiches were served to all. Anne Charlotte stayed in her father's lap, then ventured to Mrs. Hale's side and allowed Mrs. Hale to prepare her a cup of tea so fortified by milk that it appeared to be entirely white.

As soon as the boys polished off the last of the biscuits, Mrs. Hale looked to the clock. "We need to leave. It has been continuing to snow, and we do not wish the coachmen or the horses to be caught out in a storm too late."

Lord Banbridge went to the window. "I had not realized it was snowing quite so hard. If you wish, you could stay the night. I'm sure we can find a nightshirt for Timothy, and there would be room in the nursery. I can prepare rooms for you and Miss Georgiana, or a room if you would rather share. We do not wish to put you out, but as you have said, a night ride in the snow and ice could prove dangerous."

Mrs. Hale joined Lord Banbridge at the window. "It is quite deep. I have not seen a storm like this for some time."

"I believe it was Christmas five years ago."

"Yes, I believe you are right," said Mrs. Hale. "We will accept your hospitality rather than endanger your servants."

Lord Banbridge rang the bell and informed the footman of the change of plans. He turned to the small party. "Will your housekeeper worry about you?"

Mrs. Hale shook her head. "No, I gave her the night off, and she went to her sister's."

"Then there's nothing left for us to do but find a way to amuse ourselves. Miss Georgiana, do you play?"

Georgiana shook her head. "One would think I did, but I can barely scratch out a tune. My eldest sister and my twin sister received all of that talent, I'm afraid."

"Miss Hale? I recall your playing as quite fine."

"I would hate to offend your ears. I no longer have an instrument upon which to practice."

"What?" asked Lord Banbridge. "Was there not a lovely pianoforte in your music room. Was it damaged?"

Mrs. Hale dropped her head. "It brought a good price, and I needed the money."

"You sold your pianoforte?" Georgiana's jaw clenched.

"It was a gift to me. I owned it in whole. No need to tell your father."

"You know I would not." Georgiana took her aunt's hand in support.

Lord Banbridge frowned. "I wish you had told me. I could have helped. Let me show you to the music room, and you may be reacquainted with the instrument."

"I would not want to inconvenience you." Mrs. Hale looked up at her host.

"Nonsense. Anne Charlotte finds my pianoforte most intriguing. I believe she would enjoy hearing it played."

The little girl giggled.

"I must not disappoint her then." Mrs. Hale stood, taking Anne Charlotte's hand.

Johnathan looked to Georgiana to see if they should follow.

Instead of leaving, Georgiana walked to the window. Johnathan looked over his shoulder at the boys who were engrossed in a book on ships they found before he joined her.

TWENTY-SIX

Large flakes fell, blanketing the world in white. George should have followed her aunt from the room, however the few moments in the stable with Johnathan were not enough. Since the boys were still in the room, she was chaperoned enough, was she not?

"This reminds me of home. I am glad I do not have chores in the morning, as surely there will be more than a foot of snow." Johnathan stood far enough away to keep the image of propriety.

"Not that much. Aunt says they never have more than a few inches."

"At home, we often receive more than a foot and a half in a single night."

George turned to him. "You jest."

"Do you not have great blizzards where the wind howls, and it snows so violently that one can hardly see his hand in front of his face?"

She searched for signs of teasing in his face and found none.

"There was a storm in my youth with snow so deep we could barely get to the barn to see to the animals."

"When?" There would not be a quick answer to such an imagined story.

"November of '97, it was my tenth birthday. I shall never forget it with the drifts taller than me."

"You celebrated a birthday last month?"

"Not exactly celebrated. I dare say only your grandfather knew."

George stepped back. He was nearly ten years her senior. She'd known he was older but they never discussed age. "You must think me terribly young."

"Does my age bother you?"

Most women married men a few years older than them. He was the same age as Phil's husband and she was not two years younger than her sister. "No. It is not so unusual."

He stepped closer. "I am glad to hear it."

"I am rather disappointed you did not tell me of your birthday in your letters."

He held the fingers of her right hand in his. "It was an oversight. With everything happening in Town, it seemed rather unimportant. May I ask, when is yours?"

"April third."

"You'll be eighteen?" He leaned closer as if asking a secret.

George swallowed. Unable to answer under the gaze of those very blue eyes of his, she lowered her face.

Johnathan slid a finger along her jaw sending the most delicious tingles down it to where he stopped at her chin and lifted it. "I believe that is the perfect—"

A loud clatter caused them to jump apart.

"Back you fiend!" Timothy brandished a fire poker as one would a sword, coming uncomfortably close to Johnathan's face. "Step away from her. You are acting most ungentle-manly."

Lord Banbridge rushed into the room. "What is going on here?"

"This man was about to ravish my cousin." Timothy jabbed the poker at Johnathan. Who jumped back.

Aunt Elaine gasped.

Heat rushed up George's face and she stepped further from Johnathan. Ravish? Where did he learn that word and how did he misunderstand its meaning. A near kiss was far from ravishment. If that is indeed what it was. Was it? She should not have allowed his touch. She raised her hand to where her jaw still buzzed. Oh, but what sensations filled her. She forgot entirely about the boys in the moment and only Johnathan existed.

"May I have the poker?" Lord Banbridge's jaw twitched as if he was trying not to smile.

Timothy handed over the poker without breaking his glare aimed at Johnathan.

"Now what do you mean by ravish?" asked Lord Banbridge.

"They were about to kiss!" Patrick shook with disgust.

Was it possible to burn to ashes from shame? George pressed her back against the window hoping it would cool her.

"Thank you, boys. I believe it is time for you to go up to bed. I've already sent Anne Charlotte up."

Patrick responded immediately and left the room.

Timothy stood with his arms crossed. "This American must be punished. He cannot take liberties with my cousin."

Aunt Elaine covered her mouth with her gloved hand. Perhaps George might not be punished too severely for nearly forgetting propriety.

Still holding the poker, Lord Banbridge bent until he was eye to eye with Timothy. "It is very valiant of you to protect your cousin. Would you allow me to meet out his punishment?"

"Will you challenge him to a duel?"

Out of the corner of her eye she saw Johnathan stiffen.

Aunt Elaine coughed a strangled sort of sound.

"No, besides being illegal, I do not believe that is the proper punishment."

"Will you punish him?"

"I will."

Timothy cast one last glare at Johnathan before marching from the room.

Lord Banbridge returned the poker to the fireplace. "Mr. Whittaker, will you join me in my study?"

Johnathan left without a word.

Aunt Elaine sat on the settee, no longer bothering to hide her amusement. "Come. I believe we need to talk."

"We did not—" George shuffled toward her aunt. "I—we—did not—"

"Obviously not." Aunt Elaine smiled. "You looked positively mortified. Take my fan, your cheeks are still burning."

George pressed a hand to her warm cheek. "I can never—Oh."

"As you know, I do not have a daughter, but I am not so old as to have forgotten my youth. First, I must know, do you wish for Mr. Whittaker's attentions?"

She fanned faster as the heat rose again. "Yes. He asked if he could court me before I came here."

"Am I correct to assume that my ignoramus of a brother does not approve?"

"He does not know." With effort, George set the fan in her lap. "Father was so angry and just declared I should come here. We did not dare ask. Johnathan and I have been writing."

"Ah, that explains your determination to get the post so often. And the many letters from your grandfather."

"He writes too."

Aunt Elaine laughed. "I am sure he does. Does the earl know you are writing?"

"I have not told him. However, Grandfather seems to know everything."

"That he does. Now for my next question. Were you about to kiss?"

George bit her lip. Was she? The tingles which raced along her jaw already faded to a memory. Were they a prelude to the touch of their lips? "I do not know. I could not think. He was standing close. I wanted him to."

"Hmm." Aunt Elaine sat back. "I see. And here I thought I was the one who needed a chaperone."

"What?" George raised her head.

"I thought you would follow us into the music room. Surely you suspected that Lord Banbridge and I…"

"Anne Charlotte was with you."

"And fortunately, you had the boys. We are a pair."

"Is staying the night wise?" asked George.

"We have little choice at this point. We shall have to chaperone each other, it appears." Aunt Elaine giggled, the sound starting as a tiny bubble and building to a full laugh.

George could not help but to join in.

Perhaps at some future date, Johnathan would laugh about this evening and the denied kiss. Lord Banbridge handed him a brandy as punishment.

"I am duty bound to ask if you dishonored Miss Georgiana under my roof."

"I did not intend to. We were only talking."

"Talking can lead to much more."

"I have asked her to court me."

"I wondered as much. Lord Ryeland is eager to put you forward."

"Unfortunately, Sir Lightwood is not."

"Understandable. If your petition to the Crown is success-ful, he loses a fortune he has coveted for many years. You should know as his neighbor I hold him in no esteem. Even less so witnessing his neglect to my dear Elaine since her husband's passing." Mrs. Hale's Christian name slipped so easily from his tongue as to leave little doubt about the lord's feelings for the lady. "We are in a similar position when it comes to romance it seems. However, given Miss Georgiana's age and innocence, I must insist that she is not to be trifled with under my roof."

"Agreed. I have nothing but sincere feelings for her."

"Still until there is an understanding, at least sanctioned by her grandfather, you will keep your distance."

It rankled to have another man call him out for his behav-ior which was barely above reproach. If the moment ended in a kiss, it would have been the nearest of touches. Enough to know if she returned his affection. Johnathan lashed back in the only defense he could think of. "I should say Mrs. Hale is to be under some protection as well."

"Not quite. As I am willing to propose as soon as she will allow me the conversation. One we were on the verge of starting after having sent my daughter off with the nurse."

"My apologies."

Lord Banbridge chuckled. "I assume that in all the history of interrupted interludes in England, yours is of historic proportions. Timothy was genuinely distraught. I've never met such a dedicated chaperone, and I found my first bride after three Seasons in London, so I met more than a few chaperones."

"I promise not to—"

Lord Banbridge held up a hand. "I will not stand in the way of love. So make me no promise other than you will not dishonor Miss Georgiana."

"Of course."

"And you will assist me in finding a few minutes alone with my Elaine, so I may ask for her hand."

"I am acquainted enough with the situation to know if you marry Mrs. Hale, that Sir Lightwood will do little to provide for her son, including schooling. Since Mrs. Hale has no champion, I feel compelled to ask if you will care for the boy."

"Felton and I have known each other for many years. His character is as poor as it ever was. Be assured, I will provide for Timothy the same as Patrick until he reaches maturity. I cannot do more than that."

"Such an offer is more than generous and more than I expected. I will do what I can to provide you with time with Mrs. Hale."

The glass clinked as Lord Banbridge set it on the silver tray. "Then we should go rejoin the women before they have a chance to undermine our plans and go into hiding."

TWENTY-SEVEN

As soon as the sun rose, Aunt Elaine insisted on returning home. The carriage was called for a hasty departure. Upon their return, her aunt retired to her room. Unusual when there were tasks to be done. Nettie arrived only minutes after the family finding the entire house to be cold. After setting the fires to rights, George collected the best of her knitting for her sisters, father, and grandfather. Small gifts were better than a letter. Small gifts were all that were ever exchanged.

As for Johnathan's gift, she did not have a scarf worthy of him. After sorting through the projects twice, she went in search of a skein of yarn she saw last week. In frustration, she finally knocked on her aunt's door.

The door opened far enough to see her aunt's red-rimmed eyes. "What do you need?"

"Is something amiss?" George struggled to think what it could be.

Aunt Elaine shook her head and opened the door wider. "Nothing more than me behaving like a schoolgirl. Was I needed?"

"I was in search of a skein of yarn I saw last week. It is a bright blue. I thought—"

To George's surprise, tears welled up in aunt's eyes.

"I have ruined it," said Aunt Elaine as she opened the door fully.

On the bed sat a rumpled mass of bright blue yarn full of curls and crinkles indicative of a project gone awry. Aunt picked up the tangled wool. "I wanted to give Lord Banbridge something for Christmas. I hoped to bake for him, but then I saw his Christmas pudding this morning when I snuck into the kitchen in search of a bit of toast."

That explained the tray sent to their room full of fresh buns and steaming chocolate.

"Our pudding is so pathetic. I might as well be a beggar going door-to-door today."

"I forgot it is St. Thomas day. Do we have anything prepared?" George had never been in charge of the annual gifts for the poor who traveled door to door.

"I have the barrel of apples you convinced your sister to send and gloves enough for those who do not have them. Not many come out this far from our little town."

"That would explain why no one has knocked."

"I should be thankful that I am as well off as I am. We have food enough to eat even if it is not as fine as I once ate. The roof is not leaking anymore and we can warm enough rooms to not have to live in close quarters." Aunt Elaine sat in the chair near the window and wound the yarn around two fingers to start a ball.

"What were you making?"

"A scarf, but I was trying a pattern I learned years ago at school, and I did not remember it correctly."

"I thought of making Johnathan a scarf, but I am afraid I will not have time before he leaves even if I knit all night. And if he comes to call, I cannot knit then."

"Call?" Aunt Elaine's head popped up. "You do not think they will come to call, do you?"

"I hope Johnathan does."

"We are not prepared." Aunt set the yarn aside. Tears threatened again.

Alex was better at calming people. What would her sister say? "They will not come for a few hours yet. My sister Alex makes lists when she has too many things to think about."

"A list. Yes. I need a gift."

"And you have four days until Christmas."

"I need to change to receive visitors and plan some food."

"My sister sent me a recipe for my cook's apple pudding. If we start soon, it can be prepared."

Aunt Elaine nodded. "I must change. Fitz—, Lord Banbridge, er, I want to—"

George understood the sentiment all too well. "We can help each other after we make the pudding. I saw some cinnamon on the shelf."

Nettie was more than happy to not add extra work to her day and gave up the larger table for the ladies to use.

George peeled and cored the apples. "I have an idea for a gift for you to give Lord Banbridge. A concert."

"What?"

"Play for him on his pianoforte."

"How can I practice? I have no instrument."

"When Alex was recuperating, she longed to play. However, could not leave her bed. Mr. Green, her nurse's husband, took a long board and traced the keyboard of my grandfather's pianoforte on it. Although it did not make noise she could move her fingers on it and imagine. When she was recovered enough to sit, she played us a Mozart concerto which she taught herself on what she called her piano-silent."

Aunt was silent as she crumbed the stale bread. "I could practice some older pieces that way, I suppose. I kept my music."

"And music is a gift everyone can enjoy. Anne Charlotte will be in raptures."

A blush bloomed across her aunt's face. "She is a delightful child."

As predicted, Johnathan and Lord Banbridge came at the appropriate hour. Aunt Elaine appeared much calmer than George felt as the men entered the parlor. Patrick also came and was led away by Timothy. Aunt Elaine and Lord Banbridge sat in the seats nearest the window leaving the settee for George and Johnathan. The arrangement was ideal for two private, yet chaperoned conversations.

Johnathan sat next to her allowing space between them. "We would have been here earlier, but Lord Banbridge insisted we wait for the proper time. I am not sure which one of us watched the clock closer. At least he has your tradition of St. Thomas Day to keep him occupied."

"And what did you do?"

"I spent time with the children. I miss my nieces and nephews, so I found it refreshing. Patrick found a book about the Americas and spent quite some time quizzing me. There is much I do not know as I have never traveled more than twenty miles from my home before traveling to England. I could tell him nothing of plantations and little of the natives. I believe he finds me a great disappointment."

The conversation fell into an easy cadence. Nettie brought in tea and informed Aunt that the boys were taking theirs in the kitchen.

Johnathan took a bit of the Apple crumb pudding. "This reminds me very much of the one your cook made."

"It is her recipe." George did not disclose that she and her aunt made it. Lord Banbridge might overhear and what would impress Johnathan might mortify her aunt if revealed. George glanced at her aunt to find her leaning forward in her chair as did Lord Banbridge. Had his chair moved? It seemed much closer to her aunt than she remembered.

"They seem very much enamored of each other." Johnathan moved an inch closer. His hand brushed hers as he moved.

"It does appear so." Her words came out too breathy. Aunt was not the only one enamored.

"I am glad of it. I have worried about your aunt's welfare if your father loses his place in line for the earlship and is forced to return here."

"I have thought the same thing. I pray you do not mention their relationship to my family. If my father were to learn before things are settled—" she braved setting her hand between them on the settee.

"He would interfere. You have not told your sisters?" Johnathan's hand covered hers as if it was the most natural action to take.

Warmth greater than that from the fire radiated up her arm. "No. I do not know when father will be at Kellmore and if he will read my letters to them."

"Do you write to your father as well?" His fingers danced over her hand, sending the most agreeable sensations up her arm.

George tried to appear unaffected as she answered. "As I must."

Johnathan chuckled, an action that seemed to have very little to do with the words passing between them. "He was not happy to discover that the earl would be descending on him for the festivities."

"Father much prefers when we go to The Willows for Christmas and New Year's day. Then he does not have the expense of hosting."

"So I gathered. Although I believe I am more of a problem to him. He cannot throw me out since you grandfather owns Kellmore."

"When will you return?" Her fingers responded to his and explored. Not all of his calluses faded, giving evidence to his hard work.

"I depart in the morning."

"Early?" She drew a question mark.

"At sunrise, I'm afraid." He caught her fingers softly in his hand, stilling them for a moment, but sending other feelings dancing through her.

"So I will not see you again?" There would not be other moments to sit touching and enjoying each other's nearness. Sharing in this way could not happen in a letter. Even if she possessed the words to write of the feeling, she could not, lest they be intercepted.

"If you allow me to call at such an unfashionable time. We can have our farewells in the morning."

George looked at her aunt, deep in conversation. "I believe I can gain her approval."

"That suits me very well." Johnathan clasped her hand inside of his.

Across the room, Lord Banbridge stood. "I am afraid we have pushed the bounds of propriety by staying so long."

"It was no bother at all." A schoolgirl blush bloomed on Elaine's cheek.

Johnathan stood as well. "I wish we were in Massachusetts. Society is not so strict."

"Hardly anyone comes here. You are unlikely to be discovered if you overextend your stay." George took Johnathan's offered arm to walk him out of the room.

"While that may be true, I gather there are several women in the area who keep a close eye on his lordship's comings and goings. He does not wish to harm Mrs. Hale's reputation. More than he has."

"You have discussed this."

"We have." Johnathan put on his thick wool coat and like Lord Banbridge, prepared to leave.

Patrick appeared with Timothy begging to stay longer. His objections were overruled.

Johnathan took advantage of the commotion and leaned close to George's ear. "Until tomorrow."

"Tomorrow."

George watched with her aunt as the men departed.

"I suspect you are going to ask for permission to have Mr. Whittaker call quite early. As he is departing the area, I see nothing wrong with it. Now if you excuse me, I have a piano-silent to practice. If you think you can make something with the blue yarn you are welcome to it."

While there was not time to make an entire new scarf, there was more than enough to embellish a plain grey one. Providing one stayed up most of the night near the kitchen fire to see her work. Still, it did not seem adequate. George stared at her creation and sighed. Well past midnight, there was nothing to do, but to wrap her meager offering. As she picked up her scissors a daring idea struck. Would Johnathan appreciate it? She acted before she could talk herself out of the most forward thing she had ever done.

As much as he wished to stay in Yorkshire longer, Johnathan knew he must return in time for the celebrations at Kellmore. Fortunately, the quiet night broke into a cloudless morning with not a touch of red in the sky boding well for his travels.

As the sun crested the horizon, Johnathan bid farewell to his host with vague promises to meet again when Parliament resumed. Frost clung to leafless branches, fence posts, and road as he made his way to Lightwood Manor. With no way to properly care for his horse, the stop would be necessarily brief.

The front door opened as soon as he arrived. Georgiana, wrapped in a woolen shawl, stepped out carrying a sack.

"Go back, I'll come in." Johnathan dismounted and removed the sack with the gifts from her family as well as his own. Would she like the miniature Lady Philippa insisted he have made? She assured him that the small portrait was an appropriate gift for a courting couple. He wished he could stay long enough to watch Georgiana's reaction to opening the gift.

"No. It is much too cold. I do not wish your horse to suffer so that we may have a few precious seconds together."

Johnathan took her offered bag, exchanging it for his. "At least we are alone."

"But not unwatched." Georgiana inclined her head toward an upstairs window.

Timothy stood with arms crossed, glaring down at them.

"Your champion is guarding you well, I see." The dream of a chaste kiss turned to mist just as his words did in the frigid morning air.

"He considers it his duty. Only my aunt's interference kept him inside."

"I see." He reached for her empty hand. "We have only a few weeks until you come to Town. We shall have time to speak then."

"Where shall I write you, in the meantime?"

"Your grandfather intends for us to return to London no later than the first week of the new year. There is still much to do with the petition.

"That sounds rather dull."

"My expectations for excitement are rather low." He tugged her hand bringing her a little closer and quickly brushed a kiss on the top of her head. "I shall miss you."

A shout echoed from the upper window.

They turned to find the window empty.

"Hurry before you face a fireplace poker."

Johnathan mounted his horse. "One day Miss Georgiana, I will kiss you properly and it will be worth every threat of being run through."

Georgiana's mouth popped open to a perfect "O". It took all his will power to stay astride his horse and not fling himself off and gather her in his arms. Instead, he nodded and urged his horse into a walk. At the gate, he turned to find her still watching and waved.

As the day grew colder, he wished he took the opportunity to kiss her, then he would at least have a warm memory.

When he and his horse could go no further, Johnathan stopped at an inn. After a meal of edible nondescript food, he retired to a room not much larger than the sagging bed. As much out of boredom as curiosity, he opened the sack Georgiana entrusted him with. A letter lay at the top. His name written across it.

> Johnathan –
>> Open when you are alone.

His smile grew as he broke the seal. A lock of hair tied with a blue ribbon fell out as he unfolded the letter. He scooped it up and cradled it in his hand. A gift shared only by lovers. He regretted the missed kiss even more.

> Johnathan,
>
> How inadequate this gift must appear when measured against the regard I would wish to express for you. Is it the fashion in America for a lady to part with a curl of her hair as an emblem of sincere

affection? I sincerely hope that such is the case as I lack the words to express its meaning.

The other night when we were separated, my aunt inquired whether we were upon the point of... The intimate expression of feeling that my nephew was preparing to duel you over. I confessed that I could not say with certainty what might have transpired. Had such been the case, this token would carry a meaning that I trust your understanding heart would comprehend without my need to speak more plainly.

I pray that Providence will watch over your journey homeward and that you may find every happiness this Christmas season. I count the days until we may meet again.

Most faithfully yours,

Georgiana

She loved him. Though she had not uttered the words, the lock of hair and the letters told him more deeply than her eyes did that evening in Lord Banbridge's parlor. The miniature seemed inadequate now. The only proper gift to give Georgiana would be her father's blessing. Unfortunately that was likely to prove more difficult as the earl's quest to name him heir. Yet obtain permission he would.

TWENTY-EIGHT

Johnathan,

    1815! I hope you are celebrating the new year with much happiness now that the Treaty of Ghent is signed. Lord Banbridge says that it will be weeks before the news reaches America, but that it should help your petition as we are officially no longer at war.

    I have a great secret to share with you. Which I may since by the time you read this letter, the news of it cannot harm anyone. Lord Banbridge and Aunt Elaine are to be wed by special license on Twelfth Night. He proposed on Christmas Day while I was out in the garden with the boys. They are very happy. We are closing up Lightwood Manor. Only Cook and her husband, and the best mousing cats will stay. They are rushing the wedding so that Timothy can return to school with Patrick in a fortnight. Lord Banbridge sorted all the particulars out with the headmaster when he gathered Patrick from the school Timothy is too excited to contain himself, as is Elaine.

    For now, I am to move to Lord Banbridge's with my aunt as she does not wish for father to get word of her change in circum-

*stances until after she is wed and protected. Lord Banbridge says
he will bring us both to Town, along with darling Anne Charlotte
when Parliament resumes. This means that I shall be in Town by
mid-February. Weeks earlier than I planned. I have written to my
Aunt Healand to advise her of the situation. I am not sure what she
will advise as you are also living at Grandfather's house on the square
and for us to be courting and living under the same roof will cause
a scandal.*

*After the nuptials are complete, I'll write to Philippa as well.
Alex's last letter says she has plans to take Jane to Bath after
her birthday to see the home grandfather purchased for her. Father
approved the trip and Jane is in raptures. (I write this forgetting you
may well know this as you were likely with them.)*

*Elaine is pleased that we shall arrive in Town well before the start
of the Season, as Lord Banbridge has promised her a new wardrobe.
His kindness to her knows no bounds.*

*As for your kindness, I appreciate the book as I believe I will
have leisure time this next month. Even more dear is your miniature. I
hold it dear, though the artist missed the intensity of your eyes—*

At a knock on the door George set down her pen. "I'm
blowing out the candle."

The door opened. "May I come in?"

"Of course, is something wrong?"

"I'm all nerves. So many thoughts I cannot sort them out."
Aunt Elaine brought in a tea tray. "May I talk them out with
you? I brought tea and the last of the plum pudding."

"Would you rather talk in the parlor?"

"No, I want to cozy up on the bed like I did with my cousins
when we were girls."

"You have cousins?" George was not aware of any family.

Aunt set the tray on the bedside table and climbed on the
bed. "My mother had a sister with three daughters. Each

summer, we would visit. I attended my first ball with my cousins. A year later I met my Horatio. We discussed it once, you know."

George could not remember any conversation about meeting Mr. Hale. "Discussed what?"

"Me getting married again. Horatio was insistent we talk about his possible death. With the war, we knew him not returning was always a chance. I told him I would never fall in love again." Aunt sipped from her teacup. "He left me two letters. One to read if the worst happened and one to read if …"

George waited patiently for her aunt to continue.

"If I were to marry again." Aunt pulled a pristine letter from a hidden pocket. "I am scared to read it. I thought I made my peace with being a widow. I was content enough with Timothy. Then, Lord Banbridge has me feeling the way I thought I never would again. I know I have Horatio's blessing so to speak, but I cannot bear to read it." Aunt Elaine set the letter between them.

"Shall I then?"

Aunt nodded.

"What if it contains private sentiments?"

"Please?"

George broke the seal. And read.

My most beloved Elaine,

It is with thoughts of the most complex nature that I pen these lines, knowing that should you read them, you have at last resolved to enter again into the matrimonial state. I can scarce describe my joy that you have found courage to embrace happiness once more. I earnestly hope that the gentleman who has secured your affections proves himself deserving of such a treasure, possessed as he must be of every virtue that might recommend

George tried in vain to hold in a giggle at the thought. Elaine laughed until tears came to her eyes. She motioned for George to continue.

Aunt Elaine laughed again.

"I agree. Any man who gets on with Father is not the right choice for a husband."

After they both calmed enough to drink a few sips of tea, George continued:

and your second—each sacred, each complete, neither diminishing the other.

I remain, even in death, with the deepest affection and most earnest wishes for your felicity,

Your devoted,
Horatio

They sat in silence for a long minute. George sipped her tea while her aunt reread the letter. With deliberate slowness Aunt folded and smoothed the paper.

"He had quite a way with words, did he not? I feared he would make it more difficult for me to marry. Instead he gave me permission to love Fitzwilliam too."

"Do you love Lord Banbridge then?"

"I do. When I was a girl, he was the most handsome man in the parish. But by the time I was out he was already affianced. Which was only right as he is so much older than I. That of course, was not love. Even I knew it was an infatuation of youth. Fitzwilliam only remembers me as a young girl whom Felton despised. It was last summer that he became aware of me. Felton wrote him to ask if he would rent out the last of the Lightwood's fields at a high rent. He came by and quizzed me. I was terribly impolite. Turned him away. Then I discovered he quizzed Timothy and I was livid. I marched over to his house and made a cake of myself. I yelled like a fishmonger."

"Surely not."

"I may have even used a few words I heard down at the docks." Aunt Elaine covered her mouth. "I ran from the house and vowed never to speak to him again. He, of course, did not take no for an answer. I am terribly glad that your presence finally gave him a chaperone for propriety."

"Can you imagine how furious father will be when he discovers that sending me here facilitated your nuptials?"

"No more angry than he was when Fitzwilliam negotiated a reasonable rent. Soon after, I started receiving money in the post. I thought at first Felton sent more money. I was stupid enough to mention it in a letter.... You know your father."

"He cut off more funds. Did he not?"

"I would not have made it through without Fitzwilliam's care."

"You are not marrying him out of gratitude?"

"No." Elaine blushed then covered her mouth in a giggle. "I deeply love him. If I did not, I could not enjoy his attentions so. I must admit that if we had not been granted a special license, I would be in danger of having a very wicked time with him."

George gasped.

"I forget you have never kissed a man. I should not say such shocking things."

"Is a kiss that—" George waved her hand, unable to put words to her thoughts.

"Beautiful? Powerful? Intoxicating? They can be with the right man in the right place. That is why we as ladies are encouraged to wait until an engagement to receive such intentions."

There was a warning in her aunt's words. Perhaps it was better that Timothy guarded her so with a poker and watched from the window. As she was sure there had never been a man finer than Johnathan Whittaker.

TWENTY-NINE

The early morning shouts could only mean one thing: Sir Lightwood had returned.

Today was Johnathan's last opportunity to ask for permission to formally court Georgiana before accompanying the earl to Town. He had not dared on Christmas Day, lest an argument ruin the festivities for everyone. The next morning, Sir Lightwood left in a huff after Viscount Endelton stopped him from berating Jane for an imaginary infraction.

Johnathan hoped Sir Lightwood would be in something less than high temper for this conversation, but it was unlikely that the day would improve Sir Lightwood's demeanor—for Sir Lightwood was rarely given to anything but anger around Johnathan.

Johnathan made two steps out of his door when he noticed Jane on the other side of the landing, trembling with Sir Galahad in her arms. The only way for the dog to exit was through the servants' stairway. This meant Jane would risk being seen by her father if she crossed the landing. She likely did not dare let the dog go, lest he take the front stairway, as he often did.

Johnathan waved Jane back and continued toward the main stairway. At the top of the stairway he whispered. "I will ask Sir Lightwood for a meeting in his study. You can take care of our friend then."

Johnathan clattered down the stairway, gaining Sir Lightwood's attention.

"You're still here?"

"Ah, Sir Lightwood, just the man I wanted to see. Do you have a moment?"

"What could you possibly have to say to me?"

"Perhaps we could go to your study?"

Sir Lightwood huffed, but led the way toward the study. Johnathan closed the door behind him—not so much to keep the conversation private but as to guarantee Jane's safe escape with Sir Galahad.

Sir Lightwood turned and jabbed a finger at Johnathan.

"Now, what do you have to discuss? Do you have something more to take away from me than my inheritance?"

"You must know that is not my aim."

"It may not be your aim, but it is my father-in-law's. He wishes to oust me so that I might never be earl!"

Johnathan could not argue with the truth of that statement. "I have sought an audience with you on quite a different matter."

Sir Lightwood folded his arms. "Enlighten me."

"I wish to court your daughter."

"Alexandra? By all means—take her far away."

"Not Miss Lightwood—"

"Jane? You may have Jane. She isn't—"

Thinking it best to cut off the diatribe before it continued, Johnathan interrupted. "I was speaking of Miss Georgiana."

"George?" Sir Lightwood called his daughter by the masculine form of her name. "I should say not. She is the only one of my remaining daughters who can make a good match, until Rose is of age. She is a true beauty. George is not for you, Yankee. The only way you could provide for her is if I cannot. You must be mad to think you can have my only means of securing a future the earl is determined to steal from me. Alexandra is useless on the marriage mart—what type of man would have her? And Jane... Jane is so mousy that no man would want her. You can have either of them if you wish for one of my daughters since that damnable duke has ruined my ability to force them to marry. But he never said I couldn't forbid them—" a cold calculating curve of the lips that resembled a smile grew on Sir Lightwood's face. "Ha. The duke only said I couldn't force— not forbid."

Sir Lightwood all but laughed at the revelation that gave him power. "No, you may not have Georgiana. You may have leave to court either Jane or Alexandra. You have asked and I have answered. I am their father. I still have that power. Georgiana is not yet of age and must abide by my decision. Now be gone. Get out of my study and out of my home."

"I will leave your study as you wish. But as for leaving Kellmore—I will not leave until the earl does."

Sir Lightwood yelled a rather colorful expletive as Johnathan hurried out the door.

Jane stood at the edge of the breakfast room.

"Thank you for distracting Father," she said as he neared. "He told me he would kill Sir Galahad if he found him in the house again. I did not think he would come back with Grandfather still here."

At least his argument with Sir Lightwood did some good for the family.

"Sit with me and eat?" asked Jane. " I'm afraid the others will not be down for some time, and I do not wish to be alone."

Johnathan had little appetite, but knew it was better for Jane not to face Sir Lightwood alone, especially after his ill-fated conversation. He made himself a plate and sat across from her.

"I heard your argument with my father. I am very sorry. I do believe Georgiana would be quite willing to court you as well."

"Without your father's blessing, I cannot."

"If we were identical, we could trade places, and then you could court her all you wanted."

"That would be an interesting solution. I beg you not to tell Georgiana of this. I shall try again."

A muffled yell, swallowed by a thump, came from the study down the hall.

"Oh dear, what now?"

The door slammed open, and Sir Lightwood yelled for his steward. Receiving no answer Sir Lightwood stomped down the corridor and into the breakfast room.

"Have either of you seen my steward?"

"No, Father. He's been given some time at home with his newly born son."

"And who gave that order?"

"If you would like, I can rouse the earl," said Johnathan.

"Figures! But how am I to take care of this then?" Sir Lightwood waved a letter. "There's been a disaster in Yorkshire that must be solved immediately."

Jane gasped. Johnathan wished to console her, but he knew it was not Georgiana who was in danger.

"My sister has gone and married—and closed up the house—both without my permission!"

"Aunt Elaine is married?" asked Jane.

"Yes. The bumbling Banbridge has swiped her from me. He has all my lands!"

Johnathan did not point out that those lands were, in fact, rented to Lord Banbridge—a fact he knew only from Georgiana.

"And what of Georgiana? Where is she?" asked Jane.

"Likely in the shelter of Banbridge. Although she knows her place, she's at Lightwood Manor. I was going to stay for the day, but I must leave immediately for Yorkshire. Find someone to ready my carriage!"

"Poor George," sighed Jane. "We have no way to warn her."

The possibility of leaving now on horseback crossed his mind. He would reach Banbridge first, but then what? Short of abducting Georgiana, that is how the law would see it, there was little he could do. Banbridge knew Sir Lightwood, hence the marriage by special license. By the time Sir Lightwood arrived in Yorkshire the boys would be tucked safely away at school. Banbridge was no fool. Georgiana would be safe.

"I'm sure she'll be well enough off. Lord Banbridge is the good sort. He is hardly one to leave Miss Georgiana alone. And I would say, in a round of fisticuffs, Lord Banbridge would easily win—if it comes to that." It wasn't much reassurance but it was all he could give.

"Are you sure?"

"I resided with the man for two days. And he was much besotted with your aunt. He will let no harm come to your sister."

"I should go upstairs and write to her immediately. My letter will not beat Father there, but perhaps it will do some good."

Jane rushed from the breakfast room, leaving a half-eaten bun on her plate.

As for Johnathan, he had absolutely nothing of interest to write to Georgiana—because his quest failed.

The candle flickered and the inn's wobbly desk threatened to spill her ink with every word George penned.

Dearest Jane and Alex,

If you have not yet set off for Bath, I wish you to with all haste. Father will be some days in returning to you, as he is likely following me to London. I shall explain forthwith, but I feel some urgency that you remove yourself from Kellmore as I have never witnessed father in such a rage as he is over our aunt's nuptials. Though the reason the wedding has set him into such a frenzy, I do not know.

I have already sent a letter detailing the wedding, so I shall waste no ink and paper on the beauty of it. I also included joy for Alex's birthday in the previous letter. I hope you have received it as there is no joy in this tale.

Father arrived two—no three—days ago and was granted admittance to Lord Banbridge's parlor. I shall spare you the cruelties father spewed at his sister. Lord Banbridge, much to his credit, barred Father from the house. Of course, father did not quit the village. We did not see him again until yesterday morning as services commenced at the parish chapel. Father arrived disheveled and intoxicated. I shall spare you the scene that unfolded. The curate's wife spirited our aunt away. Father realizing our aunt left, turned on me. Only the interference of Lord Banbridge kept me safe from father's temper.

Lord Banbridge has kindly offered to send me to London to stay with Grandfather with all speed.—

She could not bear to write the next. How her stomach lurched at the reek of drink that clung to father's rumpled coat. The congregation turned as one, their faces a collection of startled "Ohs" and raised eyebrows.

"Sir Lightwood, you forget yourself." Lord Banbridge stepped between George and her father.

"Forget myself? I forget nothing!" Father lurched forward, nearly colliding with a pew. "You think you can steal my sister and corrupt my daughter with your—"

"Papa, please." The words escaped Georgiana's throat as barely a whisper. The last time she called him Papa, mother had been at his side.

His bloodshot eyes fixed on her with such venom that she stepped backward into a column. Father grabbed her by the arm. "Come with me now, daughter."

"That is quite enough." Lord Banbridge stepped forward, his jaw set as firmly as the stone columns supporting the parish church. "I cannot allow you to handle your daughter thus while you are in this state and neither can these good people. Shall I call the magistrate? You are in God's house, sir, and you will conduct yourself accordingly. Remove yourself at once."

Father blinked as if noticing for the first time he was in the church. He dropped George's arm and fled.

George omitted the conversation leading to her leaving in the dead of a clear cold night in hopes that by the time the ruse was discovered, she would be beyond her father's reach. As traveling companions she had a coachman, three footmen, one of which whom had the arms of a blacksmith and could barely fit his clothes, and two housemaids who were being dispatched to Lord Banbridge's London residence to ready it for the arrival of the new lady of the house.

One of the maids came into the inn's dimly lit bedroom with a pitcher of water. "Miss? The coachman wishes to leave at five in the morning. Ye best be getting into bed."

George concluded, signed and sealed the letter, leaving instructions that it be posted at the first opportunity.

CHAPTER THIRTY

Lady Healand and the earl said their good nights after an early dinner, leaving Johnathan to his own devices. The last several days in London were quite pleasant, other than the smoke-filled fog that wound through London's streets. The recess with no soirees, dinners, or balls meant they were quite free to keep country hours while in Town. He settled into a chair to read the 1812 parliamentary minutes before retiring.

He had scarcely finished the third page when a heavy pounding on the front door broke the silence of the house. Johnathan closed the book and listened as one of the footmen answered the door.

"His Lordship has retired for the evening. You may call in the morning."

"But I must speak to my grandfather."

Georgiana? Impossible. Johnathan jumped from his chair and rushed to the door where the footman was still trying to decide if he should allow a cloaked woman accompanied by a liveried footman into the entry.

"Georgiana?"

Her eyes met his.

What the devil was she doing here? And at this time of night?

Johnathan ordered the footman to admit her and send for the earl and Lady Healand at once. In the flurry of trunks and footman Johnathan and Georgiana were unable to give but the briefest of greetings before Lady Healand appeared, quickly followed by the earl.

As the fire still burned in the library, they gathered there to hear Georgiana's tale over a pot of tea. There was a moment of stunned silence as she ended her recantation of events which landed her on the doorstep in a lightly falling snow so late that night.

The earl was the first to speak. "I sent my carriage back to Kellmore to take your sisters to Bath as soon as we arrived in Town. Likely they are enroute already. No need to worry on their account. Unfortunately, this is the first place your father will look for you."

"I do not know what father wanted other than to remove me from Lord Banbridge's protection. I believe sending me to Yorkshire was meant to be a punishment. Lord Banbridge's spectacular manor house hardly qualifies as punishment, as I have no responsibility beyond entertaining his daughter whenever I wish. Father can hardly force me to stay at Lightwood Manor on my own since he expects me to have a brilliant Season and news of my living without a chaperone would ruin his plans. What reason would he have to remove me from Town?"

A similar conversation occurred in this very room only days ago. Lady Healand glanced Johnathan's direction. He took a deep breath before answering. "As long as I am here, Sir Lightwood has reason to remove you from this house."

"Why?" Georgiana tipped her head.

"I asked your father for permission to court you. And he refused."

Georgiana's mouth popped open but no sound came out.

"He gave me leave to court either Alexandra or Jane, but not you."

"I do not understand." For the first time in the conversation, Georgiana blinked as if tears might form.

The earl took his granddaughter's hand. "I believe he thinks that you have the best chance of making a good match and since he is firmly set against Johnathan having a future here in England he intends to forbid the match."

"He cannot. He has an agreement with the Duke of Aylton."

"An agreement that says he cannot force his daughters to wed," said the earl.

Lady Healand set her teacup on the tray. "However forbidding a daughter in marriage is not the same thing, nor was it part of the agreement."

Georgiana's shoulders slumped. "We are not yet at the point of marriage. It was only a courtship."

As he suspected, she was unprepared for the full commitment.

The earl looked from one to another. "If you were prepared to wed, I could think of a solution."

"What grandfather?"

"The same as your aunt. Gretna Green."

Georgiana and her aunt gasped at this suggestion.

Whomever Gretna was, she could not be that bad.

Lady Healand shook her head. "Not this time of year. Traveling to Scotland in the dead of winter is hazardous at best. Not to mention the damage to her sisters' reputations. I have been reproached many times for my choice to marry over the anvil."

If he had not been confused before, Johnathan was completely befuddled now. "Pardon, who is Gretna Green?"

His question elicited a giggle from Georgiana and a laugh from the earl, lightening the melancholy filling the room.

Lady Healand answered his question, "Gretna Green is not a person. It is a Scottish village just beyond the border, where the matrimonial laws prove rather more accommodating than our own. Young couples of ardent attachments flee there for immediate nuptials. The local blacksmith may perform the ceremony without benefit of banns or parental permission."

"An elopement then?" How could the earl propose such a thing for his own granddaughter?

"It is one suggestion," said the earl.

"I cannot do that. Father will take all his anger out on Jane. And I promised I would be at her side this Season. And Johna—Mr. Whittaker—is to charm the daughters of those whom he needs to vote for him. If he is wed that cannot happen."

He had not thought of the aspect of their marriage standing in the way of his petition. Obviously Georgiana had thought much about the matter.

"We need another option. One that keeps all of my nieces from Felton's temper and allows Johnathan and Georgiana to have social interaction. For they cannot live under the same roof," said Lady Healand.

"We did at Kellmore," said Georgiana.

"The eyes of the ton are not on Kellmore. And that was before Johnathan stared in the eyes of so many of this Season's debutants. A prospective Earl does not come along every year," said Lady Healand.

"We discussed the possibility of my taking a flat before the Season. Will that not suffice?"

"It is still not ideal. It would be so much easier if you were here. And we have not found one suitable in the vicinity."

"Could I not stay with Phil?"

Lady Healand tapped her chin. "The viscount's mother and sisters are also in residence. Miss Moriah is to be introduced this Season, I believe. If there is room, it would be a good solution to the present problem. Still, Johnathan would need to take a flat before Jane arrives."

The earl yawned. "It is too late to send around a note tonight. I will do so first thing in the morning. I do not expect Felton before then. Even if he followed you immediately, his carriage is not up to such a quick journey, and he is unlikely to pay for the fastest horses."

"Come," said Lady Healand. "They have made up your room next to mine. We shall settle the rest in the morning."

The earl accompanied his daughter and granddaughter out of the room.

Alone, Johnathan stared into the fire. Elopement? The word echoed in his head, bouncing all of the other words associated with it; dishonorable, ruined, and words that would make his mother cringe. Georgiana deserved a better marriage than that. She also deserved a choice. She had known so few men. It was only fair she meet some this Season.

CHAPTER THIRTY-ONE

Y ou're here!" Phil pounced on George's bed long before George was ready to escape it.

"And you are far too happy for this time of day." George fluffed her pillow.

"You love mornings. I cannot believe I find you still abed."

"I have also spent the past three nights in inns with rickety beds and long days in a carriage."

"So Grandfather said. However, I am to have the rest of the story from you."

"And I am in want of a bath. It was too late for one last night."

"Then you can tell me everything while I comb out and wash your hair. Do you think the cooks will spare us some vinegar?"

George shuddered. The chance she picked up lice in the inns was greater than not. She and her sisters had spent long hours ridding themselves of the itchy little creatures who had no care for rank or status. She threw back the covers. "I'll tell everything as long as you kill every last one of them."

Two hours later, both sisters were satisfied, Phil with an account of George's adventures, and George with a head declared free of nits.

Phil picked at a scone the maid brought up. "I wish we could have you stay with us. But we are meant to leave in the morning for the Duke's house party. Rather his wife's. He loathes the things, but she insists that she has one. Michael and I are invited as the Duke's guests so he can avoid some of the more rowdy goings-on. I would never venture to take any of my sisters to the Duchess's parties as debauchery is on the menu."

"The Duke allows this?"

"He stops what he can. I imagine that if he did not attend that it would be much worse."

"What am I to do? Where can I go?"

"Why not join Alex and Jane in Bath? Father should not be upset by that. You will be far from Johnathan and at no expense of Father's."

"I had not thought of that."

"Father is more likely to pursue Marguerite than come after you."

In unison, the sisters laughed a bitter laugh.

"I believe Bath is the answer then. I best speak with Grandfather to make arrangements." George put on her shoes.

"I'll speak with Grandfather. You speak with Johnathan. I saw him after his Christmas travels to Yorkshire. He will not relish you leaving again."

Johnathan was in the library, his nose buried in a book. George observed him from the shadows of the corridor. His eyes crinkled at the corners. A thin line creased his brow. She stepped through the doorway and his eyes rose from the book and met hers—she was lost and found at the same time.

How was it possible that Georgiana looked more beautiful each time he saw her?

Elopement.

The word floated through his head. This time not accompanied by the ugly echoes. With effort he pushed the word back out of his mind.

"Are you off to your sister's then?"

"Phil is making arrangements for me to go to Bath."

He stood and came to her. "You're not leaving with her?"

"Phil cannot have me since they are leaving Town."

"How long?"

"I assume until the beginning of the Season."

He reached for her hand and brushed her fingertips. "That long?"

"It is no longer than we planned."

"I hoped..." He rubbed the back of her knuckles.

Georgiana turned over her hand, giving him access to her palm. "I thought we would have an opportunity to talk at least a few times."

"We can still write letters."

"No." Georgiana pulled her hand away and stepped back. "Father said you cannot court me. I need to abide by his wishes. Perhaps then he may change his mind."

"But—"

"Please. My sisters and I have fought against Father since Mother died. Learning to garden, bartering with the butcher, sneaking Sir Galahad in and out of the house... So much. We have not, as the Bible says, honored our father. I have thought about this much since hearing a sermon on the subject last spring. After Father's rampage in the church, I wonder if my constant defiance was making matters worse."

"So you will give up our letters?"

"I will honor my father's wishes in hopes of softening his heart. Once the Season begins, we can speak with my father together and make him understand we wish to court."

"And if he does not?"

Georgiana turned her face back to him. "Then there is always our friend Mrs. Gretna Green."

Before he could react, Georgiana whirled out of the room. Good thing too, if she stayed a minute longer he would have been tempted to take advantage of their lack of chaperone and kiss those upturned lips that dared speak of elopement.

THIRTY-TWO

Alex folded another petticoat. "I cannot believe you leave for London in two days. Our time has gone much too fast."

"You can still come with us," said Jane.

"No." Alex rubbed her hip. "I cannot travel again. I believe the waters are helping. This Season is for you and George to enjoy. One was enough for me."

George wrapped Johnathan's miniature in his handkerchief. "Will you be terribly lonely?"

"I have several new friends I have made at the baths."

"And they are all as old as grandfather," said George.

Alex threw a ribbon at George. "Not all of them. The Countess of Dunningham is not two years my senior. She is to stay here until her confinement, while her husband is in Town for the parliamentary session."

It was not right, Alex living alone. Well, she would not be completely alone. Green and her husband moved here to Bath with Alex, and there was a new cook and two maids. While servants were people, and Green far more personable than most, they still were not those whom Alex could interact with socially. Alex as a hermitess was not a lovely picture. "You will promise to go to every music recital you can?"

"I've promised ten times over to do exactly that and to attend services." Alex folded another shift. "Let us finish this and then we can partake of the waters. Father could be here as early as morning to collect you both."

According to the landlord, the flat was everything that a young gentleman in Town for the Season could want, including quarters for the valet and a cook who set out a breakfast each day. It was not a home. Only a place to sleep. Johnathan sat on the bed. At least it was comfortable. The chair in the small parlor room was not. Johnathan dreaded the hours he must continue to study almost as much as he dreaded the time he would spend in insipid conversation with each peer, his wife, daughters, and sons. Fortunately he only needed the patriarch or heir's support and influence.

March was time to prepare fields for planting. Watch over cows, sows, and nannies as they progressed to increasing the livestock population. Time for taking inventory of the winter stores to see how far they could be stretched. Sitting in a club placing bets on things such as raindrops, discussing politics with men who never saw war—only read about it in the papers—or strategizing crop rotation with men who never planted a seed was becoming increasingly ridiculous. Each day, more gentlemen arrived with their wives and daughters in tow. Each day, there were more people to meet and impress.

Johnathan lay back on the bed and stared at the underside of the canopy. The entire venture was exhausting without being physically wearing. How his father would laugh if Johnathan could tell him how much he desired to chop a cord of wood. Even mucking out a stall would be welcome at the moment.

This was a mistake.

He did not belong here.

He should have refused his grandpa's wish.

Georgiana.

She was the only reason to endure.

Georgiana.

Would she understand if he could not continue?

If only they could talk. She should arrive in Town sometime this week. But he must wait for an invitation before calling on her at the townhouse he called home these last several months. Lady Healand promised a small dinner party including him, within the week. In the meantime he was due at White's. The earl had secured a private meeting room for them to meet each day at 1:30.

He could do this, if for no other reason than Georgiana.

THIRTY-THREE

ather's voice droned on as his antiquated carriage bounced along the road to London.

With Jane, George faced the retreating road. Father had not stopped speaking for the full two hours since they left Bath. Alex was correct, traveling would not be kind to her health. By the time they arrived in Town, George would need a cane to exit the carriage and ascend the stairs to Grandfather's townhouse.

The only bright spot in the diatribe, thus far, was the revelation that father would stay in separate lodgings. The news did not come as a surprise as Father had been tossed out of Grandfather's townhouse last Season. Since Father did not rent a flat large enough to accommodate two daughters, and with Aunt Healand being his sole option for a female chaperone, allowing them to stay with their grandfather was his only choice, not to mention the sought after Russell Square address of the townhouse brought better opportunities.

"As for that cousin of yours. He is not to court you Georgiana, although I gave him leave to court Jane."

"I do not understand. If he asked to court me, why give him permission to court Jane?" George asked the obvious question.

"Because, Jane is unlikely to make a match since she chooses to dress like a scullery maid and talks even less. Another Season of paying for gowns so a daughter may be a wallflower. You, Georgiana, though not as refined or beautiful as Philippa, have an excellent chance at making a match from the many potential suitors. If Mr. Whittaker is going to steal my inheritance, the least he can do is take one of my two less marketable daughters off of my hands."

She should not have asked. Jane turned her head to the window.

"Stop your crying girl. It makes your skin blotchy and red."

Jane sniffled.

Father pounded on the roof of the coach to signal a stop. "I think I shall ride. I do not need to be subject to your nervous sniveling."

As soon as her father left. George soothed her sister only to have Jane calm her fears.

"I know you have deep feelings for our cousin. I shall not interfere. Though he is kind, I have no depth of emotion toward him any more than I did for our dear brother. No matter how Father pushes, I would not wed him. I believe Alex feels the same."

Her grand plan of honoring father had not softened his heart. What would Johnathan say? Two months of no communication did not mean that she had not thought of him daily, no, hourly. Though she had not sent him letters, it had not stopped her from composing them in her mind. The little miniature was in danger of having the paint worn off. "I miss him."

Jane squeezed her hand. "I know you do. I saw those far off looks."

"Do you think there is a way to gain Father's blessing?"

Jane did not answer.

No one could.

THIRTY-FOUR

ince arriving in England, Johnathan had sat in the earl's pew each Sunday morning. For the first time, he debated his place. There was room for him next to Miss Jane and Georgiana. Sir Lightwood was not present, yet. If he were to come, Johnathan did not want to be the cause of a scene like the one in Yorkshire which propelled Georgiana to Town in January.

Lady Healand beckoned him over, making the decision for him. It would be rude to refuse her. "My brother does not attend with us."

Johnathan sat next to Georgiana. If only it was not at church so they could talk. However, being so near the front, a conversation would not go unnoticed. The strict formality of the church in London had them standing and sitting at various times. The only benefit of which was the opportunity to brush his hand against Georgiana's. She inched her hand closer, giving him hope that she was as overjoyed to finally see him as he was her.

Another scripture was read. Johnathan allowed his mind to wander. He missed his church at home. It was not as regimented. Although like here, many people attended more for social reasons than spiritual.

Another reading from the Common Book of Prayer. Another song. The choir was quite lovely. He always enjoyed hymns, like the stained-glass windows, the music gave him a feeling of awe for God.

The benediction was offered and all rose to leave.

His fingers brushed Georgiana's again. "Miss—"

"Mr. Whittaker." It was not Georgiana's voice, but the earl's. Johnathan turned to converse with him.

"You are invited for the afternoon. We expect Viscount Endelton and his wife as well."

"Of course. May I escort Miss Georgiana to your home?"

"Only if Jane is with you."

A chaperone, as expected. He turned back to the sisters. "Are you up for walking? The day is brisk, but I thought I saw sunshine light the windows during the last hymn."

"If it is still pleasant outside, and if Jane is willing."

Jane nodded and the trio left the church. All signs of sunshine vanished, replaced by a cold drizzle. Jane pointed to the earl's coach. "Come, there will be room for you as well."

Once again, any chance at an intimate conversation was dashed. However, being seated next to Georgiana in close quarters was not unpleasant in the least.

It was not until after a small repast that Johnathan and Georgiana were able to sit in the corner of the library under the watchful eyes of the rest of the party and converse with a modicum of privacy.

Georgiana studied her hands as they twisted her handkerchief. No, it was his. The one he loaned her in the garden so many months ago.

"Are you shy around me now?"

"I just do not know what to say, or where to begin."

He could start with the weather, or the sermon, but Johnathan cared little about either. "Do you still want to speak with your father to see if he will relent?"

"I have little hope of him relenting. He lectured Jane and I much of the way from Bath. He is determined that I make a brilliant match as he is determined that you should never be Earl of Whitstone."

"As we assumed. I cannot tell you how much I wished I could have conversed with you these last two months. I confess I have composed several long missives to you."

She raised her eyes to meet his. "May I read them?"

"I thought it best to burn them lest they be discovered, but I can tell you of the contents." Johnathan ticked off on his fingers. "One, a shameful amount about the weather. Two, more than one diatribe over the state of the English political system. Three, details of meetings with your grandfather's solicitor, which end with the same 'we must wait for the messengers to return from America,' and, four, the genealogist is still not convinced that the heir is your father, and likely not myself either. And finally, how glad I am to have a quieter social season than when I came in November."

"That is all?"

"There were many questions about you. How do you like Bath? Did you partake of the waters? There were also deeper questions that I find myself reluctant to ask with so many who might overhear."

A giggle turned cough from Jane proved his point.

"Yes, I partook of the waters, and Jane and I agree they taste perfectly dreadful. We also bathed in the pools with Alex. They are in a cave and so very warm. Quite lovely."

"Do they help Alexandra?"

"She believes so. Peggy the first accompanies her, which is of course given to float," Georgiana's eyes danced. There was more to that story. "But it is much easier for her to get in and out of the pool. She claimed she would stay in for hours if given the chance."

"And what else did you do?"

"There were ever so many concerts at the assembly hall. We rarely went on dancing nights. Still we were out at least two nights per week, sometimes three."

They conversed for some time discussing those daily details that made up their lives during the past two months. Conversation Johnathan did not mind if the others overheard. Jane joined them for a few moments to give her version of a particularly odious violinist.

After an hour, the sun made another appearance sending the rain elsewhere.

Johnathan leaned close. "Do you think we require a chaperone for a turn in the garden?"

Georgiana looked at the windows. "I should think not. The whole of it can be seen from the house."

They left as soon as they gained permission. The garden was not very large as townhouse gardens were wont to be, being no wider than the house. Yet it offered more privacy than Johnathan hoped for.

He led Georgiana to the single bench.

"Oh it has a puddle on it. Grandfather must have sat here often."

"We shall have to content ourselves with walking about then."

"Oh look, something is budding." Georgiana brought him to a bush he did not recognize.

"What is it?"

Georgiana trailed a finger across the bud and over the stem. "I am not familiar with this plant. Perhaps if its leaves were out, I might be able to identify it. I'll have to ask the gardener."

Johnathan took her hand from the plant. "I do not wish to

curtail your joy over the bud, however we have only a few moments in which we can talk freely, and I wish not to lose them discussing matters that can be spoken in company."

"Why do you think I brought you to this bush? It is the furthest that can be seen out of the window without undue straining."

"Clever girl. Now may we speak of us?"

"Of course."

"I have much to say on that matter." He trailed a finger up her arm.

"I do as well. I do not care if you are the earl or not. Status does not change my feelings."

"I am glad of that. Would you feel the same if I voluntarily did not become an earl?"

"What do you mean?"

"I am having problems reconciling myself to some of the practices of Parliament."

"In what way?"

"Some of the laws they pass seem to me to punish the poor for being such." He did not want to dive deeply into the minutes and laws he had read.

"Could you change these laws if you were in Parliament and oppose them?"

"I have thought much on that. Honestly, I do not know precisely how my own government works, but here it seems very much a matter of 'since you are my friend you will vote this way, and because I like you, I will vote that.' I am not saying that there are not times when it is obvious that men vote the way their mind and heart lead them, but—" He let the sentence hang.

"If your heart is weary and your mind uncomfortable, then you must not compromise who you are. I would be extremely disappointed if you were to become something you are not in trying to please the rest of us."

He clasped her hands to his chest. "I only want to please you."

His heartbeat raced beneath her palms. How was George supposed to react to such a declaration? She tried to read his eyes. Her gaze dropped to his lips. Realizing where she looked she met his eyes again. The bright blue deepened and grew darker, drawing her in.

She could respond without words. She raised up on her toes and her lips met his. Firm, warm.

A heartbeat later, she pulled back. His lips bowed into a smile.

"I should not have, if we were seen…" Georgiana stepped back and glanced around.

"If we were seen, I would be forced to marry you. An outcome which I embrace with my whole being."

She pulled her hands from his. "It would bring disgrace to my sisters."

"Considering there is no shout from the window and no one is rushing out of the house, I believe you are safe from being forced to marry me." He crossed his arms.

"Oh! That is not what… I mean, I would like to… Oh mushy apples! I did not mean to slight you or repent of my boldness. I quite enjoyed—" George waved her hands as the word kiss refused to come out of her mouth.

Johnathan caught her hand. "I quite enjoyed it as well."

Heat rose in her face. "I do not believe we are supposed to admit that."

"I understand your dilemma. However," He tucked her hand over his arm. "It might be best if I escort you back inside as I am quite tempted to kiss you much more thoroughly."

George's eyes widened at his declaration, and her mouth grew slack.

Johnathan's lips thinned and he turned his head as he all but dragged her back into the house. Whatever had upset him now?

Once inside the door, George pulled her hand away. "I am not a racehorse. Why did you rush me so?"

Johnathan stepped back. "If you do not understand, it is best I do not explain. Please join your aunt and sister, I will return shortly."

Most peculiar. George opened the library door and looked back over her shoulder. Johnathan hurried to the stairway. Very odd indeed. Unfortunately, she could not hardly discuss the events with Jane.

While they were outside, their party had grown as Phil and Michael arrived. Which would explain why no one rushed outside after her brief kiss. Likely it was unwitnessed. George hurried over to her sister and brother-in-law to welcome them.

As she greeted Phil, her sister whispered in her ear, "We need to talk later."

Maybe she was not so fortunate after all.

Much to the enjoyment of all, Father did not appear by the supper hour and conversation flowed freely. However, as they concluded the meal, the butler entered to announce Sir Lightwood's late arrival. Grandfather excused the ladies to go to the parlor as soon as Father entered the room.

Aunt Healand ordered the door shut as soon as George and her sisters were all safely inside. "I would rather not hear any of the conversation from the dining room. Once again, your father pushes the bounds."

The three sisters did not need to be told this obvious truth.

"Jane, will you play for us?" asked their aunt.

Jane who played nearly as well as Alex, sat at the pianoforte and played a song from memory.

Phil motioned George to the settee furthest from the door. George thought it best to beat her sister to the questioning. "What news have you?"

"None of my news matters at the moment. I thought I saw you kiss Mr. Whittaker in the garden. But it happened so quickly that I could be mistaken."

Heat bloomed in George's cheeks.

"That is what I thought. Fortunately, Grandfather, our Aunt, and Jane were all facing Michael at that moment. You must be more careful."

"You will not tell, will you?"

"I do not see the need to. It was of such a quick duration that I doubt if a woodpecker could have been quicker. I assume it was your first?"

"Phil. Please do stop. I'll be in high color when the men join us and Father—"

"Does not approve. I know. We shall have to work on him."

"How? I stayed in Bath these past two months and out of obedience did not write a single letter to Johnathan. Yet he still berates me as if I were a child." Until that moment it had not occurred to George that since her father never knew of the letters, he did not know of her sacrifice.

"Now I have a husband to help us." Phil patted George's hand. "We also have the duke who finds a great deal of pleasure in vexing our father, because he enjoys defending me."

"He does? I had not heard of anything."

"Only yesterday, his Grace happened upon Father at his club. He did not say a word but Father took his leave forthwith. Michael and Richard thought it a very good joke."

"You call the duke by his Christian name?"

Phil covered her mouth with her hand and raised her brows. "Michael does all the time and I am afraid it has rubbed off. The duke is the kindest of men."

The door to the parlor opened, and the men came in. Judging from the thunderous look on Grandfather's face, the time apart had not gone well.

Father sat across from George and Phil. "I am informed you have not been invited to a single ball."

"My sisters are on the list for the Duchess's ball. The invitations always go out the day after Easter, which is a week away yet. It is early for invitations to most functions. Families are just returning to Town." Phil's answer came off with all the authority of the viscountess she was.

Father opened his mouth to reply, then shut it.

"As I told you at Christmas, leave the invitations for my sisters to Aunt Healand and myself."

"You have no right to tell your father what to do."

Phil closed her eyes for a moment and took a deep breath. "As the wife of a Viscount, I have more doors opened to me. Allow me to do this for my sisters."

Father scowled. No doubt he detested the reminder that his daughter ranked higher than him. "Just be sure to find them proper English husbands."

"I will not find them husbands. I will see that they are properly introduced and that they are not ensnared by rakes or fortune hunters."

George and Jane's dowries, though no less than Phil's, were hardly enough to turn any but the most desperate of men to seek after their fortune.

"You just keep her away from that American." Father's comment was loud enough to be heard by everyone in the room. Obviously he had not softened toward Johnathan.

THIRTY-FIVE

The Duchess's Ball was every bit the crush that Johnathan had been warned it would be. The card room was full as was the ballroom. He worked his way around the ballroom hoping to find Georgiana as he had not seen her since Easter Sunday and the intervening days became dreadfully long. He sent flowers around on her birthday, but was excluded from the family celebration as Sir Lightwood was in attendance. That man at least would not be at tonight's ball.

The first person he recognized was not whom he expected.

"Mr. Dalrymple, I did not know you were in Town."

"I only arrived a few days ago. Do you know if any of our mutual acquaintances are here?"

Loath as he was to admit Georgiana's presence, politeness dictated his truthfulness. "I believe Miss Jane and Miss Georgiana Lightwood are in attendance, and I saw Lord Godderidge in the card room when I passed. So I assume his wife and daughter are also here."

The news cheered Mr. Dalrymple more than Johnathan was comfortable with. "Good, good. Have you met my friend Lord Montgomery the Earl of Dunningham?"

"No, we are not acquainted." They made the proper introductions. Johnathan learned the man had recently been in Bath and owned a townhouse only a few doors down from Alexandra, whom had become his wife's particular friend.

Turning, he narrowly avoided bumping into Miss Simesson, who had likely stepped into his path. Mrs. Simesson stood close behind her daughter. With moves to match a chess master, Miss Simesson maneuvered for a dance. The supper dance was offered, Johnathan declined as it was already claimed. Or so he hoped. The set after next was determined and he moved away as quickly as he could. He needed to find Georgiana and secure the supper dance.

He greeted Lord and Lady Banbridge, who looked as in love as newlyweds deserved to be. They pointed him in the direction of the Lightwood sisters, whom they had just left.

Three quarters around the room, he located Georgiana and Jane discreetly fanning Lady Philippa.

"Mr. Whittaker." The name sounded odd from Georgiana's lips. "Would you mind finding Lord Endelton for us? My sister feels faint."

Philippa waved him off. "It is but a little thing, just the crush. Please do not alert my husband. It might alarm him."

"What if I escort you to the garden or obtain a glass of punch?"

"Anything with a bit of ice would be lovely."

Several minutes later, Johnathan returned with three glasses. Philippa looked no less pale. "Are you sure I should not locate your husband?"

Jane set her cup aside and fanned her sister more vigorously. "Please do, I think he should escort my sister home."

"No, I am your chaperone, you cannot leave before you have danced. All I need is a bit of air."

Johnathan offered his arm. "We will return shortly."

Once outside, Johnathan located a bench. Philippa breathed deeply of the cooler night air. After several minutes she stood. "See, all I needed was a few moments."

Johnathan had enough female relations to believe otherwise. If he was correct, his dear cousin needed several months. However, since no announcement had been made, he tucked his suspicions away. "Shall we find your sisters?"

"I suppose we must. I much prefer the garden. It is where Michael and I met. Nothing scandalous. Alex and Peggy had a falling out…"

"Georgiana told me the story. I did not realize it happened here."

"That is why I am loath to find Michael. It was a very trying night for him."

"Might I suggest we find you a seat near a window?"

With Philippa's agreement, they returned to the ball and found both sisters dancing a set.

"You need to ask my sister soon, or she may not have a dance available." The sparkle in Philippa's eyes softened the tease.

"I intended to do just that."

"I will be well here by the window. And my husband will come find me within the hour. This set has five minutes left at least. Go and find others to dance with while you wait."

There was wisdom in her command. It must not appear that he was partial to Georgiana. Soon he secured three other partners for the evening and returned as the set ended. Engaging first Jane for a set, then Georgiana for the supper dance.

Ouch! George pinched her lips together to keep from yelling at the man who stepped on her toes for the second time. If he had not been watching another female, and paid any attention to where he was, he may well have avoided her toes all together. The final notes played saving George's toes from further abuse.

Jane was already at Phil's side. Michael had joined them. Phil still looked pale and tired. George opened her mouth to ask if they should leave.

Jane pinched George's arm and whispered, "Do not ask her."

George rubbed at the spot above her elbow. "That was not necessary."

"I believe it was," whispered Jane. "She and Michael just settled on leaving directly after supper. Another question might change the situation."

Johnathan joined them carrying a cup of iced punch. "Lord Endelton, I see my services to my cousin are not needed further."

Phil took the cup. "Yet, still appreciated. I hope it will not inconvenience you. We will be leaving as soon as supper is over. We do not wish you or Georgiana to rush on our account."

If George counted correctly that was only two more sets away.

"You must excuse me as I have promised this dance to—"

"Miss Simesson?" At Phil's uncordial exclamation, everyone turned to an impeccably dressed blonde who laid her hand on Johnathan's arm.

"Lady Endelton, you do not look well. Please tell me you are not planning to upstage the evening as you did last year." There was not a single note of kindness in Miss Simesson's voice. "This must be your sister. The one who was exiled to live on the moors."

With clenched teeth George returned the nod. How did this woman know she'd been in the north country? Could she be the anonymous letter writer?

Miss Simesson's gaze swept over Jane's unembellished grey silk gown. "And goodness me, you brought a maid with you."

Johnathan disengaged Miss Simesson's hand from his arm. "I am afraid, Miss, that I am no longer inclined to dance with you."

"But a gentleman never breaks a promise to dance."

"And a lady does not abuse a gentleman's closest friends in his hearing and not expect some sort of consequence." Johnathan turned to Jane whose face was as white as milk. "Miss Jane. I believe we shall have that set I promised you now."

Jane took his arm and was led away from the rude woman.

Miss Simesson sneered more than smiled. "Do not watch the man too closely Miss Georgiana. He will never be yours. Your father will never allow it. You must set your sights elsewhere."

George glared at the obscene woman. "For someone who has only just gained my acquaintance, you speak rather decidedly about matters you know nothing of."

"Don't I? Your father is loose with his tongue when he plays cards with mine. They have many plans. Mark my words, if anyone is to be the next Countess of Whitstone it will be me."

"You sent that letter."

Miss Simesson's smile contained more venom in it than all the adders in England.

"Miss Simesson." Michael's voice was almost as imposing as his more famous cousin. "I believe it is best you leave us. My cousin is likely to side with me if I ask you to be removed altogether."

As Miss Simesson walked off, George was sure she heard the woman hiss. George's own partner came to claim the set and she was separated from her sisters.

After the set was over, George hurried back to Phil and Jane returned with Johnathan. Her sister's color was much improved. Johnathan bowed to Phil and Michael before offering George his arm.

The waltz was announced.

Johnathan led her onto the floor. "I hope you are not displeased to have to spend the entire dance with only myself."

As much as she wanted to ask about the odious Miss Simesson, whose name she was familiar with from last November's letters, George was determined to enjoy the waltz and not mention the encounter if he did not. "I find it impossible to be disappointed. I feel as if I hardly see you."

"You miss me then?"

"Of course I do."

"Then I am fortunate that I am told it would be a great offense if I did not call on you tomorrow."

"You will be received with open doors."

Johnathan led her into a turn ending in a little hop. The movement bought them in line with Mr. Dalrymple and Isabel. The two couples nodded cordially.

"I was surprised to see him when he asked me to dance earlier."

"I did not see you dance with him."

A thrill shot through her. Johnathan had watched her. "Your partner must have been beautiful."

"I consider myself fortunate to have secured a dance with you."

George smiled up at him. "I saved the supper dance for you."

Johnathan smiled back. The warmth of his gaze filled her from her toes to the ribbon in her hair. He was the only one she ever wanted to have look at her in such a way. "She was not nearly as beautiful as you."

THIRTY-SIX

ounding on the door of his flat roused Johnathan from a dream he wished could be reality.

The valet entered his bedroom moments later. "The Earl of Whitstone asked that you meet him at the club in one hour. He also sends his condolences for the news in the morning paper.

"Condolences?"

The valet pointed at the newspaper in his hands and a particular article on the lower part of a page.

Incident at Dartmoor.

Johnathan read in disbelief. Seven of his fellow countrymen killed, another sixty injured. The war was over. Why were they still incarcerated as prisoners of war? Were they not supposed to go home? Details were vague, blaming the unarmed detainees for the guards firing into the crowded prison grounds. If his countrymen were escaping, why would they have been loitering about the walls? Gambling? No sane man would have stayed, even in this island country. The statements of Captain Thomas Shortland seemed incomplete at best.

Johnathan slumped into the chair nearest the window. There were no names. Did he know any of them? He had not even realized there were prisoners from the war there. Had anyone spoken of it on the voyage over? He searched his memory. Yes, there was a discussion of prisoners of war, but not specific locations. Not that he paid much attention to the preparations the men on his ship were making for the talks in Ghent.

The treaty was signed four months ago.

How?

Why?

A church bell rang. He needed to get up.

His valet entered. "My apologies. I have waited as long as I dare. But I cannot delay any further as you have an appointment with the Earl."

More flowers than George imagined filled the parlor. Jane received two bouquets. George a surprising four. Johnathan sent flowers to both of them. Simple ones that meant no more than friendship.

George searched for cards in the other three bouquets. The man who stepped on her toes, had the decency to apologize. His note being short and to the point.

Aunt Healand took the card when George passed it on. "Interesting. I wonder how many ladies of the ton have received the self-same bouquet and card."

"I shall count myself fortunate I did not dance with him." Jane smelled her flowers. "I do not understand why Mr. Dalrymple would send me flowers. We hardly spoke during the dance other than the mention of the differences between home and Town. Do men send flowers out of pity?"

Aunt Healand took the card from Jane. It only identified the sender, no other sentiment was added. "Not unusual for flowers to only come with a calling card. We shall see if he comes calling. Georgiana, who sent your other flowers?"

"I am at a loss. Neither of them has a card. I've searched every bud."

Aunt rang the bell, and a footman answered. He was tasked with searching for lost cards.

Aunt sat in the most comfortable seat and picked up her needlework. "Now girls, we wait."

The earl's carriage stopped in front of the solicitor's door. Hardly what Johnathan expected for the morning meeting.

"Shall we see what was so pressing he could not put the news in a letter?" The earl exited first.

As before they were shown into a not overly tidy office and were offered a seat and refreshment.

The solicitor sat behind a desk and opened a folder. "Yesterday a ship arrived from Boston. I must commend you on having me send two men. As only one returned."

"And the other?" asked Johnathan.

"My fault for sending a single man. He fell in love with an American and is not returning. He did, however, send his report." The solicitor took a paper from the folder and handed it to the earl.

"I have made you a copy. As you see, both men agree that Mr. Nathaniel Whittaker was indeed the son of the Third Earl of Ryeland and thus the original heir to the title. I have a letter here signed by Mr. Whittaker confirming that he has pledged his allegiance to the United States and disavowed the crown which solidifies the legitimacy of your father's claim to being the Fifth Earl. I shall retain a copy of the document, and the original is included as evidence with your petition."

Johnathan sat wordlessly, though his mind was more than full. He had not thought the men would return so soon. It was possible to make the voyage in less than two months either way. And their business could have concluded quickly. Grandfather had nothing to hide. Disappointment filled him. A growing part of him hoped the visit would prove unsatisfactory, thus putting an end to the petition without the necessity of him declining. After this morning's news, the idea of pledging allegiance to a king, a man, who by some accounts was mad, and the Prince Regent, who possessed all the morals of a common barn cat, was morally repugnant. The Incident at Dartmoor was a massacre on his countrymen. How could the Crown do anything other than immediately apologize?

The solicitor pulled out another paper. "I have already sent a copy of this to Mr. Fawkes. This, according to Mr. Whittaker, is a complete list of his wives, children, grandchildren, and great-grandchildren. While it is obvious that Johnathan would not be first in line for the title, none of his relations are willing to take it either and have signed affidavits to that effect." He handed over more papers and added three sealed letters. "These letters are for you, Mr. Whittaker."

The earl shuffled the papers. "In your opinion is there anything to keep the petition from proceeding?"

"Not from the information I have gathered. I believe Mr. Nathaniel Whittaker's accounts and the witness of the man I sent will be adequate to establish the validity of Mr. Johnathan Whittaker's claim. There will be no challenge from that front. However, Mr. Fawkes has yet to deliver his final findings. I see no reason why you should not see that the petition is added to the parliamentary docket." The solicitor's words dropped as a gavel.

Why did becoming an Earl, a well-respected man of society, a man who could affect reform, feel like a prison sentence?

THIRTY-SEVEN

At home hours were nearing a close when the butler announced their first visitor. Mr. Dalrymple.

Where was Johnathan? He promised to come. Grandfather had left early and said something about Johnathan. He must be detained. Grandfather was still out as well.

Mr. Dalrymple spoke to everyone generally of the weather, last night's ball, and how London air smelled of smoke. After precisely fifteen minutes he took his leave with no particular attention to Jane or George. Puzzling, since he had sent flowers. Didn't that usually indicate some sentiment, even if only an apology for bruised toes?

Aunt Healand checked the corridor to ascertain if they were alone. "I've sat through enough at home visits and I have never had one such as this. All these flowers and only one visit, and you'll pardon me saying so, but Mr. Dalrymple did not appear nervous, nor did he express particular interest in Jane."

Jane walked to her flowers and breathed in the scent. "Since I have no interest in him, I did not mind. It is peculiar that he sent them. Our conversation was not out of the ordinary. And his only compliment was on my sensible dress, which I am sure was not a complement at all."

The grey-almost-lavender dress Jane wore today was typical of her dresses with no added lace or frills.

George moved to the window and parted the curtain. No carriage in front of the house. No Johnathan. And no clue as to the origin of the other two bouquets of flowers. She turned to study them. While she enjoyed pruning and growing mother's roses and flowers, she had never taken a particular interest in the language of flowers. "Jane, what do pink roses mean?"

"They could mean the beginning of a relationship."

"Not much of a beginning when I am unaware of the sender."

"They could also mean he finds you graceful or elegant."

George pulled a daisy from the bouquet from Johnathan. "And this collection has so many different flowers that send quite a muddled message, does it not?"

"Not so varied. A daisy is for innocence, and you like them. Primroses are for consistency. I am unsure about some of the others, but myrtle is for marriage."

George turned away to hide her blush. "And what do the ones you were sent mean?"

"Friendship, kindness. Nothing of romance." Jane tapped the vase from Mr. Dalrymple's offering. It is as if he sent these just to send flowers to any lady of his acquaintance. I must ask Isabel if she knows more."

"Do I dare ask about my last flowers?"

Aunt Healand spoke up. "Red and white roses? How can you not know when you have been caring for your mother's roses all these years?"

"Tending roses and knowing what they mean have nothing whatsoever to do with one another."

"Red roses mean passionate love." Jane's answer came out in a reverent whisper.

George sat down hard. "I am confused. Why would someone send those messages with no card?"

Jane circled the table where the flowers stood. Once, twice, again. Then she started to giggle.

"What?"

Jane held one hand over her mouth trying to stop the laughter as she beckoned George with the other.

"What is it?"

"Look, they all came from the same florist except Mr. Dalrymple's and the man who stepped on your toes."

"Probably not that many places to choose from."

Aunt Healand laughed. "I cannot even count the number of shops where a man can purchase hot house flowers. And a few men like the Duke of Aylton have homes that boast an orangery and grow their own."

"So, it would be highly unlikely for four of six offerings to have similar origins?" Jane smiled as she did whenever she was correct.

"Precisely."

Johnathan sent them all? George could not voice the question. Especially when he had not appeared during the usual hours. "If will you excuse me, I think I shall take a turn about the garden."

It was late afternoon when Johnathan and the Earl returned to his townhouse. Visits to various clerks had been accomplished followed by a stop at White's where several of the Earl's friends toasted the good news that the petition could go forward. No one mentioned Dartmoor. Though a few turned their papers over to hide the story.

All the while Johnathan fretted.

Before he could tell the Earl, he must talk with Georgiana. It took several dropped hints to get the Earl to invite him back to the townhouse. The butler informed him the ladies were in the parlor.

With a speed that his tutors of the past few months would frown upon, Johnathan rushed to the parlor. Jane sat at the pianoforte and Lady Healand dozed in a corner chair. Georgiana was no place to be seen.

Jane stopped mid-stanza. "Johnathan?"

"My apologies for appearing so late and not waiting to be announced."

"George is in the garden." Jane straightened her music. "As soon as I finish this piece, I will join you. Aunt would be upset if I did not provide proper chaperoning."

"Is it a long piece?"

"Only if I make too many mistakes." Jane played the first few notes, the last one being most obviously wrong. "Oh it might take some time."

Johnathan rushed out of the room to the sounds of a discordant cord. He owed Jane a better bouquet of flowers and a box of sweets.

George sat on the bench in the corner twirling a daisy. Since none grew in the small space it must have come from the flowers he sent. She looked up as he approached.

"You received my flowers."

"If Jane is correct you sent me three sets. Two of them with no card."

He rubbed the back of his neck. "I did. I wanted to make sure I chased away any other suitors you might have had."

"You need not have worried on that account. Only Mr. Dalrymple came."

"Dalrymple? What was he doing here?"

"We do not know that any more than we know why he sent Jane flowers that meant friendship."

Johnathan gestured to the empty side of the bench. "May I?"

Georgiana tucked her skirts closer to her and nodded.

"Jane is giving us a few moments alone. I do not wish to waste them and we must speak."

She set the flower between them and looked into his eyes.

For a moment, he forgot his purpose. Then the newspaper headline flashed through his mind. "Do you read the newspaper?"

"Jane does on occasion. Why?"

"Have you heard of Dartmoor Prison?"

"No."

In as delicate of terms as he could manage, he relayed what he knew.

"The war is over between us? Why were they there still?"

"I do not know. England has ships enough. There has been no one I could ask."

"Is that where you have been?"

"No. We visited the solicitor this morning, and then your grandfather stopped at the club to celebrate with his friends."

"Celebrate what? It does not seem like a day to celebrate."

"The messengers sent to my grandfather returned with the news that they were hoping for and the petition can proceed."

Georgiana studied his face. "You did not celebrate, did you?"

"Only enough to satisfy your grandfather." Johnathan clenched his hands tighter and focused on his whitening knuckles. "I cannot become an earl. I do not know how to not accept the title either. I will disappoint so many people."

A light touch on his arm was followed by Georgiana's whole hand and she leaned closer. "Johnathan?"

He continued to stare at his hands.

"Please look at me."

He turned enough to see the side of her face.

"If you will not look at me properly, at least hear what I say. As you seem to have forgotten our previous conversation."

Her statement was enough to convince him to look at her fully.

"I said this before, and not far from this very spot. I am not interested in you because of a title nor do I wish you to take it if you will be miserable."

"I know you said as much, but do you mean this? Do you realize I cannot stay in England if I turn away this petition of your grandfather's?"

"Why not?"

"Other than living as one of your grandfather's tenants. I have no way to make my way in this country. In my heart I am only a farmer. All the lessons in all the country are not going to make me into a fine gentleman."

"You acted like one at the Duchess's ball."

"Learning to dance does not make me a gentleman any more than swimming makes me a ship."

"Considering one fine gentleman stepped on my toes often enough that he sent flowers as an apology, dancing has nothing to do with being a gentleman. And you have always acted as one even the day you stood all wrinkled and travel worn at Grandfather's door and faced down his butler."

"That does not change my lack of another vocation. How can I hope to marry you if I cannot provide anything but a leaky roof over your head? Even if your grandfather grants me a place to live, your father could take it away once he inherits."

Georgiana took his hand. "It sounds like you are trying to count your harvest before the planting is done. We will talk with Grandfather—"

"Not today. He is so happy. I cannot face him today. He will tell me it is only the news of Dartmoor and I will feel differently in a fortnight."

Georgiana gave him a soft smile. "That he will do."

The back door opened with more noise than usual, and Jane clomped out of the house. "Aunt sent me out. She says she had not heard poorer playing in many a year, and if I play another note, she is liable to smash my fingers with a book."

Johnathan stood. "I would not have your fingers damaged on my account. May I take you to Gunters for an ice? Many thanks are due."

"Only if George comes along to chaperone. It would not be proper without her."

"Would tomorrow afternoon suit?"

Jane looked at Georgiana before answering. "Yes. It will."

The acceptance raised Johnathan's mood considerably.

THIRTY-EIGHT

ll the best made plans went awry. George stared into the library's dying fire. More people than chairs occupied Gunter's. Most of the gentlemen they passed that afternoon barely stopped short of giving Johnathan the cut direct as he mumbled their greetings. She heard the word Dartmoor more than once in whispers. She'd tried to read about it as today's papers would likely contain more information than yesterday's, but the papers were not in the breakfast room.

Jane, being an excellent chaperone in public, had not left Johnathan alone with George long enough to even ask if he had spoken with Grandfather. And if all of that was not enough, they returned home to find Father calling.

Of course he was in a heated discussion with grandfather that centered around the advancing petition.

Needless to say that when Father looked out the window to see Johnathan returning with both Jane and George, Father's cup of anger reached the boiling point and overflowed, spilling onto everyone in the household.

No one was in high spirits when they departed for Lady Millburn's annual musical. Father had not been invited, so at least the evening was spared any further time in his dour company.

Johnathan did not come either. Too late, George discovered his lack of invitation. To her delight Elaine was there with her husband. Lord Banbridge kept his promise, her aunt's wardrobe was exquisite, so different from the woolen dress her aunt wore the day George knocked on the door of Lightwood Manor.

George made it through the evening with all of her thoughts elsewhere. With every gentleman she looked at, she found herself wondering what skills beyond the ability to write his title on a document or write out a cheque did any of these men have?

They all attended Oxford or Cambridge, so they were well read. A good preparation for Parliament if she understood correctly, but little else unless they intended to go into the Church. There were a few in attendance in uniform coats, but if there was no war, could they provide?

Against all these men, Johnathan's ability to farm at least meant his family was unlikely to starve wherever they lived.

When they returned home, Jane pled a headache and went to bed. Knowing her sister would need complete silence and darkness. George chose to wait until Jane slept to retreat to her room.

Grandfather entered. "Am I disturbing you? I thought you would all have gone to bed."

"No, I was only pondering."

"May I pour you a glass of sherry? I came down for a nip of brandy."

"No, I drank too much raffia at the musical. What has you awake at this hour? I thought you did not accompany us because you were tired."

"Truthfully, my hearing is not what it once was and music is particularly unenjoyable." Grandfather poured his glass and sat in the chair opposite George.

"Your hearing? You never said anything about not hearing."

"Conversations are not very difficult for me yet. Now tell me, what has you awake and sitting alone?"

"Jane has a headache."

"You could take one of the other rooms."

"Thank you, no. I missed my twin too much when I was in Yorkshire. The thought that someday we will permanently not share a room haunts me."

"Do you not wish to marry? Judging by the number of franked letters in my name, I thought you had some sort of understanding with young Whittaker."

"We do wish to marry, but the thought of leaving my sister alone hurts. Jane says she is reconciled to our separation, although she wishes Sir Galahad came to Town."

"That would cause Felton a right fit would it not?" Grandfather sipped his drink. "What is worse, he may have the last laugh when all this earl business is over."

"How? I thought the information from the solicitor meant that the petition was proceeding."

"I received a message from the genealogist. He wishes to meet on Monday."

George rubbed the side of her head where her own headache was forming. "I thought Johnathan's genealogy was clear."

"You have spoken about the petition?"

"Yes."

"Of course. It will affect your life as much as his, if I am not mistaken. In time, you will fill the role of countess as well as your grandmother did."

Obviously Johnathan had not yet spoken with grandfather. She must speak carefully to not betray that confidence.

"You approve of us marrying, then? Father is quite against it."

"I would not have suggested Gretna Green, if I felt otherwise. Although I do see the issues with that course. I have yet to find a way to shield Jane from your father's wrath."

"The only way is to get Father to agree to my marriage or wait for another four years." Both options were unsatisfactory. She could wait. But if Johnathan returned to America, would he ever send for her? Would she go? Yes.

Grandfather finished his drink. "I wish I had an answer for you. If I find one, I shall let you know."

"I will do the same."

Grandfather left, leaving George alone to her quandary.

THIRTY NINE

he truth will set you free."

The verse from the eighth chapter of John read by the priest was not an unknown one to Johnathan. Nor was this the first time he heard it from a pulpit. Arguably, this was the most ornate pulpit he'd seen. His eyes traced the carvings as the words turned over in his mind. He must speak to the earl today.

Hours later, he sat in the earl's study, willing his knee not to shake as he sat.

"You know I have no power to grant that you can marry my granddaughter?"

"I did not wish to speak to you about Georgiana."

The earl raised a brow.

"When I first arrived at The Willows we spoke at length and you asked me if I thought I could remain in England all of my life. My answer is the same now. I could. We toured your estates, and you asked if I could manage them. I still believe I could. Then you asked if I could swear fidelity to the King. At the time, I thought it might be possible, yet I have doubts. The unease I felt with the idea expanded until it occupied most of my time and questions as I studied. After reading the minutes of Parliament, hearing of the Prince Regent's debauchery from many sources, and the reaction of the peers to the slaughter at Dartmoor, I have concluded that I can never in good conscience kneel to an earthly king."

The loudest noise in the room was the ticking of the clock. Johnathan counted the tics and tocks. At the count of eighty-one, the earl leaned forward.

"I cannot say this is unexpected. I have watched you question and struggle with the concept of the House of Lords. I am disappointed, but part of me feels I would be even more disappointed if you did not follow your conscience."

"I so wanted to save your earldom from Sir Lightwood. I wanted to protect those who live on your lands. I wanted to —"

"Marry my granddaughter?"

"That was part of it."

The earl took a folded paper from his drawer. "What do you make of this?"

Johnathan read the letter. "Mr. Fawkes wants to see us?"

"On a matter of urgency. There were some places in the pedigree that had holes in them. Perhaps he found another heir. Last night I worried about the possibility. This afternoon I am ready to embrace it. Let us not mention anything of this conversation until we meet with the genealogist in the morning."

"Georgiana and I have already spoken of it, as I cannot see a way to marry and provide for her if I do not continue and become an earl."

The earl nodded. "I thought as much. Ask her to keep this private, too. Not even Jane for now. If you love my granddaughter as much as I believe you do, we will find a way."

"But I have no way of making a living."

The earl stood and walked around the desk. He laid a fatherly hand on Johnathan's shoulder. "We shall think on that for the time being. Now we must return before the ladies think something is amiss."

"Thank you for understanding."

"Thank you for being honest. It is too bad your honesty fell on the side it did. You might have made the best earl England has ever seen."

The scripture was true. Though there was much to be resolved. The heaviness that grew on his shoulders over the past months dissipated. He was free, in a manner of speaking.

Phil and Michael arrived shortly before the dinner hour unexpectedly. Aunt Healand left the parlor to make the necessary adjustments to the evening meal.

Phil motioned to her husband to sit near the door before she corralled her sisters into the far corner. She set one hand over her middle and leaned close. "We came so I could tell you that I am leaving Town tomorrow."

"Leaving?" asked George and Jane in unison. "Why?"

Phil smoothed her dress down in the front. "So in July you can be Aunt George and Aunt Jane."

Jane gasped.

George whooped.

"Hush!" Phil covered George's mouth with her hand. "This is not news to be bandied about."

"Does Alex know?"

"I told her at Christmas when I first suspected."

"And you did not tell us?" Again, the question came in unison.

"I could hardly write such news in a letter and telling Jane without telling you felt wrong."

"Do Rose and Father know?" asked Jane.

"They will know when I start my confinement. I will tell Grandfather and aunt tonight."

"This is why you were ill at the Duchess's Ball?" asked George.

"I believe it was the crush. Other than some moments in the early days I have been well."

Michael loudly welcomed Aunt back into the room. Grandfather and Johnathan entered a moment later. Phil excused herself and went to her husband. They spoke quietly by the door before asking for everyone's attention.

Michael could not pull his gaze from Phil's as he spoke. "We know what we are about to say is not exactly proper. However, we feel you should know the truth when my darling leaves for our country home in the morning. It seems that The Earl of Whitstone will soon have a new title…"

Phil grinned. "Great-Grandfather!"

The celebratory joy wove throughout the evening. No one took particular notice when Johnathan led George through the garden door at dusk. A few steps from the door he stopped.

"I spoke with your grandfather about abandoning the petition. He is disappointed, but not upset. He asked that I not let my feelings be known until after we meet with the genealogist in the morning."

George took his hand in hers. "You did not need to tell me tonight."

"I did. You are the most important person in my life. He knows I would tell you. He approves of our potential union."

George glanced through the near window into the well-lit room, everyone was looking toward the entryway, so no one was watching them. She moved closer to Johnathn. "Yes, he expressed that in January. But it will do us little good without my father's consent."

"Nor without a way for me to support you. I have no employment or money to purchase land to farm. Even if such land were available."

"Please —" George's thought was cut off by her father rushing out the door.

"I have told you that you could not court her." The scent of stale ale wafted off of him.

"We were only talking and only feet from the door." That explained why everyone was preoccupied a moment ago.

"With your hand in his. I will not stand for it!" Father yanked George away from Johnathan.

Michael, Grandfather, and two footmen joined them after hearing the ruckus.

"Sir Lightwood, come inside. The whole of Russell Square need not hear you." Michael moved between Father and Johnathan. The footmen followed suit, boxing Father in, until he had no choice but to go inside.

"Might I suggest the ladies go to the parlor?" Grandfather's question was taken as the direction it was meant. Aunt Healand, Phil, Jane, and George went to the other room, but left the parlor door cracked open.

"Did Father say why he came?" asked George.

Jane led George to a chair. "He said something about never being an earl. Then said Johnathan would not either. That is when he saw you outside."

"I've called for tea," said Aunt Healand. "No telling how long this will go."

George sighed. "I wish I could go in there and tell Father to stop this foolishness. I want to marry Johnathan."

Jane laughed. "I thought you would never admit your feelings."

"I've been telling you so for weeks."

Jane pointed her finger at George. "Not so forthright. You have been hinting at it."

"I've told you plainly."

"No, you haven't. You just stare at his miniature and sigh."

"Do not."

"Girls! Anyone with two eyes can see that George has fallen for Johnathan, you do not need to fight about what is obvious."

Phil suddenly gasped, moving her hand over her middle and silencing any rebuttals to aunt. "He kicked me."

Aunt Healand gasped.

Jane exchanged a look with George. They had both seen more puppies, piglets, kids, and kits born than most gently bred women.

"I know that it is not proper for me to discuss such things. But you are my sisters. And I must tell someone."

Aunt Healand, trying to remind them of propriety, asked, "Promise me you will keep it among your sisters only?"

"I wish I could take you both to the country with me."

Jane did not wait a tick before answering. "I will go. I have endured enough of the Season. If George marries, I know I could not survive an event on my own."

George grabbed Jane's hand. Her sister could not live with their father forever. "Enough of the Season? We have only had two weeks of ours, and we have not been to Almack's yet. You cannot give up so soon. There must be someone for you."

Tea arrived. Aunt Healand poured.

Phil took her cup. "You are unlikely to receive vouchers after they ripped mine up last year. I did not find Almack's as superior as I thought it would be."

Aunt Healand handed Jane her cup. "Better off not applying for vouchers. Those old birds are not about to admit they were wrong last year. As for another Season, you are welcome to be my guest when you are ready. Besides, London isn't the only place one can find love. I certainly did not. You may find someone who suits you where you least expect it."

The tension in Jane's brow faded. "Or perhaps I will enjoy being the doting aunt far too much to care."

George looked to the door. "It is far too quiet. I wonder if Father has left."

Jane shook her head. "If you listen carefully, you can hear muffled voices."

"I believe Father is a bit intimidated by Michael. Perhaps that is why we don't hear his usual yelling."

Setting her cup aside, George walked to the door. "I almost wish they would yell so I would know what transpires."

Could the silence be good?

FORTY

either the earl nor Johnathan spoke on the ride to the genealogist's office. Sir Lightwood's drunken revelations of last evening gave them both much to think about. If Georgiana's father was correct…

Johnathan could not begin to comprehend the implications. As for the earl, it was as if he aged ten years overnight. However, the source of the information was highly suspect. Sir Lightwood was so inebriated that he had sunk into complete oblivion and a deep slumber. Some time in the night he roused enough to be escorted out by the footmen.

Mr. Fawkes greeted them at the door and led them into the same chaotic office they visited last time. The solicitor was present. He greeted the earl in his usual manner, with no indication, outside of his being in the room, that anything was amiss.

Against one wall stood a large board with a genealogical graph attached. On the left side was a branch starting with Nathaniel Whittaker née Ryeland. It was the same line the solicitor had shown them the previous week leading to

Johnathan. On the far right was Sir Lightwood's name. Across the top was written "Whitstone Earldom." The Second Earl of Whitstone was listed immediately below the title.

Mr. Fawkes spread his arms wide. "This has been the most complicated genealogy I have worked on in my career."

If the man expected congratulations, he should have not told others about the information.

The earl stepped closer to the board inspecting his own name. "I have heard speculation that you have completely upended the line of succession."

"Yes, very exciting. I have been bursting with the news for days now."

The earl turned to face Mr. Fawkes. "Enough that you told it throughout the taverns of London?"

Mr. Fawkes took a step back. "I've told none outside this office. The notes I sent you and your solicitor were deliberately vague, lest they be intercepted."

"Then you have those in your employ whose tongues wag like old ladies."

"Surely not."

"Sir Lightwood came to my house last night with the news that not only was he not to inherit, but I should be deposed as well."

To his credit Mr. Fawkes registered shock. "I—I—I—"

This standoff would not help anything. Johnathan pointed to the tree. "Perhaps it would be best if you explain the particulars, then we can determine the source of Sir Lightwood's information."

Mr. Fawkes picked up a pointing stick. "If you will have a seat, I shall explain the succession and where it went awry."

The genealogist took a long drink from his teacup before proceeding. "As suspected, I found more family on Sir Lightwood's line. However, it appears he is a clear heir to the title of baronet."

Perhaps Sir Lightwood had been wrong last night in his drunken ramblings.

"However, as I will show you in a moment, the heir to the barony is not next in line for the title of earldom." Mr. Fawkes moved his pointer to the fourth Earl of Whitstone. "Were you aware that your cousin was the product of the fourth earl and his second wife?"

"Yes. The first wife and all the children died. Mumps I believe, or measles."

"Almost correct. The oldest son, Thomas who was thirteen, survived but was rendered completely deaf by the illness. I had a devil of a time locating him. The Fourth Earl set him up in the country on a small estate with a good couple to care for him. When he was of age, the boy inherited, a bit more than a gentleman's farm, enough to keep him in a matter of gentility without drawing undue attention. Thomas Ryeland kept his surname which helped with the genealogy. Although he was deaf, he married and had six children. Including three sons, who lived to adulthood. The oldest stayed on the farm, the second joined the ministry and the third purchased a commission and died on the continent." Mr. Fawkes tapped the board where each of the names were written.

"We will only concern ourselves with the eldest, Thomas Jr. As you see he had four children that lived to adulthood. The oldest inherited the farm, which has continued to do very well. He even managed to send his son to Harrow. Unfortunately, Thomas Jr. passed in January. His son Theodore has returned home from school. The boy will be fifteen in June, and he is unaware that he is the rightful heir to the earldom."

Silence filled the room.

"So all this time I've not been the earl?"

"The fault does not lie with you. The fourth earl went to great lengths to conceal the memory of his deaf son and first wife. He moved from Kellmore to The Willows permanently.

I cannot find that his second wife ever knew of the boy. She believed the whole of the first family tragically passed. Only the solicitor knew. When the fourth earl passed, Thomas was alive and running a profitable estate as a gentleman. He should have been the fifth earl. He was well read and wrote a fine letter. However, even if Thomas Ryeland's existence was known, because of his deafness the crown may have passed him over as heir. The Fifth Earl kept correspondence from King George where he was acknowledged by title. I can find no evidence the Fifth Earl was aware of his cousin's existence either."

The earl took advantage of a pause in Mr. Fawkes narrative to comment. "If deafness is enough to keep Lords out of Parliament, then half the lords over sixty would be released."

"Yes, yes, you see my point. Thomas Ryeland was the rightful heir, not his younger half-brother Nathaniel, nor his cousin, your father."

"I am at a loss as to how to proceed. It seems I've been living a lie my entire life." The earl's voice shook.

The solicitor stepped forward with a leather-bound folio "I have taken the liberty of writing up a synopsis of Mr. Fawkes findings. Given young Theodore's age and your own. I suggest the best way to reconcile the wrong is to have him tutored under your care until he reaches his maturity. It will also give him time to finish at Harrow and continue on to Oxford or Cambridge and thus be better prepared for his future. I believe there is a courtesy title the boy can be given immediately to help with the transition."

The earl took the folio. "I hope the matter can be clarified quickly as it still must be a matter of parliamentary procedure."

Mr. Fawkes cleared his throat. "This is not the first time I have discovered an error in genealogy that affected one's status in the peerage. The other ones were only barons, and a viscount. Both times the matters were taken care of swiftly and quietly to ease the embarrassment of the crown. I assume you will experience the same. I wish you Godspeed."

Once they were alone in the carriage, the earl leaned his head back and sighed. "Last night I never dreamed Felton would be correct. I hope you'll remain my guest. It seems we have a new cousin to meet. I am sure you can navigate him through the first bit better than I can."

"The poor boy. I can imagine his surprise."

"I'm afraid you may not. As a gentleman's son of no rank, he would have been the least of the students. When he returns to school after his mourning, he will have a new place and some will resent it. His new life will not be easy."

"You have done well as my mentor. You will be better as his."

"For now, it is up to others to determine the exact course this will take. I am hopeful I will not be penalized by the crown, as I was not involved in the deception." The earl shook his head. "I cannot think on it too much. Shall we turn our energies to your problems?"

"Mine?"

"Georgiana."

The one word summed up all that was wrong and right in his life.

 To see the chart Mr. Fawkes made please visit :
https://loringrace.com/the-colonists-petition-genealogy/

FORTY-ONE

Georgiana ignored the knock on the door as she had since Grandfather returned home Monday last with Johnathan and shared the discoveries of the genealogist. The days evolved into the most shocking routine. Gentlemen of various ranks arrived on the doorstep far earlier than courtesy allowed and continued in a steady flow until grandfather left for his club or Parliament.

Other than Lady Banbridge, only the oldest of Aunt Healand's friends came during at home hours and Johnathan had not come round at all. He sent a note the morning after the meeting, which George read a dozen times a day.

…Owing to my present suspended status, I think it best to allow the earl to meet with those whose advice could clarify the matters. I see little choice for my future, but to arrange passage home…

The letter contained several sentiments that she kept close to her heart, but no further plans for marriage or hope that he would ask her to accompany him to America.

The butler opened the parlor door and announced the Duke of Aylton and his cousin Viscount Endelton.

Jane dropped her needle work and she stood to greet the guests.

Aunt Healand being much more composed addressed them. "Your Grace, Lord Endelton, welcome. The earl is in his study if you would like to speak with him."

The duke indicated they could continue on as they were before sitting in the chair Aunt Healand offered which, save her own, was the finest in the room.

"I have already spoken to Whitstone. I told him that by unanimous vote he is to keep his title. An envoy, including myself and Whitstone will leave tomorrow morning to inform the new Lord Ryeland as to his new status. The lad is being awarded the courtesy title of Viscount Ryeland by order of the king."

"We thank you for the swift handling of this matter and your kindness in coming to inform us." Aunt Healand offered tea.

"My purpose is not to tell you that which you will surely learn, but to see if I may help with other wrongs that have been committed. You no doubt know that besides bearing the title of your brother, Michael is my cousin, and he is consumed with concern as to his wife's condition and is spending far too much time fretting."

Michael opened his mouth to protest but the duke silenced him with a look. Michael fretting over Phil, this was not news to the family. Michael came nearly every day for reassurances. Jane offered multiple times to go to her sister.

"As you may know, once Michael starts discussing a subject, it is difficult to turn his mind elsewhere. And not only is he talking incessantly of his wife—which I find to be somewhat charming—his only other subject upon which he ruminates is, and I quote, 'poor George.' This brings me to the next problem. According to the Duchess who is at the center of all that happens in the ton, the two of you managed what took your sisters twice the time in being snubbed by the ton. This of course was not of your doing, but with your place in society being in question, most followed my wife's lead and snubbed you. That is my fault as I showed partiality toward your family. Which I do not regret. I only regret that my wife chose to show her disapproval of you only to spite me. Which would have been settled quietly if only your father had not appeared at Almack's this past evening."

"What?" George covered her mouth. She had not meant to interrupt his Grace.

"I was not there, but the duchess was." Odd how the duke never called her his wife. "It is unclear how Lightwood entered the establishment, as he has no voucher. Nevertheless, he put out quite a spectacle inviting all the men to come wed his daughters by any means they could in the most vulgar terms. In particular, he challenged them to capture you in marriage, Miss Georgiana, so you could not marry the, and I quote, 'upstart colonist.'"

Father likely used other terms to refer to Johnathan and the Duke was editing his comments. Just as shocking as Father's escapade, was the fact that the formerly reticent Duke continued to speak.

"After Lightwood's actions last summer with your sister, I thought I put things to rest. I hold Lady Philippa and Miss Alexandra in the highest esteem. Although we are barely acquainted, Michael tells me that you are of the same fine cloth as your sisters. So I propose that I intervene to spare both of you possible ruination, as I feel that at least part of you being in such a position is my fault for not checking the duchess."

Aunt Healand gasped. Jane, who kept her eyes on the fallen needlework the entire conversation, moved closer to George.

"I have already been much more indelicate than I wish to be. However, due to the challenge your father issued last night, this house is being watched closely by those unscrupulous enough whom would try to catch either of you alone. Far too many servants, even on this square can be bought. Therefore, we have a plan." The duke turned to Michael to explain.

"Lord and Lady Banbridge are to be willing accomplices. They will leave in the morning for their estate under the guise of needing to see to something or another. They have invited Johnathan to travel with them. The two of you will leave here in my coach, with or without Lady Healand, as she wishes, to attend to my sweet Phil. At Luton, both parties will stay at the same inn. In the morning, Lady Banbridge's maid and George will switch places. My coach will continue on to Terrace Hall where Phil shall have the solace of Jane. George will continue northward passing Lord Banbridge's estate and on to Gretna Green, where his lordship will witness your nuptials with Johnathan. Meanwhile, Whitstone and the Duke will be on their way to meet the future Earl of Whitstone and thus Grandfather remains blissfully unaware of his granddaughter's nuptial plans so he can honestly claim he knew nothing about the elopement."

"Considering my father was the first to propose such a plan, that will hardly be believable." Aunt Healand took a biscuit from the tray. "I am not fond of the position you have put me in your Grace, I am either to be an accomplice to a marriage I fully approve of or pretend to be surprised."

"My sincere apologies Lady Healand. I would have asked you to leave the room…" the Duke's smile lacked all sincerity. Obviously, Lady Healand's help was necessary to carry off the deceptions as trunks must be packed.

"Oh fiddle-diddle. You knew full well what you were doing. I think it best that I go to Philippa as well."

"Has Johna— I mean, Mr. Whittaker agreed to this plan?" asked George.

The duke sighed and picked up his teacup. "There is the rub. The man has a willful independence, which in most circumstances I admire. I gave him a living, which is mine to grant and he refused. He is at least pondering a place managing one of my estates."

"If he will not marry me, then why such an elaborate plan?"

The Duke grinned like a cat who caught the mouse that vexed the cook. "Because he wants to marry you and is more downcast than my cousin. I am sure you can dissolve his reluctance at the theater tonight."

"Theater?" Aunt Healand looked from Michael to the Duke.

"No Season is complete without a visit to the theater. Of course, you, Lady Healand and Whitstone are invited. The Duchess will not be in attendance."

Aunt Healand tipped her head. "I assume that is your way of telling the blaggards that my nieces are not available at any cost."

"I knew you understood me." His Grace raised his teacup as he would for a toast. "I shall see you this evening. The Earl has already agreed to come as a celebration so you have no need to convince him."

The Duke of Aylton and Michael took their leave.

George hardly knew what to say as the men quit the room. Jane clasped her hand. "Did I just imagine that conversation?"

Aunt Healand sighed a bone deep sound. "I am not entirely sure. I thought his Grace was known for his foul temper."

"Alex always claimed he was kind. We must believe her now," said Jane.

Must she? It seemed the Duke of Aylton enjoyed meddling in other's lives simply because he was not happy with his own. However, George was not entirely opposed to the plan.

Only after arriving at Drury Lane, which Johnathan still was not sure if it was a street or a building, did he discover that like Lord Banbridge he was also a guest of the most ill-tempered duke of his acquaintance. Also, the only duke he knew. The selfsame duke who only that morning offered Johnathan what the man called a 'living'. One could not simply give another person the position of preaching. Being a preacher was something a man must have in his heart. Father's friend Gideon Frost told him so. And Mr. Frost should know, since he had been a minister of God's word for some years before leaving his denomination over differences.

Despite what the Duke of Aylton offered, Johnathan could not become the preacher at a church he did not belong to nor agree with some of the fundamental theological elements.

Johnathan followed Lord and Lady Banbridge up the stairway. Leaving would be beyond rude. The Duke of Aylton met them at the door to his box. "Lady Banbridge, Lord Banbridge, and Whittaker. I am expecting a somewhat full box tonight. The front four seats are reserved. Banbridge if you and your lovely wife would sit in these center seats. Sorry Whittaker, I'm afraid you shall have to take that one in the corner."

His Grace may claim to be trying to help, however even Johnathan knew that being relegated to the darkest corner like an errant schoolboy, was not a good thing. It would have been more fitting for Lord and Lady Banbridge, as Georgiana's recently wed aunt was constantly touching her new husband who was not above sneaking a kiss whenever he thought he was not watched.

A moment later the rest of the Duke's company arrived.

"Lord Whitstone, Lady Healand, Miss Jane, Miss Georgiana."

Johnathan's heart sped up to a quick trot. He stood when the ladies entered.

The duke continued as if nothing out of the ordinary was occurring. "Welcome. I'm afraid I quite miscounted seats. Miss Georgiana would you mind terribly sitting in the back row.

Georgiana turned, her eyes grew wide as they met with Johnathan's. Her lips curved into a smile. "The back row suits me well."

Johnathan could not help his smile which came as quickly as his revision of opinion of the Duke. "I am not sure I understand all of his Grace's plots and plans. However, they make life interesting."

"I'm beginning to think he is one of the most brilliant men in the country. Look at him next to my grandfather. There will be few who would continue to give Grandfather the cut direct now. Then with my sister on the far side of my aunt, the duke is clearly saying that my sister, and by extension me, who is in his box, are not to be trifled with despite the inappropriate declarations of our father."

"You know of those?" Johnathan tried to keep his voice calm. When he'd heard the rumors, only Lord Banbridge's interference kept him from confronting Lightwood.

"Not in detail. However, I am not a stranger to my father's outbursts or linguistic choices."

"You should not be subject to —" Without words to finish the thought, he took her hand in his. "Did the Duke tell you of his scheme to take us northward?"

"Yes. He says you are not in favor of the plan."

"You told me visiting Gretna Green would disgrace you and your sisters."

"Not with Lord and Lady Banbridge as our escorts. They add a sense of legitimacy to the affair. Proper escorts. Proof we are running to Gretna Green only because my father leaves us little choice."

"This is not what you wanted."

"I am not sure what I wanted. I am not like Isabel. I have no dreams of a certain wedding dress, or a flower filled breakfast after pleading my troth. I did hope to at least be asked to wed."

Johnathan stared at her in the dim light. For the first time he realized there was someone singing on stage. He racked his mind. They discussed marriage several times. Even discussed their admiration for one another. Laughed over his misunderstanding of Gretna Green not being a person. Never once had he actually asked her to marry. Court, yes. Wed, no.

The aria concluded and the gaslights glowed brighter for intermission.

Johnathan did not let go of Georgiana's hand. "It seems I have been very remiss. I intend to remedy this as soon as we can find a moment of privacy."

"Not likely to get any privacy now. Everyone will come to see the Duke in his box."

"May we leave?"

"I understand there are refreshments down in the lobby."

"There were last time I was here."

"You did not write of the refreshments or the theater."

"Neither of us are good at writing details of our lives. Shall we go seek some lemonade?"

"Yes, we should take Jane." Georgiana motioned to her sister.

A flash of disappointment flicked across his mind. However, it was the proper thing, and this was a public venue.

After the intermission, the second half of the theatrical performance passed without Johnathan taking in a single word or song. How was he to get a moment alone? It must happen before they left in the morning. Before they set off for their elopement.

He escorted Georgiana to the Earl's coach. They were the last to arrive. He was preparing to hand Georgiana up when the duke put a hand on his shoulder. "I need to speak to Whitstone about a matter that cannot wait. Would you take my carriage and see Miss Georgiana home? I do not think there will be room for all of us."

"But—"

"My coachman will take you directly to the Whitstone's townhouse. If you dishonor—" The fearsome glint in the duke's eyes hinted of a punishment worse than death.

Johnathan swallowed the knot in his throat and nodded.

"Go on then. I expect you no more than a minute after we arrive."

Georgiana's eyes were large, but she went with Johnathan willingly.

The Duke's coach was the height of luxury. Johnathan sat across from Georgiana. Both of them ran their hands across the seats.

"Have you ever felt anything so luxurious in your life?" Georgiana traced the golden stitching on a pillow.

The floor of the coach was immaculately clean. Before he could think too long about it Johnathan dropped to his knees and took Georgiana's bare hand between his. She set the cushion aside and gave him her other hand.

"My dearest, I have been terribly remiss. Our courtship has been all comings and goings. I always intended to ask for your hand as soon as your father— well he has not, and things have been arranged so quickly—"

Georgiana moved her hand and placed a finger on his lips. "I've lived that as well."

She removed her finger with such slowness it left a warm tingle.

"Georgiana Lightwood. Will you be my wife? I am not sure what our future holds or even if it can be here in England.

We have yet to discuss the possibility of America—"

She touched his lips again, this time with hers. A brief kiss, not much longer than their first, before pulling back. "I will marry you Johnathan Whittaker and I will follow you to the ends of the earth if necessary."

Their lips met again. Johnathan moved his hands to hold her face and slipped them into her hair. There was absolutely something far more luxurious than the coach's cushions. No, two things. Her hair and her lips. Some day he would tell her that. But not now.

Without letting her go he moved a kiss to her jawline and slid upon the seat next to her to hold her better. The carriage turned a corner, the movement pulling her away from him.

Georgiana looked at him with wide eyes. Her chest moved up and down as she too caught her breath.

"I know we are to travel together for most of the way." Johnathan held her hands between them. "However I think it best if I ride my horse and meet you at the altar."

"Anvil."

"What?"

"A blacksmith will marry us. Over an anvil."

For a man considered by most to be a backward colonist, a blacksmith shop seemed more fitting than a London cathedral. "I will meet you over the anvil. And the next time we kiss, you will be my wife. Which is somehow fitting since our first kiss was halted by fireplace poker."

"How about the time after the next time?"

Before he could respond Georgiana's lips met his again. Just as he pulled her into his arms to do a proper job, the coach came to a stop. He leaned his forehead against hers. "Until the anvil."

"Until the anvil."

He handed her out the door and she turned back once she was firmly on the ground. "I love you Johnathan."

EPILOGUE

George had never previously visited Viscount Endelton's ancestral home, Terrace Hall. Holding her husband's hand she peered out of the window. "I cannot believe it has been more than a month since I last saw Jane. Before, when I was away from her, it was such agony."

"I'm glad to have kept you from too much pain. However, it would be best if you did not tell her she was not missed." Johnathan kissed her hand.

George swatted at him. "I missed her. Just not as much as—"

Johnathan moved his attentions to her neck. She pushed him back.

"Do not start kissing me now. What will Jane think if I exit the carriage all mussed and disarranged?"

He turned her hand over and kissed the inside of her wrist sending a thrill straight to her heart. "She is likely to think you had a difficult journey. However, Philippa will think that I have been ravishing you as only a husband should."

He started to work his way up her arm.

"Stop. We have shocking enough news without Phil giggling at us."

Johnathan dropped their linked hands to his lap. "I still could take the steward position His Grace offered."

"No, you are a farmer at heart. You won't enjoy keeping books, even if you can oversee the harvest. You belong in Massachusetts, and I belong there with you."

"Positive?"

"I'm glad we are waiting until my niece or nephew is baptized before we leave so I can see the entire family."

"You need to say a proper farewell to everyone."

George grazed her lips across his. "I have the best of all husbands."

"Remember that a year from now?"

The coach stopped and Jane rushed out to meet them. Before she exited the carriage. George turned to her husband. "I will remember a hundred years from now."

Johnathan held back Georgiana's hair as she expelled what he thought was an empty belly into a bucket again. When she finished, he wiped her face with a damp cloth. The seas had been calm for the first three days of their voyage. According to the captain, fair days were uncommon for the first of October and with the defeat of Napoleon they wouldn't have to hide from every ship they saw. Once she got used to the movement of the ship, they should have a lovely two months at sea.

Georgiana leaned back resting her head in her hands.

Johnathan moved the pail aside. "This will end in a few days as you get used to the ship. My first week on my voyage to meet you was difficult. More than once I ran retching to the railing. I wondered if I should cast myself overboard as well. Then I got my sea legs, so to speak, and it was much better. This will end, you will see." Now was not the time to tell her of the storms which weakened his resolve.

"I do not think it will."

He stroked her hair. "You will get your sea legs, just as I did."

She shook her head. His powerful wife who chased pigs and climbed trees was brought low by the movement of the sea. Believing she was done for now, he helped her onto the bed. Glad for the relatively large cabin the earl insisted paying for, while not very large, it was private. He moved behind her holding her against his chest, hoping that having her head higher than her traitorous stomach would help. He continued to wipe her brow with the cool cloth, knowing from experience that it helped.

Soon Georgiana's breathing slowed. She reached up and held his hand in place against the side of her head. "That feels good."

"I wish I could do more. This will pass."

"It... Will... not..."

"It only feels that way. I thought so too."

"You... Were... Not—" She paused between each word, struggling with the swaying and rocking from the waves." With... Child."

"Of course not, I—" Her words sunk in. "Child? We are having a baby. Are you sure?"

Five months of marriage and now she was with child? He shifted her in his arms to look at her face better in the dim light of the oil lamp.

Georgiana's soft smile brightened the room. "I am sure. The week of the harvest fair, I felt ill. The smell of apples made me gag. Even if I wanted to, I could not have gone near the press. Phil told me she felt the same when she first started expanding. Only she couldn't stand the smell of cheese. I would have asked my Aunt Elaine, since she is increasing, but I could not put such a question in a letter. Cook, who has six children of her own, confirmed it. She gave me peppermint tea, but I have been unable to keep it down."

"I'm going to be a father? A father." The truth sunk in slowly. That also explained the number of hard ginger biscuits the Kellmore cook sent with them. He wouldn't eat another one.

"And I shall likely be ill this entire voyage." She moved her free hand to her midsection.

"I will do everything I can to help you." Johnathan had no idea what he could do. But he still wished to be of use. At a time like this he feared husbands were of little use, but still he could try.

"I know you will. I would not have married you if I thought you would do anything less." Georgiana's voice grew softer as she spoke. Her hand holding his unclenched without breaking the link.

Johnathan held her as she slept, praying she could rest and hold down enough food to sustain her and their child. And if he was very fortunate, his grandpa would live to see his next great-grandchild.

April 10, 1816

Dear Jane,

It is another cold and rainy day. We have had quite a few of those this spring. Something Johnathan claims is quite unusual. On to better news. At dawn on the morning of April 6, we welcomed Hannah Jane Whittaker into the world. I named her for Mother and you, my dearest sister. Her eyes are blue like Johnathan's, and she has only the thinnest smattering of hair. I wish I could draw half as well as Isabel to send you a proper picture. When she sleeps she is as an angel. She met her great-grandpa this morning. He reminds me of our grandfather in stature and kindness. I wish she could meet all of you.

You may tell Phil my daughter can match her son for lusty cries and unrequited hunger. I will write to her in due course. Johnathan has written grandfather. I assume our letters shall arrive at the same time. I will send a note to Father, though I don't expect him to acknowledge me or a granddaughter.

Sorry this is so brief. Hannah is hungry again.

All my love,

George

THE END

HISTORICAL NOTES

This book was so fun to research. Like Johnathan, I read or skimmed the Journals of the House of Lords, only I read 1814 and 1815. It was fun to see what sort of things they discussed. Interestingly enough there were more divorces than I expected to be on the dockets. I put a link on my Pinterest board for this book. If it is between scrubbing toilets and reading the Journals of the House of Lords… Well, who am I to give reading advice?

Most pieces of legislation created during the 1814-15 session were repealed within a few years. Some contained perks reminiscent of what sometimes find their way into legislation today. One example was a purchase of an estate for Lord Nelson. By modern sensibilities, I can see the damage some laws, specifically the Corn Laws, caused. However, there was one act that stood out to me: The Apothecary Act. This act was the first step to training and licensing of medical personnel in England. The law stayed active until 1989, although it went through several revisions. It still would be some time before germ theory was proposed, and leeches discontinued as a cure. The Apothecary Act was a first step in establishing reliable health care.

For Johnathan, and to a lesser degree the Lightwoods, this book begins amidst the War of 1812. I placed Johnathan on the same voyage as the delegation, including John Quincy Adams, for the peace talks. The negotiations started on August 1, 1814 in The Sovereign Principality of the United Netherlands, which as a political entity was the short-lived foundation for the Netherlands we know today. However, if you wish to visit where the Treaty of Ghent was signed, make sure you book travel to Belgium.

One of the forgotten events of the War of 1812 was the Dartmoor Massacre. The British refer to it as the Dartmoor Incident. While I placed the Massacre on the correct week in Johnathan's story, I can't prove that there was an article in the London papers the morning after the massacre. I have located an article dated four days later from The Morning Chronicle (London) dated April 11, 1814. However, the details in that article were extremely biased against the Americans and cited the wrong day for the incident, which would have been even more alarming to an American living in London.

From today's perspective, with more information than Johnathan would have known, I would write a newspaper article this way:

Massacre At Dartmoor

Returning American POWs after the ratification of the Treaty of Ghent [December 24, 1814 UK and February 16, 1815 USA] slowed from a trickle to a full stop when Napoleon escaped from Elba and returned to Paris in March 1815. In April of that year some 5,000–6.000 American POWs remained at Dartmoor Prison awaiting freedom.

Dartmoor Prison was particularly suited for its purposes and housed at various times over 6,000 American prisoners and another 3,000 French. Conditions were miserable and the food worse. The POWs were in a political tug of war they likely knew nothing about, as the ships meant to take them home were re-tasked to fight Napoleon, and inspectors were barred from the prison where conditions grew worse.

About 6:00 pm on 6 April, 1815, Captain Thomas Shortland discovered a hole from one of the five Dartmoor prisons to the barrack yard near the gun racks. Some prisoners were outside the fence, noisily pelting each other with turf, and many more were near the breach at the gambling tables. The signal was sounded for the prisoners to return to their cells. However, Shortland was convinced of an escape plot and rang the alarm bell to collect the officers and have the guards ready. Prisoners, who should have been free men, came to see what was happening. A prisoner broke a gate chain with an iron bar, and a number of the prisoners entered the prison's central square. After attempts at persuasion, Shortland ordered a charge which drove some of the prisoners inside. Those near the gate, however, hooted at and taunted the soldiery, [USA! USA!] who fired a volley over their heads. The crowd yelled louder and threw stones, and the soldiers—without orders—fired a direct volley which killed seven and wounded another sixty, thirty severely. The soldiers continued firing at the prisoners, who were struggling to get back inside the barracks.

Finally the captain, a lieutenant and the hospital surgeon (the other officers being at dinner) succeeded in stopping the shooting and started caring for the wounded.

The incident was examined by a joint commission, Charles King for the United States and F. S. Larpent for Great Britain. They exonerated Shortland, who was rewarded with a promotion. Though no blame was assigned, the British government paid compensation to the American families of those killed and pensioned the disabled.

POWs who returned to the United States predicted the Dartmoor Massacre would remain a day of infamy in the memory of all Americans.

Today, for most of us, the War of 1812 is a footnote in history that produced the Star-Spangled Banner.

One side note that is not included in the book is that Jane Austen anonymously released Mansfield Park in 1814. You may recall that Fanny married her first cousin. I made George and Johnathan third cousins once removed, which is much further. In fact, you could be living next door to your fourth cousin and not even know it. Twice in the last few years, I have met fourth cousins living in my neighborhood.

AUTHOR'S NOTE

The Heirs & Heroes is the first series I have written where at least one character does not fall within the Wilsons's extended family tree. Samuel Wilson and his family are introduced in Waking Lucy, my first published novel. Since then I have managed to slip at least one character into every series that is somehow distantly related to this family. While I am sure that Samuel and Lucy can trace their ancestry back to England and likely the Mayflower. Which means that someone, quite possibly Mrs. Green, is a distant cousin, it is too much of a complicated tree to follow as I would need to travel up several generations and back again.

I have, however, made a character link to the second book I published, Reforming Elizabeth. Some of my readers may remember Gideon Frost receiving advice from Mr. (Nathaniel) Whittaker, an older man in his congregation. Mr. Whittaker tells a story of love and loss, spanning decades of his life, including his leaving his home in England where he was destined to be an Earl.

And lest dear reader you think there was no link to Lucy and Samuel, Johnathan remembers a blizzard on his tenth birthday. That would have been November 1797, the same blizzard that is featured in the first chapters of Waking Lucy. I should note here that I have no proof there was, or was not, a blizzard that week in November. It was my first book, and I was not as historically accurate as I try to be now. Although given my research on 1816, I can say it would be difficult to prove or disprove such a storm due to lack of weather records.

ACKNOWLEDGMENTS

I may do way too much genealogy. Still it took me a while to figure out exactly how to make all of the family connections in this book work and have the cousin relationship distant enough for modern sensibilities.

As always, thanks to Tammy and Nanette who are so willing to help make all my projects better and to read for all my mistakes. I would never make it through a day without Mara whose messages keep me on task. Thank you wonderful ladies.

Big thanks to Julie for fitting me in and for the excellent edits. And to my wonderful proofreaders who are not to be blamed for any remaining errors. Thank you all!

My husband encourages me every crazy step of the way and puts up with all my messy spreadsheets, and lack of cooking as my imaginary friends eat better.

And all gratitude to my Father in Heaven for putting these wonderful people, and any I may have forgotten to mention, in my life. I am grateful for every experience and blessing I have been granted.

Visit me at https://loringrace.com/

ABOUT THE AUTHOR

Lorin Grace was born in Colorado and has been moving around the country ever since, living in eight states and several imaginary worlds. She holds a degree in graphic design which comes in handy with creating book covers. Currently, she lives with her husband, and a dog who is insanely jealous of her laptop.

When not writing, Lorin enjoys creating graphics, visiting historical sites, museums, painting furniture, and reading. Three of her books, her debut novel, *Waking Lucy* (2017), *Mending Fences* (2018), and *Not the Bodyguard's Baby* (2020) have won Recommend Read awards in the League of Utah Writers Published book contest.